Seduction at Sea

Octavia's face flamed at Sheffield's remark. "Let me out of here."

He made no attempt to stop her. "Before you go, would you be so kind as to pass me a bottle of brandy from the chest behind you?"

She hesitated for a moment, then handed him the spirits with an exaggerated shrug of her shoulders. "Go ahead, then, drown whatever it is that you are running from—and yourself along with it. Good night, sir."

"Good night, miss," Sheffield murmured, his head bending closer to hers.

Octavia swallowed hard. "Sir, I warn you, I'll not stand for any more of your nonsense. If you try to kiss me again—"

There was a low rumble of amusement in his throat. "Kiss you? That was not a kiss back there, my dear. *This* is a kiss."

His lips came down on hers, firmly but gently, sending both shivers and sparks down her spine. He tasted of fiery brandy and the salty tang of the sea. It was like nothing she had ever imagined. For a moment she found herself responding to the heat of his embrace. She melted into his chest and tilted her head back, allowing him to deepen the embrace, if only for an instant. . . .

The Storybook Hero

Andrea Pickens

A SIGNET BOOK

SIGNET
Published by New American Library, a division of
Penguin Putnam Inc., 375 Hudson Street,
New York, New York 10014, U.S.A.
Penguin Books Ltd, 80 Strand,
London WC2R 0RL, England
Penguin Books Australia Ltd, Ringwood,
Victoria, Australia
Penguin Books Canada Ltd, 10 Alcorn Avenue,
Toronto, Ontario, Canada M4V 3B2
Penguin Books (N.Z.) Ltd, 182–190 Wairau Road,
Auckland 10, New Zealand

Penguin Books Ltd, Registered Offices:
Harmondsworth, Middlesex, England

First published by Signet, an imprint of New American Library,
a division of Penguin Putnam Inc.

First Printing, October 2002
10 9 8 7 6 5 4 3 2 1

Chapter One

"Good Lord, given the circumstances, you might at least have made a semblance of an effort to appear in a respectable state." The speaker's patrician nose wrinkled in disgust, as if he could actually catch a whiff of the dregs of brandy and musky perfume from all the way across the room.

The figure sprawled in the worn wing chair made no effort to smooth the creases in his rumpled cravat nor to rearrange his long legs in a more decorous posture. "And what circumstances are those, William? The prospect of a warm family reunion?"

The Marquess of Killingworth gave an exasperated snort as he turned away from his youngest brother and caught the eye of his other sibling. "You see? Bloody waste of time, inviting him. I don't know why we bothered. Uncle Ivor must be daft to have thought he might accept."

"Come now, William," murmured Thomas Sheffield, Viscount Alston, in a voice designed to put out the sparks of anger beginning to flare in the marquess's heated gaze. "You promised to keep a cool head. Remember the reason we are here." Taking the ensuing silence as a grudging acquiescence, he sighed and went on. "And you, Alex. You might try not to goad him on. It *has* been a long time. Too long. It's good to see you"—he paused as he regarded the bloodshot eyes, sallow complexion, and state of dishevelment that spoke all too clearly of a night spent in reckless carousing— "though I wish I could say you are looking well."

"Always the peacemaker, Tommy." Alexander Sheffield noticed the cufflink dangling from the cuff of his wrinkled shirt and slowly fastened it in place. "Don't bother."

The marquess shrugged in impatience to indicate things were going exactly as he expected. "Well, will you come?" he demanded. "Or are you too busy wenching or gambling or God knows whatever else it is you do that seeks to sink the family name in further reproach."

"William," warned Alston.

His younger brother only laughed. "Oh, I have much too thick a skin for any of Lord William's stinging set downs to have the least effect."

The marquess's lip curled in contempt.

"But," he added in a slow drawl, "I admit to an overwhelming curiosity as to Uncle Ivor's summons. And seeing that the chance to dine with my affectionate family occurs so rarely these days, I do believe I shall make an appearance." If truth be told, the fact that it would also irk his eldest sibling to no end was perhaps the deciding factor.

"Very well. But if you think to bring another"—the marquess nearly choked on the word—"doxy masquerading as a lady acquaintance into my house, I vow I shall throw you bodily from the premises."

That *had* been a rather shabby thing to do, reflected the youngest Sheffield. He must truly have been four sheets to the wind to have come up with such a stunt. He had nothing against his sisters-in law. In fact, he liked them quite a bit. But then again, he had no trouble getting along with females.

"You might try pressing your coat and finding a fresh set of linen," continued the marquess. "And you might—"

Alston put a hand on his brother's shoulder. "Tomorrow at seven, then, Alex?"

The figure in the chair nodded, his unruly long dark locks falling to obscure the flash of pain in his eyes. His hand shot out for the glass on the side table, and he drained the amber contents in one quick gulp. "Oh, seeing that it has been quite some time since either of you visited town, let me know if I may be of any assistance in suggesting some entertainment. Madame Violet has a particularly lovely assortment of females—you do still favor big breasts, William?"

Alston propelled his older sibling through the door before the growl of rage reverberating in the marquess's throat could reach a roar.

As it fell shut, Alexander Sheffield poured himself another brandy.

Sheffield paused before reaching for the familiar lion's head brass knocker. He usually avoided Grosvenor Square—not that his usual jaunts tended to take him anywhere near such a bastion of propriety. The imposing town house, home to four previous Marquesses of Killingworth, had changed not a whit since his first stay, when he was a lad not yet out of leading strings. His throat tightened for just a moment as he recalled larking through the hallways and sliding down the banisters with William and Thomas—and Jack, of course.

Damnation, he knew he shouldn't have come.

But it was too late to turn tail now. He reached up and rapped with rather more force than was necessary. Almost immediately, the heavy varnished door swung open.

"Why, good evening, Mister Alex." The reedy butler, already a fixture in the house in his father's time, gave a quirk of a smile before composing his angular features into their normal impassive expression. "Welcome home."

"I doubt that I am," he muttered under his breath as he allowed the elderly man to relieve him of his greatcoat. To his dismay, he could feel a strange flutter in his stomach.

"The others are in the drawing room. Shall I—"

"I haven't forgotten the way, Evans. And no, thank you, I shall announce myself."

The butler inclined his head a fraction. "As you wish, sir."

Once again, he hesitated slightly, his eyes drifting of their own accord to the gilt-framed portrait of the first earl hanging at the head of the ornately carved staircase, then to the massive crystal chandelier dangling in the center of the entrance hall, missing several baubles due to having served on occasion as target practice for four unruly boys. With a mental shake, he banished such thoughts and forced his steps down the polished parquet hallway.

"Ah, Alexander!"

His Uncle Ivor, the Earl of Chittenden, moved from a spot by the crackling fire and extended his hand. "I appreciate your coming."

Sheffield felt his throat constrict. He said nothing as he shook hands.

His two brothers rose from their seats. A cousin, his uncle's only son, laid aside the book he was perusing and looked up as well.

"Alex," murmured Alston in greeting, a tentative smile on his face.

The marquess glowered and gave only a curt nod.

His cousin Richard, following his father's lead, also came over to greet him. "Good to see you, Lex. It's been too damn long," he murmured, leaning in close to Sheffield's ear as he gave him a firm handshake.

"I believe you are acquainted with your sisters-in-law, are you not?"

Sheffield nodded and sketched a bow toward the marquess's wife, Augusta, and Alston's wife, Olivia.

For a moment, there was an uncomfortable silence.

"What can I get you to drink?" continued his uncle in a hearty tone that sought to dispel the underlying tension in the room.

"Anything, as long as the bottle is full," muttered the marquess.

Their uncle shot him a dark look, then went on. "Sherry? Brandy?"

Sheffield shrugged. "Whatever you are having."

The earl returned with a glass of sherry and motioned for him to take a place in one of the wing chairs by the fire. Sheffield accepted the drink but ignored the invitation to be seated. He merely polished off the contents in one gulp and shifted the glass from hand to hand, his lips curled in a willful belligerence that challenged any reproach.

"Let us not waste time with strained civility, Uncle. Why did you ask me here?" he blurted out.

His uncle's brow furrowed slightly, but he kept a smile on his lined face. "Plenty of time to discuss business after dinner."

"Ah, you mean we should spend some time in convivial family chatter?" The mocking tone of his voice could hardly be mistaken.

"Well, at least you have had the decency to appear before us in a pressed coat and properly tied cravat," muttered William.

"Oh, Squid is capable of starching a neck cloth or polishing a boot, if he is so directed."

His brother's brow furrowed. "Squid?"

"My valet."

"A deucedly queer name for a gentleman's man, but then again, you might—"

"An interesting moniker. And just how did he come to be called that?" interrupted Olivia, seeking to deflect the barbs being tossed by her elder brother-in law.

Sheffield's lips quirked slightly. "Because he was accorded to have rather slippery tentacles in his former line of work."

There was a snort of disgust from the marquess, while Olivia ducked her head to hide a grin.

"Actually, the ladies prefer to call him 'Angel' for his cherubic looks," continued Sheffield. He paused to pick at a thread on his sleeve. "And from what I hear, he *does* transport them to heaven—"

"For God's sake, hold your tongue! Have you forgotten there are true ladies present, and not your usual sort of company?" snapped the marquess.

Augusta didn't attempt to repress an amused laugh. "Come now, William. Have a sense of humor. Can't you see that Alex is merely trying to pull your cork? Besides, we are hardly schoolroom misses here, that we cannot sully our ears with anything more bland than the state of the weather or the latest modiste."

"But I *was* referring to true ladies, dear brother," went on the marquess's youngest sibling, a wicked twinkle in his eye. "I assure you on the several occasions we have exchanged places, Squid has comported himself in a most gentlemanly manner. *Most* gentlemanly. Why there is more than one wealthy widow in Brighton who is no doubt pining the departure of the blond Mr. Sheffield—"

The marquess's fist came down upon the table with a resounding bang. "That is *enough*, I say."

On that note, dinner was announced.

The meal was a strained affair. Despite the earl's attempts to keep conversation flowing, seconded by the efforts of the two ladies, a number of awkward silences punctuated the clink of crystal and the scraping of silverware. Sheffield hardly spoke a word, responding to the questions from both his uncle and his sisters-in-law with little more than monosyllabic replies. It was to everyone's relief when Chittenden finally pushed back his chair and suggested the gentlemen forego the ritual of port and cigars at the table so that they might all retire to the drawing room to take their coffee.

The earl cleared his throat after the cups were passed around, signaling that he was at last ready to discuss why he had gathered them together. "I believe you are all familiar enough with family history to know that my wife's mother, your grandmother, had a younger sister," he began, fixing all three Sheffield males with a pointed look. "This sister fell in love with a Russian count attached to their embassy here in London. They married, and when he was posted home, she naturally returned with him."

"Yes, yes," grumbled the marquess. "We have all heard stories of our great-aunt and her adventures in that cursed land of ice and bears. Interesting perhaps, but I don't see what it has to do—"

"Perhaps if you allowed Uncle to finish we would find out." Sheffield regarded his eldest brother through the amber contents of his brandy glass. He alone had chosen to remain standing, and as he leaned nonchalantly against the carved mantel his eyes found the spot on the intricate acanthus molding where he had once carved away a scroll of leaf with a new jackknife. "But then you always think you know it all, don't you, William?"

The marquess opened his mouth to reply but was waved to silence by his uncle. "Might you try not to act as if you were six instead of thirty-six, William?"

The marquess clamped his jaw shut.

"And Alex, at twenty-nine you are no mere boy any-more either. I ask that you not try to intentionally pro-voke your brother."

Sheffield lowered his eyes and took a long swallow of brandy.

"Well, then, as I was saying, your great-aunt went to live in Russia. Though she never returned for a visit, her son Nicholas spent a year at Oxford when . . . Jack was there."

"I remember him," interjected Alston. "Jack brought him down one weekend to visit. You were at Eton, Alex, so you didn't meet him, and, William, you were away shooting at a friend's estate in Scotland. He was a nice chap."

"Yes, a nice chap. He, too, married an English girl—Lord Brougham's youngest daughter—before returning home." He paused and let out a heavy sigh. "I received some bad news a week ago. Nicholas was killed in a skirmish near the Polish border some months ago."

"A pity," murmured Alston.

"Aye," agreed his uncle. "But that is not the worst of it." He removed a letter from his coat pocket. "This arrived on its heels. It is a letter from Nicholas's wife, and it contains some very disquieting news. It seems she mistrusted her husband's relatives enough to fear for her young son's safety. She appeals to us for help in remov-ing the boy from Russia until he has reached his majority."

The marquess's brow furrowed. "Why does she not bring him here herself?" he asked. "Or appeal to her brother."

"She was quite ill when she wrote this. Apparently an epidemic of influenza swept through their estate. Your great-aunt was among the first to succumb." He stopped to take a swallow of brandy. "I met Brougham yester-day—the countess did not survive either."

There was a rustle of silk as the two ladies shifted uncomfortably on the sofa. The marquess made a slight grimace as he took a swallow of port, while Alston stared into the dregs in his coffee cup. Only Sheffield showed no change in expression, but his eyes remained locked on his uncle's grim visage.

"So the sole survivor of that branch of the family is their only son, Nicholas's namesake. A boy the age of twelve."

"I am sure we all agree that it is a terrible pity," remarked Killingworth. He tugged at a corner of his immaculate cravat. "But surely the concern is more Brougham's than ours. After all, he is her brother."

"The new Lord Brougham will not bother to lift a finger. He is an indolent fool, caring only for cards, claret, and whatever willing female will tumble into his bed," snapped the earl.

Alston darted an involuntary look at his younger brother.

"What is it you are suggesting, Uncle Ivor?" asked Sheffield softly. "That we should take responsibility for the boy?"

"His mother and grandmother were English, and he is of Sheffield blood. He belongs here, with his family, so that we may care for him and see to it he may live to take up his rightful inheritance."

"It's impossible," said the marquess. "Why, even if we agreed that it was our duty to help, it can't be done. Haven't you seen the newspapers these last few days? Napoleon is cutting a swath through Austria, and many here are sure he means to march on Russia as well. The country will be in chaos. By the time we could hire someone willing to brave the risks, it would be much too late. Besides, who would be mad enough to undertake such a dangerous task, no matter how much money is offered?"

"Actually, I wasn't going to suggest we hire someone, William."

The marquess was speechless for a moment. "You can't mean, that . . . that you want *us* . . ." he sputtered.

Sheffield looked faintly amused.

"That's precisely what I meant, though 'us' is rather broader than I had in mind." He turned to his youngest nephew. "Actually, it is *you* I planned to ask, Alex."

There were several murmurs of shock. Ignoring them, the earl went on. "You have always shown a gift for languages, and I happen to know that you picked up a working knowledge of Russian from the mathematics professor who spent a term at Oxford. Why, your tutor at Merton—"

"Alex was sent down from Oxford," barked the marquess. "In disgrace. In case you had forgotten."

"You certainly haven't," countered his uncle, and the marquess had the grace to color slightly. Turning back to Sheffield, Chittenden went on. "Your tutor felt you were one of the brightest students he had ever taught."

Sheffield picked at a thread on his jacket cuff. "As William says, that was in the past. Long in the past."

The earl fixed him with a penetrating look, one that mingled both exasperation and sympathy. Under such scrutiny, it was Sheffield who finally looked away.

"What on earth made you think I might agree to such a proposal?" he asked softly. His usual cynicism quickly reasserted itself, and he gave a curt laugh. "Obviously it would solve a great number of problems—William would be free of the burden of my quarterly allowance, and the rest of you would no longer have to fret about what blot will fall next on the family name."

"I thought you might say yes because I remember a young man who had just the sort of pluck and resourcefulness to bring off something like this."

"That man died ten years ago," said Sheffield harshly.

"Did he?" answered the earl quietly. "My memory must be getting addled in my old age—I thought only Jack died."

Sheffield gulped the remaining contents of his glass and thumped it down on the mantel hard enough to set several of the silver candlesticks to wobbling.

"It's not fair to ask—" began Alston.

"It's much too great a risk—" blurted out Olivia at the same time.

Their voices were overridden by the marquess's own protest. "You must be mad, Uncle Ivor. To think that Alex"—he hesitated a fraction, his gaze raking over his youngest brother—"could be counted on to act responsibly. The first whiff of vodka or flounce of a skirt and he'd forget all about our young cousin. Pluck and resourcefulness you say? More like recklessness. God knows, this family is aware that he has more than enough of *those* qualities!"

A muscle twitched on Sheffield's rigid face, and he paled slightly.

Thomas reached out a hand to restrain any further words. "That's enough, William."

"Yes—I have never understood why you all blame Alex for—"

"I don't need you to fight my battles, Augusta," said Sheffield coldly. "Neither do I need your pity."

His sister-in-law fell into a wounded silence.

"Naturally I'm overwhelmed by your confidence in my abilities, dear brother," continued Alex, his tone changing to one of obvious sarcasm. "Actually, you should be voicing a hearty encouragement, knowing the chances are good that I would follow Jack to the grave."

"I . . . I have never said I wished such a thing."

Sheffield's lips curled in a mocking smile. "No," he agreed. "You have never said it. You are much too much a gentleman to voice what you really feel."

"For God's sake, none of us would wish for any harm to befall you, Alex. I think you know that," cut in Alston.

"Do I now?" Sheffield walked slowly to the side table and refilled his glass nearly to the brim. Downing it in one swallow, he made a point of filling it again before speaking. "My thanks for such an enjoyable evening *en famille*, but if you will excuse me now, I have a pressing engagement." He made an elaborate show of consulting his pocket watch. "And since I pay by the hour for the favors I receive, I should not like to be even a minute late." A thin smile toyed on his lips at the yelp of outrage from the marquess. "Don't bother getting up, William—I know the way out."

"Think about it, Alex," counseled the earl as his nephew stalked toward the door. "I shall send the late countess's letter and several other documents to your rooms, that you may consider the matter more carefully."

There was no answer but the thunk of the heavy oak falling shut.

A crackle of what sounded like gunshots pierced the frigid air, causing the solitary figure at the railing to start

with alarm. It took a moment for the young lady to
realize that the sounds were not made by any firearms
but by the frozen canvas of the topsails as the crew set
the big merchant ship into motion. She pulled her
shabby cloak even tighter around her willowy form and
watched as the heavy oak hull gathered way and the
bustling dockyards began to recede. The freshening wind
bit through the thick wool, but rather than retreat to the
cramped confines of her tiny cabin, she chose to remain
on deck for a while longer. The prospect of having to
endure the mindless chatter of the embassy secretary's
plump wife for the entire voyage was enough to set her
already unsettled stomach to churning.

Besides, she thought with grim humor, she had better
get used to the cold.

The port-side watch sprung into the rigging nearby
where she stood and scrambled aloft to obey the series
of orders bellowed by the officer on deck. Intrigued by
the strange terms, as incomprehensible as Hindu to her
landlocked ears, the young lady watched with great interest as the men swung out precariously on the yard-
arms and let out another billow of sail.

"Excuse me, miss, but you would be better off below,
out of harm's way."

Though the officer's voice was polite enough, the
meaning was clear. For a moment she was tempted to
ignore the veiled order, but thought better of setting
herself at odds with those in command so soon. With a
last look at the winking lights of the Isle of the Dogs,
with London a mere haze behind it, she made her way
across the rolling deck to the main hatchway.

Below deck, the combination of murky darkness and
fetid air caused the bile to rise in her throat. With lurching steps she managed to locate her cabin and stumble
to her narrow berth.

"Don't worry, dearie, you'll soon get used to it," came
a shrill voice, more irritating for its grating cheerfulness.
"Most everyone is dreadfully sick for the first few days,
though I must confess I seem to have been blessed with
a strong stomach. You'll recover—unless you are one of
those unfortunate few who never find their sea legs and
remain miserable for the entire journey. Why, I traveled

to India with Joseph in the spring of 'ninety-five, and let me assure you, *that* was a voyage to remember. . . ." Mrs. Phillips launched into what promised to be an interminable account of the trials of shipboard life.

Miserable? Ha, that was an understatement, thought Miss Octavia Hadley as her insides gave yet another heave. It was a good thing she had more than enough practice in letting wave after wave of whinings or complaints wash over her with as little effect as the salty chop was having against the thick wooden hull of their vessel.

As Mrs. Phillips droned on, Octavia couldn't help thinking back over the last half year. It was too bad that neither her father nor herself had ever given much thought to what would become of her when he was gone. Oh, she had known he was by no means a wealthy man, but she had never comprehended the true state of his finances. Once the innumerable creditors had been paid off with the proceeds of the sale of their snug cottage, there was scarcely enough for an outside passage on the mail coach to London.

Dear Papa, she thought, blinking back a tear. A more interesting or kindly companion she could not have asked for. She might, however, have wished for a tad more concern for the real world rather than that of the ancients. Greek and Latin—along with a host of other languages—were all very well, but she would have gladly traded the lot of them for a roof of her own and a modest stipend for bread and books.

That the only relative willing to offer her a place turned out to be an ill-tempered cousin looking to save a few pounds a year by not having to hire a nanny was bad enough. It was her cousin's husband who had proved intolerable. The memory of his groping hands in the shadows of the nursery corridor was enough to bring on a fresh wave of nausea. At least, she thought with a grim smile, she had had the satisfaction of seeing his corpulent face twist in agony as her knee had smacked into his groin.

She must remember to thank her old childhood friend Johnnie Ferguson for that interesting bit of advice on how to deal with an aggressive male.

It was not to be expected that the odious man would

take rejection in stride, but even she hadn't anticipated the depths of his malice. Manipulated by his slanderous lies, her cousin had fallen into a fit of near hysteria, calling Octavia an ungrateful slut—and worse—for trying to seduce her noble husband. She had been all for tossing Octavia and her meager possessions onto the street without further ado. However, her husband, a smirk of virtuous honor on his face, had argued that such a course of action would hardly be a Christian thing to do.

He had gone on to say that while it was impossible for Octavia to remain under their roof, he had taken it upon himself to find an appropriate position for her— one that would not offer her the temptation of such scandalous transgression. He had heard word that the deputy minister at the embassy in Moscow was in desperate need of an English governess for his ward, the third such female in as many months having fled for home.

Octavia was lucky, he added with a barely suppressed chortle. The man and his wife couldn't afford to be choosy. There was no doubt she would be acceptable, especially as she spoke a few words of the heathen language.

"Russia?" she had blurted out.

A nasty smile had spread over his face. "Yes, Russia."

In the end, she really had little choice. It was that or the streets. She was not so naive as to not know what that would mean.

So here she was on a merchant ship bound for the Baltic Sea. Her friends at the Historical Society had been aghast when she had given them the news of her imminent departure. Why, it was a land of barbarians, one of them had exclaimed.

Well, they certainly couldn't be more barbaric than her own relatives.

Besides, she had always had a spark of adventure in her, and found the idea of exotic travel intriguing. The experience should prove immensely interesting. That is, provided she survived the journey.

"MISS Hadley!" Mrs. Phillips had raised her voice to a level where it finally cut through Octavia's reverie.

"Sorry," she murmured. "I really am feeling a bit under the weather."

"I *said*, shall we repair to the main salon for supper?"

"I believe you had better go on without me," answered Octavia.

"Very well. But you had best try to keep up your strength. You never know what trials may await you in such a foreign land."

"He did *what*?" demanded Alston, nearly spilling the contents of his glass over his burgundy-and-gray-striped waistcoat.

"He embarked not an hour ago," replied the earl. "I just received the note he sent around with his man . . . Squid."

Killingworth frowned. "Can't believe he would actually undertake such a daunting journey, especially when the odds seem so great against any sort of success. Why, Alex hasn't made an effort to do aught but engage in one scandalous escapade after another. Deep play, indiscreet dalliances, the duel with Lord Eversham over that piece of mus—" His eyes strayed to where his wife and sister-in-law where seated by the fire, and he awkwardly cleared his throat. "It seems he deliberately behaves in a reckless manner, one that is designed to bring scorn on himself and his family. That he would put himself in danger for a child he has never even met—"

Chittenden fixed his eldest nephew with a withering look. "Put himself in danger? Good Lord, William, what do you think he has been doing for the past ten years? Are you so willfully blind that you fail to see that all of his actions are nothing but a tempting of fate to deal him the same hand as Jack?"

The marquess shifted uncomfortably in his chair. "It is regrettable that Alex is tormented by guilt. But if he hadn't been so damnably irresponsible that day, Jack would still be here," he said, a note of defensiveness creeping into his voice.

The crystal glass came down on the polished walnut desk with a thump that set the candelabra to teetering.

"Perhaps it is time to put that gross misconception to rest once and for all."

There was utter silence, save for the crackle of flames reducing the logs to ashes. "W-what do you mean?"

"That if guilt must fall on anyone, Jack is the one who should bear the burden of it. It was *he*, and not Alex, who was completely cupshot that day!"

Killingworth paled. "But Father was adamant about the fact that—"

"That Jack, as the Killingworth heir, could not possibly be fallible?" Chittenden had moderated his tone somewhat, but an edge of irony still shaded his words. "Yes, we are all aware of your father's pride in the noble lineage of the Sheffield family. Heaven forbid that the future marquess might be revealed as anything less than a paragon of perfection. And so, to keep his precious illusions alive, he convinced himself the blame lay with Alex. The real tragedy was that he succeeded in losing two sons instead of one."

A collective gasp sounded from the ladies while Alston turned as pale as his ecru cravat.

"What you suggest is . . . a monstrous injustice."

"Nonetheless, it is true. The accounts of the various fishermen who saw them set off all say the same thing. Jack had been drinking for hours, and it was *he* who persuaded Alex to take out the boat, even though he had been warned that a nasty storm was kicking up." The earl gave a mournful sigh. "Like all of you, Alex idolized his oldest brother, and the invitation to have a sail with him—just the two of them—was no doubt too special to turn down, despite the portent of bad weather. Think on it—you know Alex was a quiet, serious lad, who always preferred a book to a bottle of spirits. Does it make any sense that he would have been the one to suggest such an excursion that afternoon? It was Jack who should have known better!" His lips compressed in a tight line. "I always felt your father was terribly unjust in his actions after the accident. Now that you are head of the family, William, I had hoped you might discover the truth for yourself and show more compassion."

The marquess started to speak, but his uncle cut him off.

"No, wait! I haven't finished. Have you any idea the living hell your brother has endured? When the sail blew out and the boat capsized, Alex managed to catch hold of Jack's hand. As wave after wave swept over them, it was your supposedly reckless youngest brother who clung to the hull while seeking to keep Jack from being pulled under. Alex kept begging him to hold on, but Jack finally just . . . let go. As he slipped beneath the waves, he called out one last time, a plea for his brother to save him." Chittenden took a long draught of his brandy and stared into the fire. "Tell me, how would you like to face those dreams each night?" he asked quietly.

Killingworth's face was now ghostlike in its pallor. "Father never told us any of this. He insisted the blame lay with Alex. You know how Father was—no Sheffield was to make a mistake. They were not to be tolerated. Or forgiven."

"What your father could not forgive was that his eldest son, the one he had groomed so carefully to be his successor, perished rather than the youngest."

The marquess's hand passed over his brow. "How . . . How do you know what really happened?"

"It seems I was the only one of the family who ever asked Alex what really happened. In the first few days after the accident, he needed desperately to speak of it. God knows, he blamed himself enough for Jack's death—he didn't need all of you to do so as well. But your father never understood that. When he began to treat Alex as little more than a murderer, well, something inside him *did* die. From then on, he refused to ever talk about it." The earl got up to refill his brandy. "Did you never question why he turned from a scholarly young man into a wild rakehell?"

"It puzzled me," admitted Killingworth. "But I assumed he had got in with the wrong crowd at Oxford and had simply . . . changed."

Alston let out a heavy sigh as he darted a guilty look at his wife. His mouth crooked in a rueful grimace. "You have always felt that we have been too harsh on Alex. It seems you and your female intuition were right after all." He turned back to his uncle. "Why did not you tell us this sooner, so that we might have tried to make some sort of amends?"

"While your father was alive, it was not my place to do so." Chittenden's gaze shifted to the eldest Sheffield. "But you are head of the family now, William, and may set your own standards for the Sheffield family."

There was another long silence. "If I have appeared overly harsh to you—all of you—mayhap it is because I . . . I did not wish to appear unworthy of the position. I never expected to take Father's place, you know."

"Don't confuse being human with being weak, William. I have always thought you a man of good judgment and good character. Trust in your own instincts, rather than trying to emulate the actions of another." The earl gave a gruff smile. "In all honesty, I think you will be a much more admirable marquess than your father."

Killingworth bowed his head. "What the devil can I do? That is, if it is not too late to reach out to Alex."

Chittenden finished his brandy and stared for some time into the empty glass. "At the moment, I am not sure there is a cursed thing any of us might do that would make a difference. We can only pray that in setting out to save young Nicholas, Alex might also be starting a new chapter in his own life. One that will lead to something more than drunkenness and despair."

Chapter Two

*T*he wind was picking up. Off in the distance, one of the
Royal Navy frigates accompanying the small convoy of
merchantmen pitched in and out of view as the leaden
waves grew ever larger. There was the clatter of feet on
the deck as the watch was called out to take in another
reef in the sails. Overhead, the sky was nearly as dark as
the icy water, an ominous sign of the approaching storm.

Octavia clung to the railing, half hidden by the mizzen
mast, hoping to go unnoticed by the grim lieutenant su-
pervising the crew's efforts. Despite the steep roll of the
deck and swirls of salt spray that threatened to soak her
cloak, she was loath to go below. The rattle of the spars
was infinitely more welcome than the rattle of Mrs. Phillips prosing on about her experiences in savage lands,
and the buffeting gusts, though chill on her cheeks, felt
invigorating after the stale air in her cabin.

Her hopes, however, were short-lived. A sailor in the
rigging above her let slip one of the clew lines, drawing
the attention of the officer of the watch. After giving the
man a blistering set down, his eyes fell to Octavia. "You
there," he snapped. "All passengers must go below.
Can't you see a storm is brewing?"

Octavia bit off a tart reply. What a stupid question!
Of course her eyes were no less keen than his. Why was
it that men assumed a female's sensory capacities, as
well as their mental acumen, were so inferior to theirs?
She gave a sigh as she swept a windblown lock of hair
away from her eyes. It should come as no surprise, she
reminded herself, given that most of those of the opposite sex were so smugly sure of their own superiority in
every regard—unwarranted in most cases, to be sure!

Seeing that the man was about to bark again, she gathered her flapping cloak close around her and retreated
toward the mizzen hatchway. The ship gave a sudden
lurch, causing her foot to slip on the steep wooden ladder. An instant later, another twist and roll nearly sent
her headfirst into the murky darkness below. She tightened her grip and felt for the next rung.

It was clear the force of the bad weather was now full
upon them. Octavia managed to make the rest of the
descent without further mishap. Her fingers kept hold of
the ladder as she steadied her footing and peered down the
narrow passageway. It was almost pitch-black, and the
violent motion of the ship made it even more difficult
to see much of anything. However, she was sure the way
to her cabin lay ahead and to the right.

She ventured several steps forward, only to be tossed
against one of the stout oak timbers. Repressing a most
unladylike word, she rubbed her bruised shoulder and
started off again, this time keeping her body pressed up
against the rough wood. Her progress became steadier,
and as she descended another set of narrow steps, she
felt she was nearly there.

Suddenly, the ship yawed nearly on its side. Octavia
was flung across the passageway, but instead of crashing
into another beam, she found herself up against something equally as solid, but a bit more yielding.

"Well, well, what have we here?" came a slurred voice.

To her dismay, Octavia discovered that her nose—and
a good deal of the rest of her anatomy—was buried in
the rough wool of a man's coat. An arm groped its way
around her waist and pulled her even closer.

"Why, it's a female," continued the soft drawl. "And
a rather shapely one at that." The man's feet moved
unsteadily with the next buck of the hull, causing the
bottle in his other hand to thump into the cross beam.
"Perhaps you would care to join me in a little toast to
weathering this blow. I'm sure we could also . . . come
up with some interesting ways to keep each other warm
in this cursed cold."

A binnacled oil lamp up ahead cast just enough light
for Octavia to make out the lean jaw, straight nose, and
full lips of the face before her. Lips that were slowly curl-

ing into a suggestive smile. He was tall enough that he had
to stoop quite low to avoid hitting his head, causing a
tangle of long raven locks to fall over his bleary eyes.
They were blue, she noted, despite the tumble of curls. An
unusual blue, somewhere between cerulean and slate.

"Let me go at once, sir!" she demanded as she struggled to free herself from his grasp.

His arm only tightened its hold. "I assure you, it would
be a most pleasant way to forget about the storm outside."
The hull rocked wildly once more. "We could . . . make
our own waves."

What gall! How the devil did he presume to know
what she would find pleasureable? As she opened her
mouth to tell him just that, his mouth brushed against
hers and she felt his hand begin to rove lower.

That settled it. Since words were having very little effect in discouraging his amorous attentions, she decided
she would have to resort to a more convincing way of
saying no.

Her knee came up hard in his groin. Very hard.

The bottle fell from his hand and rolled away. With a
sharp intake of breath, the man sunk to his knees, then
toppled forward and rolled into a fetal position. A low
moan escaped his lips—which, she noted in grim satisfaction, were no longer curled in a smug smile.

Her rather limited experience in such evasive action
had taught her now was the time to take to her heels.
As soon as the man recovered, he was likely to be in
quite an ill humor. Unfortunately, the ship took a steep
plunge. Octavia lost her footing, and both she and the
other body slid down the pitched planking, coming up
hard against the latched door of the storeroom.

She began struggling with her tangled skirts, desperate
to be out of the man's reach by the time he was able to
move again. However, another sound from his lips
brought her up short. She couldn't quite believe her ears.

Why, it appeared he was *laughing*.

"Good Lord, where did you ever learn *that*?" he managed to gasp.

Octavia sat up on her knees. "From a friend," she
replied warily. "I was told it was the most effective way
to discourage a man's attention."

"Oh, most effective," he agreed. He slowly propped himself up against the closed door and wedged his long legs against the other side of the bulkhead to keep from being thrown about any more. Octavia couldn't help but acknowledge that it was a handsome face, despite the sallow skin and fine lines etched at the corners of the mouth. Such hints at dissolute habits were at odds with the flash of lively intelligence in those piercing blue eyes, a light evident despite the haze of alcohol. "I suppose it is a good thing I am a youngest son and need not worry about begetting an heir."

A flush of color rose to Octavia's cheeks. "That, sir, is a *most* ungentlemanly remark."

He chuckled. "And your action, my dear lady, was a *most* unsporting blow."

"I didn't realize it was a sport to accost innocent females," she countered.

The grin disappeared. "To some perhaps, but not to me. Believe me, I am not in the habit of forcing myself on a lady, no matter how deeply foxed. Allow me to apologize."

She could hardly believe her ears. "You are not angry?"

"I imagine I got what I deserved." He regarded her in silence for a moment. "Though I must admit it came as a bit of a shock. You have a good deal of, er, spirit, Miss—"

She ignored the pointed hint for her name. "A shock? By that do you mean you are not in the habit of being told no?"

The seductive smile reappeared. "No, indeed I am not."

Arrogant coxcomb!

"Allow me to offer you one bit of advice, however," he continued. "Most men will become, er, rather enraged at that little trick. You had best be as far away as possible in the short time you have."

"I'm well aware of that," she snapped. "I slipped. The other time—"

"The other time! Are you in the habit of trying to make a choirboy out of every man you meet?"

Octavia looked at him in some confusion.

"Never mind," he muttered. "And what happened on that occasion?"

Her mouth quirked upward. "I am on a ship bound for Russia; *that* is what happened, sir."

His brow furrowed. "How could he force such a thing?"

"I don't wish to discuss it, especially with a stranger," she said curtly. "As if you aren't acquainted with the way men may force what they wish upon females." His simple inquiry, however, had suddenly stirred up all the anger of the last few months that was pent up inside her. Giving vent to her feelings, she went on. "Really, what an incredibly stupid question. Are all of you men so thick that you don't see what little choice a female has in life? What rights do I have? I can own no property; I have no voice in what laws govern me; I can seek no interesting employment. And," she added for good measure, "if I were leg shackled it would be even worse!"

He looked at her with interest. "Ah, a sympathizer with the ideas of Mrs. Wollstonecraft, no doubt."

"What halfway intelligent female wouldn't be? There are any number of sensible ideas in her writings." As she spoke, it struck her that, given the circumstances, this was turning into a most peculiar conversation.

"You have an interesting point. Have you considered—"

At that moment, a monstrous wave crashed into the side of the ship, sending a strong tremor through the oaken timbers. The man winced, and his gaze searched wildly for his lost bottle. "The devil take it! My brandy," he croaked thickly. "Where's my brandy?"

Octavia was about to answer with a scathing reply when she caught sight of the rigid set of his jaw and the haunted look that had suddenly dulled the unusual blue of his eyes. Another shudder of the hull caused those eyes to squeeze tightly shut, as if in anticipation of a physical blow.

It was the storm, she realized with a start. Its effect on him was so palpable she could almost feel the tension stiffening his rigid limbs. In the flickering shadows she saw him blink once more, and in that instant, a wrenching look of raw need replaced the studied nonchalance of a hardened wastrel. Then the shadows moved once again, casting the plane of his chiseled profile in darkness.

She sensed the fleeting emotion she had just witnessed had nothing to do with physical fear. No, something infinitely more complex than that had suddenly made him seem very vulnerable and very alone. For some reason, she felt a twinge of sympathy in her breast.

"This storm is truly upsetting you, is it not?"

Another resounding crash tore a wild oath from his lips. The lamp swung wildly, then went out, leaving them in pitch-blackness.

"Sir, let me help you to your cabin. Perhaps you would feel better there." Octavia felt her way over to him and touched his arm.

He gave a low groan and clutched at the collar of his coat. "For God's sake, don't let go of me," he said thickly.

Octavia wedged herself in beside him and slipped her arm around his shoulders. "Very well, I won't let go." His head fell against her breast. Through the thick wool of her coat she could feel the racing of his pulse and hear the raggedness of his breathing. Her hand came up, threading lightly through the tangled locks, brushing them off his forehead. Beads of sweat clung to his temples, despite the chill air. "It will pass," she whispered.

He made some incoherent mutter in return, stirring in some agitation, but only to settle himself closer. One of his legs came over hers while his arms crept back around her waist. If anyone were to come along and see such a scandalous sight . . . She was thankful that the lamp had been doused and that the only sound of movement was the muffled tramping on the deck above.

Octavia had no idea how long she sat in such a compromising position, but her presence seemed to bring a modicum of comfort to her companion, so she made no effort to move. Neither did she attempt to converse. Only when the force of the storm gave signs of abating did she give a gentle shake to the man's shoulder. "Sir, I believe the worst is over. We cannot sit here all night, you know. You must get up and let me help you to your cabin."

Her words finally seemed to roust him from his stupor. He groped for a handhold and slowly pulled himself to his feet, her arm still steadying his progress.

"Which way?" she demanded.

"I . . . I'm not sure," came the vague reply.

"Well, *think*!"

He swayed slightly. "Ah . . . left."

"Then move, sir! I cannot carry you there."

He stumbled forward, leaning heavily on Octavia's shoulder. Somehow, she kept him upright, despite the constant pitch and roll.

"It's this one," he said, a bit uncertainly as he lurched to a stop before one of the tiny cabins. "At least, I think it is."

She opened the door a crack, praying that he was right. The last thing she needed was to be observed with a thoroughly foxed man hanging around her neck. Thankfully, the tiny space was indeed empty. She shoved him inside, then quickly followed and pulled the door shut behind them. Only then did it occur to her that matters would be even worse if she was seen leaving his cabin.

"Oh, damnation," she muttered to herself. At least it was dark in the narrow passageway so the chances of being caught were slim. In any case, there was little to do about it now. "Will you be all right? Do you need some assistance in removing your coat?"

He appeared to have regained control of his emotions, for the half-mocking, sensuous smile had returned. "It is a tempting offer, my dear, but I do not relish another encounter with a certain part of your anatomy." He grabbed hold of the side of his narrow berth to steady himself. "However, there are *other* parts I would dearly love to feel," he couldn't resist adding.

Her face flamed. "Let me out of here."

He made no attempt to stop her. "Before you go, would you be so kind as to pass me a bottle of brandy from the chest behind you?"

"I think you've had enough."

"The hell I have," he said softly.

She hesitated for a moment, then handed him the spirits with an exaggerated shrug of her shoulders. "Go

ahead, then, drown whatever it is that you are running
from—and yourself along with it. Good night, sir."

Whether it was the lurch of the ship or his own willful
steps, his broad chest was suddenly between her and the
door. "Good night, miss," he murmured, his head bending closer to hers. "And . . . thank you."

Octavia swallowed hard. "Sir, I warn you, I'll not
stand for any more of your nonsense. If you try to kiss
me again—"

There was a low rumble of amusement in his throat.
"Kiss you? That was not a kiss back there, my dear.
This is a kiss."

His lips came down on hers, firm but gentle, sending
both shivers and sparks down her spine. They parted,
and his tongue brushed against her own tightly shut
mouth, urging her to open to him. She made to protest,
but no words came forth as he slid inside her. He tasted
of fiery brandy and the salty tang of the sea. It was like
nothing she had ever imagined—and certainly nothing
like the fumbling advances of her cousin. For a moment
she found herself responding to the heat of his embrace.
She melted into his chest and tilted her head back,
allowing him to deepen the embrace, if only for a brief
instant.

Suddenly, she came to her senses and pushed away
from him with a small cry of outrage. "How *dare* you—"

"I warned you that you might enjoy it," he murmured
with a roguish grin.

Octavia pushed past him and flung open the door,
heedless of who might see her.

"Conceited rake," she muttered under her breath as
she hurried toward her own cabin. "Why, he is nothing
but a drunken lout. And a most ill-mannered one at
that!" How in heavens had she been gulled into thinking
he had any need of her sympathy? she wondered angrily,
though in truth she was not sure with whom she was
more upset—her accoster or herself.

The sun was bright, even though it rose no more than
thirty degrees above the horizon at the noon hour. They
had tacked into the Gulf of Finland that morning and

were in the final leg of their journey. The Baltic waters were as blue as the sky, and just as calm. A brisk wind had the ship running under full sail, its hull leaving a foaming wake as it raced along at eight knots. Octavia watched the gulls circling overhead, feeling just a slight pang of envy at their total freedom. She couldn't help wondering just what it would be like to be able to chart one's course in life, to have choices. . . . A movement near the galley caught her eye and brought her thoughts back down to earth.

Well, at least one choice she had was to avoid the odious Mr. Sheffield!

That was his name, she had learned. But since that initial meeting during the storm, she had taken great pains to stay out of his presence, no easy task given the cramped quarters of the ship. There was no way to get around his company at mealtimes, but she had studiously refrained from any more than the barest conversation that civility allowed. At least he had shown a modicum of tact by not forcing his attentions upon her, or making any sort of reference to the fact that they were acquainted with each other. On being formally introduced, he had kept his expression a mask of bland politeness. But as he bowed over her hand, the rogue had actually winked at her!

And he kept following her around, popping up at the most inopportune moments, like these, when she was alone and looking forward to some quiet time for reflection. On any number of occasions she had been forced to be rather rude, but he didn't seem to take the hint.

Drat the man.

She looked aft, with the thought of slipping up toward the quarterdeck, only to see her retreat cut off by the formidable bulk of Mrs. Phillips. *Good Lord, was nothing to go right this afternoon?*

"Ah, Miss Hadley, a lovely afternoon, isn't it?" exclaimed her cabin mate.

It *was,* she thought.

"Indeed it is." Sheffield leaned nonchalantly against the rail and fixed both ladies with a brilliant smile. He seemed to repress a chuckle at the scowl his approach brought to Octavia's face. "We look to have clear weather for the rest of our journey to St. Petersburg."

"I'm sure that is a *great* relief to some," replied Octavia a bit acidly.

"Yes, I imagine there are those who take great exception to being *tossed* and *tumbled* around."

She looked at him with narrowed eyes, and the man had the nerve to wink again.

"Oh, I couldn't agree with you more, Mr. Sheffield," said Mrs. Phillips. "Storms are most uncomfortable things." She paused to readjust her bonnet. "Sheffield, Sheffield. Tell me, you are not by any chance related to the Marquess of Killingworth?"

He raised one dark eyebrow. "Madam, do you imagine I would be on a ship bound for the wilds of Russia if I were?"

She gave a titter. "How silly of me. Why *are* you on your way to Russia, if I might be so bold as to inquire?"

Bold? Ha! Brazen was more like it, thought Octavia to herself. The lady had done nothing but try to pump information out of anyone she could corner. However, for once it might be interesting to hear the results. She, too, had wondered just what brought the man on board.

That he was no fine gentleman was evident. His clothes were presentable enough, but little things gave away the state of the owner's purse. The cuffs of his jacket were slightly frayed, and the elbows showed a bit of shine from long use. His shirt collar had already been turned, and the polish on his boots could not hide the fact that they had seen better days. Her mouth quirked slightly. Oh yes, she recognized the signs of economy quite well. Mr. Sheffield was no more plump in the pocket than she was.

And remembering his roving hands and lips, she had other reason to know he was no true gentleman, even though she had to admit such behavior was hardly a reliable measure as to one's breeding these days.

Her thoughts were interrrupted by Sheffield's reply. "I have been engaged as a tutor, ma'am."

Octavia gave a snort, which she disguised as a cough.

What in heaven's name was *he* going to teach a young man—drinking, cards, and wenching?

He seemed to read her thoughts, and a faint smile came to his lips. "I have some proficiency in languages and mathemetics," he continued. "Among other things."

She couldn't believe it! Another wink! *The man was insufferable.*

"Why, what a coincidence!" exclaimed Mrs. Phillips. "Miss Hadley is engaged as a governess, aren't you my dear?"

Octavia muttered an assent through clenched teeth.

"Yes, she is to see to the ward of one of our deputy ministers. An excellent man. My husband knows him well."

"You will no doubt find St. Petersburg a fascinating city. The French architect—"

"Oh, Miss Hadley will not be living in St. Petersburg. She is going to Moscow."

Why didn't the woman give him her bust measurements and the color of her garters while she was at it?

Sheffield's brow puckered. "Moscow?" He slanted a glance at her. "Reports have it that Napoleon means to invade Russia shortly, despite his alliance with the czar. Moscow will no doubt be his main target."

"That is hardly any of your concern." She knew it was a churlish reply, but her patience had been sorely stretched.

He accepted the set down with his usual enigmatic smile and a slight incline of his head.

"And you, Mr. Sheffield, where do you go, and for whom are you working?"

The woman truly left no stone unturned. No wonder she had mined such a wealth of gossip and trivia to inflict upon captive ears.

"I am off to some estate with an unpronounceable name, somewhere to the east of Dzerzhinsk."

Octavia had not a clue as to where that was.

"As for my employers, I am to be tutor to the only son of a Russian nobleman and his English wife."

Mrs. Phillips clucked in sympathy. "Oh dear, you must have been rather desperate to take on such a position. It sounds like an awfully daunting prospect."

He merely smiled. "Challenges are what make life interesting. Don't you agree, Miss Hadley?"

Octavia had had quite enough of his company. "If you two will excuse me, I should like to finish the chapter of the book I am reading before supper."

"And I think I shall see if I might find a cup of tea," announced Mrs. Phillips, clearly feeling she had learned as much as she was going to learn.

"Good day, Mrs. Phillips." He made a polite bow to the older lady. "And good day, Miss Hadley. A pleasure conversing with you." There was a twinkle in those cursed blue eyes. "Perhaps, given our mutual interests, we will *run into* each other during the course of our stay in Russia."

Not bloody likely. Not if she had any say in the matter.

Sheffield watched the sway of Octavia's shapely hips as she retreated toward the main hatchway. He was quite aware that certain other parts of her anatomy were just as attractive. Despite being thoroughly cupshot, he had not failed to notice the feel of her firm, rounded breasts crushed against his chest, or the lush softness of that expressive mouth—that is, when it wasn't too occupied hurling some scathing set down at him.

He could hardly blame her. To put it mildly, he had not exactly made the best of first impressions. His lips curled in a rueful grimace as he recalled his appalling behavior. He truly wasn't in the habit of groping unwilling females, especially innocent ones, even in his most intoxicated state. It was the storm. He hadn't been on a boat in ten years, not since that day with Jack. The crash of the first wave had brought a flood of terrible memories. No amount of brandy had been able to drown them out. He didn't know what he would have done if he hadn't been able to touch someone real, someone warm.

She had, however unwittingly, helped keep his personal demons at bay, and for that he was grateful.

Actually, he was more than grateful. He was curious.

If truth be told, she intrigued him. Sweet, biddable chits bored him to tears. He had the distinct feeling that those two adjectives were not ones that would come to mind when speaking of Miss Octavia Hadley. It was clear from his own dealing with her, as well as snatches of other conversations that he had managed to overhear, that she possessed a sharp intellect. Equally clear was the fact that she wasn't afraid to use it. Several pompous merchants had stalked away from an argument with her muttering darkly about damned bluestockings and unnatural females. What they had meant was, she was smarter than they were.

And she had courage and spirit to go along with her brains. Instead of falling into a fit of hysterics at finding herself in the clutches of a very large, very strong, and very drunk stranger, she had not hesitated to defend herself. Quite credibly, he might add.

Brains. Courage. Spirit. Definitely not a good combination for a female who wanted to stay out of trouble. No wonder she had landed herself in the suds. He would dearly love to have heard about just what incident had caused her exile to a mechant ship bound for St. Petersburg. He imagined she did not resort to the knee trick without extreme provocation.

However, not only had he not had a chance to pursue that topic, he had scarely been able to exchange a civil greeting with her this entire week. She had avoided him like the plague. It was a damn shame. He would probably never see her again once the ship dropped anchor, and somehow, the thought affected his spirits more than he cared to admit.

Pushing away from the varnished wood railing, he began to pace the deck. Ah, well, the pursuit of a female, no matter how interesting, was not why he was here. It was time to put her out of his mind.

But he wished her luck. He had a feeling she was going to need it.

Chapter Three

"*M*iss Hadley?"

Octavia looked around the crowded wharf for whoever had called her name. The air was redolent with the scent of pitch from the piles of spruce logs destined for spars for the British Navy. Sacks of grain were stacked hard up against bales of tanned hides and thick pelts of fox and sable. Around her was a crush of people and cultures, the long beards and embroidered robes of the Russian boyars mixing in with the felt boots and smocks of the country serfs and the European dress of the foreigners.

"Miss Hadley! Over here." A young man with a long, thin face raised a gangly arm and waved once again with a birdlike twitter. "I am Mr. Heron. I've been sent by the minister to collect you and your things. Several other members of our mission, due to arrive later this morning on the ship from Stockholm, will be traveling to Moscow with us."

Octavia managed to keep a straight face. *The poor man.* He probably suffered no end of teasing without her also cracking a smile at the joke the fates had played upon him. She returned his wave as he squeezed through a group of burly sailors and stepped with exaggerated care over a crate of live chickens.

"Have your belongings been brought off yet?" he inquired, his hand brushing perspiration across his high forehead. Despite the chill air, there was a sheen of perspiration on his pale skin and a nervous twitch to his left cheek.

Octavia pointed to the lone battered trunk at her feet that held all her worldly possessions.

"Excellent." He breathed a sigh of relief. "I'll send a porter for it right away. Would you mind terribly if I left you alone for just a short time while I fetch the bag of dispatches from London?" He pointed to the sleek Royal Navy corvette that had just dropped anchor in the harbor. Already a gig was being swung out from its davits, with a crew ready to row ashore.

"Of course. I shall be fine."

He bobbed his head in thanks and rushed off, the movement of his long legs conjuring up the unfortunate image of a large bird picking his way through a boggy marsh.

The cacophony of languages was astounding. She could pick out some Russian, along with a smattering of German and English. The rest she could only begin to guess at. Was the improbably tall blond gentleman with shoulders as broad as an ox babbling in Swedish? Perhaps the two merchants haggling over several bolts of silk were screaming at each other in Polish. Or—

Someone jostled her elbow. "Not abandoned already, I trust?"

Octavia turned around at sound of the familiar voice and glared at the speaker. "Must you always be intruding upon my peace?"

His brow came up in amusement. "Peace? Forgive me, slow top that I am, I hadn't realized how conducive this atmosphere is to peaceful contemplation."

She gave a reluctant smile. "I was caught up in just watching everything. I didn't mean to snap at you, Mr. Sheffield. And no, I have not been abandoned. The gentleman from the mission had to collect the diplomatic bag from London and will return shortly."

"Fascinating, is it not?"

"Oh yes!" She didn't trouble to hide her enthusiasm. "I have always wanted to travel."

He eyed her thoughtfully. "Most lone females would be quaking in terror at being in a foreign country, with no family, no friends. Or falling into a swoon."

"I can't afford to quake. I must work for my living," she replied. "Swooning is out, too. I forgot to pack my vinaigrette."

His blue eyes danced with laughter.

in all directions as he surveyed the bustle around him. "Tell me you are joking."

"I'm afraid not."

"Poor fellow. Well, I hope you fly along to Moscow with no trouble." He thrust out his hand. "Shall we cry friends, then, and take our leave from each other with no hard feelings for the past?"

Octavia smiled and accepted it. "Indeed, Mr. Sheffield, let us part as friends. I wish you good luck in your new position."

Instead of releasing her hand, he pulled her hard to his chest and pressed a firm kiss on her surprised lips.

"Mr. Sheffield!" she sputtered, when he allowed her to step back.

"For luck." He grinned and winked, then disappeared among a group of sailors tramping back toward their ship.

Bloody hell. She had quite enough on her mind without being troubled by thoughts of the maddening Mr. Sheffield. Why was it she couldn't seem to banish the picture of those mocking blue eyes and that sensuous smile? Really, she was acting like a schoolroom miss, mooning over some handsome face as if anything could come of it. He was nothing but a scoundrel and a rake. A charming one, but she imagined that sort of man *had* to be, else he wouldn't be successful at seduction or whatever it was scoundrels and rakes did.

She stared out of the window of the lumbering coach as it wound its way through a thick forest of towering spruce and fir. A flock of ravens landed in one of the trees up ahead and filled the air with a raucous cawing. She shivered slightly and pulled her cloak tighter around her shoulders. The sound, like the dark, unfamiliar landscape, was slightly forbidding and caused her to wonder just what lay ahead for her.

Well, whatever the fates had in store, it did not include a penniless tutor given to scandalous behavior, no matter that his stolen kisses aroused in her a certain . . . curiosity. Why, she bet he tossed out his smiles and winks as easily as a boy skipped stones across the water, and with the same careless nonchalance, unmindful of what the ripples might disturb. No doubt he had left a string of brokenhearted maids and governesses in his wake.

She, on the other hand, was much too sensible to give such a man a second thought.

"Miss Hadley?" Mr. Heron coughed hesitantly. "Is something not to your liking? You are not too chilly, or in need of a stop to stretch your legs?"

Octavia started. "Why no, I am quite comfortable, thank you. Why do you ask?"

He swallowed hard. "Well, you seemed to be, er, frowning."

"Was I?" She made a concerted effort to lighten her expression. "Forgive me. I fear I was letting my thoughts stray back to the voyage from London."

"A rough passage?" inquired one of the arrivals from Stockholm, a portly gentleman attached to the office of the secretary.

"Unpredictable," she murmured.

"I quite abhor sea trips," piped up the gentleman's wife. "One is so apt to take ill. Once you have traveled as much as I have, you will realize that the best thing in general is to quickly put any unpleasant occurrances behind you and look only to the future."

Octavia forced a smile. "Very sage advice, ma'am. I shall do my best to heed it."

The conversation turned to talk of Czar Alexander's growing rift with Napoleon, and what the odds were that the French army would march on Russia. Putting aside all thoughts of a certain individual, Octavia joined in the lively discussion, resolved not to allow any such lapse of girlish nonsense to happen again.

Sheffield turned and watched the flappable Mr. Heron lead Octavia away from the docks toward the cluster of carriages waiting along the Nevsky Prospect. The faint taste of her was still on his lips, a honeyed tang that ebbed to bittersweet as it struck him that it was most unlikely he would ever tease her with such outrageous attentions again. His mouth quirked in a slight smile, recalling her shocked expression. It was hard to resist stirring up the sparks in those flashing eyes, perhaps because she laid into him with such spirit, unintimidated to stand up for herself. No biddable young milk-and-water miss was she! He could well imagine how her strong opinions and quick tongue had landed her in trouble. Most men could not abide being challenged—especially by a female.

He, on the other hand, found it intriguing. Their snatches of conversation had hinted at a mind of sharp intelligence and unconventional ideas. There had also been a hint of something else. Beneath the icy mien of disapproval had flared, if only for an instant, a passion that surprised him. She had responded that night in his cabin to his thorough kiss. He hadn't been so far in his cups not to feel the heat course through her as she responded to his embrace. She might speak as if all men could go to the devil, but her body betrayed her.

A most interesting body it was, too. The dowdy gowns, cut high enough to choke a cleric, could not disguise her long legs and willowy curves, while the prim hairstyle did not fully tame a mass of glorious curls the color of wild heather honey. Did she really believe that nonsense she spouted about having little to attract the opposite sex? If so, it was the rare time where he might judge her opinion to be utter fustian. It was a shame there was no further chance to explore the many facets of Miss Hadley—somehow, he felt he would not be disappointed in any respect.

A farmer knocked into Sheffield's leg as he tried to maneuver a barrow loaded with sacks of grain over the rough cobblestones. With a few choice words in Russian, he motioned for the young Englishman to step aside. Sheffield complied, but his reply brought a spasm of surprise to the man's bearded face. His hand came up to tug at his forelock.

"I'm sorry, sir," he mumbled. "I didn't expect you to speak our language."

"Just enough to know when I have been insulted," replied Sheffield with a faint smile.

A quirk of humor pulled at the farmer's lips before

his face regained its stoic mien. "You are far from home?" He paused to cross himself in the Orthodox fashion. "No amount of rubles could tempt me to leave my motherland."

"Every man has his price." Sheffield then gave a small shrug. "I wonder, can you tell a stranger where one might find . . ."

In a matter of minutes, he had managed to learn where he might purchase the sort of clothing he needed, as well as where a gentleman of limited means might procure reasonable lodging. Things were going along as well as he could have hoped for, yet he couldn't help but feel a bit emptier than usual as he turned to embark in earnest on the task of finding his young relative.

By that evening he had exchanged the clothing he had brought from London for an equally modest assortment of Russian essentials that befitted a genteel but impecunious tutor. He sighed as he regarded the streak of dirt on the rough planks of his tiny garret room. The dingy sheets and threadbare blanket looked suspect as well, and he was sure he would be scratching in earnest by morning. Tossing the secondhand carpetbag on the floor, he sat on the rickety bedstead and uncorked the bottle that was hidden in the pocket of his heavy coat.

Good Lord, now that he was here, the enormity of what he had undertaken caused an icy knot to form in his stomach. Did he really expect to travel over such a vast strange country, alone and without any help to fall back on, and manage to locate a twelve-year-old child he had never set eyes on? And if he did accomplish such a daunting journey, what made him think he would be able to convince whoever was looking after the lad—or the lad himself—to let the young count quit his home in the company of an utter stranger?

Sheffield took a long swallow of the clear, fiery liquid. His Uncle Ivor must have been mad to think such a plan could work! As the vodka sought to burn through the tangle of doubt inside, he was sorely tempted to fling his plans to the devil and board the next ship for home.

What had possessed him to take on this challenge? He

was bound to fail, and fail miserably, just as he had at
any meaningful thing in his life. His jaw tightened as he
eyed what was left of his drink. His brother was dead,
his family despised him, and he had spent nearly all of
his adult life engaged in turning cards, bedding other
men's wives, and seeing how many bottles of claret and
brandy he could pour down his throat.

Oh yes, a fine hero he made.

He quickly swallowed the last of the spirits. Not bothering to remove the thick boots he had just purchased,
he fell back on the thin mattress and closed his eyes, the
empty bottle falling to the floor with a loud thump.

It was only the clatter of cart wheels and loud shouts of
the drivers that finally caused Sheffield's lids to pry
open. A faint ray of light from the narrow window fell
across his face, causing him to wince in discomfort. The
iron frame creaked as he shifted slightly.

He felt like hell.

As his hand ran along the stubble on his jaw he had
no doubt that the cracked glass above the shabby chest
of drawers would show that he looked no better. It took
some force of will to disentangle his legs from the
threadbare cover and swing them to the floor. The glint
of glass on the rough pine caught his bleary eyes.

No wonder he felt like the devil. Although, he added
to himself, usually it took more than one bottle to have
this sort of effect. The Russian stuff must be stronger
than French brandy or Jamaican rum, judging by the
cottony feel in his throat and the abominable ache in
his head.

Sheffield wished his valet were here. Squid always
knew just the right concoction for getting him on his
feet. He missed his man's sunny chatter as well, which
never failed to lighten his depressed mood on mornings
such as these. His stomach gave a lurch, as much from
the realizaion that of late, most every morning began
this way as from the pangs of hunger. He couldn't remember the last time he had bothered to eat. With a
grimace, he raked his fingers through his tangled locks
and sought his razor.

A short while later, he stumbled down the narrow
stairs, bag flung over his shoulder, and headed back
down toward the Neva. At a small shop close to the
river he joined a crowd of laborers in purchasing a
steaming cup of tea and a wedge of rye bread spread
with thick plum preserves. The heavily sugared brew
caused a pucker of his lips, but made some inroads in
settling the gnawing feeling inside him. Hunching over
in the wooden chair, he began to nibble at a corner of
the thick slice as he contemplated his next move.
Through the grimy window a sea of masts was visible
above the peaked roofs. It should be no difficult matter
to find the next merchant ship bound for London.

The sweet jam nearly stuck in his throat. What did it
matter that he was slinking back, tail between his legs,
without even trying to accomplish what he had set out
to do? Surely nobody really expected anything else
from him.

He took another swallow of tea.

The trouble was, what did he expect from himself?

Bolting down the rest of the bread, he took up his
belongings and shouldered his way out of the crowded
room. He paused for a moment, watching a straggle of
drunken sailors and thickset laborers make their way
toward the fog misting up the water's edge. But instead
of following them, his steps headed in the other direction, past the narrow canals and pastel buildings shim-
mering in the pale northern light.

Near the outskirts of the city, after numerous inquiries, he found the inn he was looking for. Cursing himself
for a fool, he tossed his bag into the dark interior of a
coach reeking of stale onions and cabbage. With one
glance over his shoulder, he climbed inside.

The cool, appraising stare would have been even more
unnerving had the eyes not been those of a twelve-year-
old. Still, Octavia couldn't help but shift uncomfortably
as she stood before the narrow desk. The young girl laid
down her pen and smoothed the sheet of paper on the
polished wood.

"Are you the latest one?" she inquired.

Octavia nodded. "I am Miss Hadley. And you are Emma?"

The girl's nose wrinkled slightly in disgust. "Who else would I be?" she said, just loud enough for Octavia to hear. "I hope you will display more intelligence than that if I am to be forced to listen to you for hours on end." The tone made no attempt to hide what she thought of governesses in general and the newest one in particular.

Octavia chose to ignore the deliberate rudeness. "May I sit down?"

Emma shrugged her thin shoulders.

Pulling up the only other chair in the attic chamber that had been turned into a makeshift schoolroom, Octavia sat opposite her new charge and cleared her throat. "Do I look to be so easily intimidated?" she asked lightly.

There was no reply as the girl picked up her pen and began to trace elaborate doodles in the margins of her writing.

She tried another tack. "As you say, Emma, we are going to be in each other's company for a good part of the day, so I would hope that we might try to be friends."

"Why bother?" shot back the girl. "You won't be around any longer than the rest."

"What makes you say that?"

Emma didn't look up from her paper. "The others hated being in such a strange place, with such different habits and speech. They said it was a land fit only for heathens or madmen. All they wanted was to go back to their homes and families. You will, too."

Octavia made a wry face. "Well, since I have neither, I rather doubt it."

The scratching of the pen stopped. "Everyone has a family. They *have* to take you, whether they want to or not."

"Not me, I'm afraid. I've already been given the boot by the only relatives I know of. Not that it matters—I wouldn't go back there for all the tea in China."

Emma fidgeted in her chair. "What did you do?" she finally asked, not able to hide her curiosity.

"Ah, let us say that I . . . Well, I had a disagreement with my cousin's husband. A serious one."

The girl thought on that for several moments. "I act disagreeably, but they've nowhere to send me. I guess they aren't allowed to simply turn me out," she said in a small voice.

A glimmer of understanding came to Octavia's eye. "Aren't you happy with your aunt and uncle?"

"They aren't really my aunt and uncle, just distant relatives," she answered quickly. "And they don't want me here. I know they don't."

Octavia made no attempt to foist any hollow platitudes about unconditional familial love on the child. "I know how you feel."

Emma eyed her warily, surprised to be spoken to on such equal terms. "You do?"

"It's not very pleasant." She picked up one of the thick leather-bound volumes that lay on the desk. "Do you enjoy Mrs. Radcliffe's writings?"

The girl's lower lip jutted out in defiance. "My last governess forbade me to touch such books. She said a well-bred young lady does not read such scandalous rubbish."

"What a prosy bore," remarked Octavia. "No wonder you headed straight for the bookshelves."

Emma stared at her in disbelief.

"Have you discovered Miss Austen's work as well? I should think you might enjoy it even more than these Gothic tales. The heroines have infinitely more pluck and common sense, not always expecting some clod of a male to sort things out."

"I . . . I don't think Uncle Albert has any of them on his shelves."

Picturing the stiff bearing and colorless features of both Mr. Renfrew and his wife, Octavia could well imagine that was true. "No matter. I believe I have a copy of *Sense and Sensibility* in my trunk. But for now, perhaps you will acquaint me with what sort of subjects you have been studying."

There was only a brief hesitation before Emma reached for the pile of notebooks on one side of the desk. "In history, I have been learning about the reign of Elizabeth. . . ."

The conversation was nearly as bland as the overcooked joint of meat. Octavia took a small swallow of wine and tried to think of yet another innocuous remark to make about the state of the weather or the color of the draperies. An earlier try at discussing current events had been squelched by a disapproving glance from the head of the table.

"That is not a subject you ladies should trouble yourselves with," announced Mr. Renfrew. "Rest assured the proper people are dealing with such important matters. The complex issues would merely serve to confuse or upset you. Don't you agree, Mrs. Renfrew?"

His wife nodded a vigorous assent.

Ha! thought Octavia. As if men hadn't been making a dreadful hash of things for the past decade and more. But she let the matter drop without argument. Given the circumstances, she really couldn't afford any slip of the tongue. She needed this job. And so she forced a smile and poked at the unappetizing morsels on her plate.

It was with great relief that she watched the stout housekeeper bustle in to clear the table and serve the pudding. Surely the interminable meal could not last a good deal longer. There was some solace in knowing it was not an ordeal that would have to be endured nightly. The lady of the house had already informed her that after being honored with an invitation to dine at their table this evening, her first in the household, she would be expected to take her meals with the rest of the help. Mrs. Renfrew had ended her lecture with a tight smile. That was how a proper English house was run, so it wouldn't do to relax the rules, she explained. Didn't Miss Hadley agree that order and discipline were what made life run smoothly?

Octavia found herself gripping her wineglass with nearly enough force to snap the stem. It was not hard to imagine what sort of life it was for a orphaned child in these surroundings—

"So, Miss Hadley, you have met your charge. What think you of your ability to keep the young person in control?" Mr. Renfrew smoothed a wrinkled hand over his severely cropped silver hair. "Be assured that you need not fear being thought too strict. The child has an unfortunate tendency toward willfulness that must be dealt with. We do not wish to spoil her."

Octavia bit back the urge to tell him that her trunk of whips and chains seemed to have gone astray during the voyage from England. "Oh, I daresay I shall be up to the challenge," she answered, striving to keep her tone neutral.

Husband and wife exchanged relieved looks. "Well, then, we will leave you to your duties, Miss Hadley. If there is anything you require, you may inform Mrs. Renfrew." He turned his attention to the thin slice of apple tart set before him, finishing it off in dead silence. Then his chair scraped back, signaling an end to the meal. "I have a number of matters to attend to in my study," he said brusquely, not bothering to see whether either of the two ladies were done.

His wife abandoned the last bite on her plate and rose hastily to her feet. "I must see to several things as well."

Octavia stood up, her hand tightening on the back of the uncomfortable straight-back chair to keep a grip on her rising temper. "Thank you for your kind hospitality," she murmured, hoping that the note of sarcasm was not too evident.

Mr. Renfrew inclined his head a fraction. "Think nothing of it," he said magnanimously. "After all, it was our duty to make you feel welcome."

Welcome indeed!

"Good evening, Miss, er, Hadley," said Mrs. Renfrew as she made to follow her husband from the room. "You look to be a capable young woman. I do trust you will be able to handle the child without needing a great deal of guidance in the matter."

Octavia didn't trust her voice enough to respond with anything more than a murmur that could be taken for an assent. It wasn't until she was climbing the narrow

stairs to her own cheerless quarters next to the schoolroom that she dared unclench her jaw. Two colder fish
she couldn't imagine. Perhaps their cruelty was uninten-
tional, but the thought of an orphaned little girl having
to endure such guardians kindled a hot anger inside her.
Knowing full well what it was like to be unloved and
unwanted, she vowed that, as long as she was around,
the child would have a friend.

Chapter Four

A great, shaggy bear was breathing down his neck, and try as he might, he couldn't seem to make his legs move. Already its stale, unwashed odor was filling his nostrils, and it seemed to be getting closer and closer. With a choked cry, Sheffield lashed out a booted foot—

"Have a care who you are kicking, my friend," grumbled the burly peasant beside him, though he did shift his bearded chin from Sheffield's shoulder and roll his considerable bulk to the other side, drawing a muttered complaint from one of the other passengers.

Sheffield rubbed at his weary eyes and tried to stretch out his cramped legs among the tangle of sleeping bodies. The other passengers seemed oblivious to the fetid air and hard wooden seats, most having settled into the journey with a certain grim resignation. The only signs of life came from a country merchant snoring loudly in one corner and a short priest whose enveloping black robes made him look like a rolled-up carpet. From out of the wrappings of wool came a litany of whispered incantations and rumbled chants. Neither man was paid much heed by anyone, save for an occasional elbow when the rasps and wheezes got too loud.

It was a rather motley assortment of humanity, Sheffield decided, his mood none too charitable after another long day on the road. But as he glanced down at his own rumpled coat and soup-stained pants, a rueful grimace tugged at the corners of his lips. No doubt he, too, must reek of garlic and sour rye.

Well, at least he must blend in!

Another rut in the rough road threw his neighbor's knee into the side of his thigh, drawing a silent oath from him. Why, he thought in exasperation as he rubbed the tender spot, could not his uncle have managed to get the name right? Russian was not the easiest of languages, but a misplaced vowel had sent him nearly a week in the wrong direction. His relatives were owners of an estate named Polyananovosk, *not* Polyananovisk. And while the endless forests of spruce and pine had been magnificent, and the wooden villages and onion-domed churches of great interest, he would have much preferred to arrive at his destination in a more direct manner.

And a more comfortable one. His hand threaded through a tangle of hair that felt as greasy as the bowl of mutton stew served at the last stop. Perhaps it had been overcautious to take on the guise of a poor tutor, rather than travel under his real name in a spacious, well-sprung private carriage with all the amenities due a member of the English aristocracy. And yet, the rumblings he had heard in the various smoky taprooms along the way had caused him to admit the precaution had not been unwarranted.

Unrest was in the air. Rumors of an impending invasion swirled around every village they had passed through. Any foreigner was eyed with suspicion—why, he had seen a older Danish gentleman dragged from his carriage and beaten to within an inch of his life just two days ago. The local peasants were not particularly concerned with the nuances of nationality and which country was the current ally of the czar. The threat to Mother Russia was from anyone not of their own blood. That England had until recently been one of the enemy only exacerbated the potential for trouble. So, as Sheffield scratched at one of the innumerable bites on his abdomen, he had to admit that the plan, however unpleasant, had been a wise one.

The coach finally lurched to a stop in the muddy yard of a small inn. Climbing over several prostrate forms numbed into oblivion by the local brew at the last stop, if the smell of their breath was any indication, Sheffield pushed open the door and stumbled to the ground. A sharp gust of wind cut through the homespun fabric of his garments, but the tang of larch and pine cleared the muzziness from his head. He stood for a moment, savoring the clean crispness of the air, before pulling the thick wool cap down over his ears and hurrying inside the inn.

Rather than stay in the smoky room, he carried his thick glass of hot tea back outdoors and walked toward a dense stand of birch, their silvery white trunks like drizzles of sugar against the darkening sky. A storm looked to be heading their way—indeed, Sheffield felt a snowflake catch on his cheek, then another. The temperature was dropping by the minute, and behind him, he heard the horses stamp in impatience to be off.

One of the ostlers muttered an oath as he struggled with a buckle of the harness.

"Nasty weather," remarked Sheffield, strolling to the other man's side.

A grunt was the only reply.

"Does it look like we will see snow?"

The man shrugged. "Whatever God wills."

Sheffield probed for a different sort of information. "Are we far from Polyananovosk? The estate of Count Scherbatov?"

The question was met by a blank stare.

"I was told it was near Kovrov."

"Oh, that is at least twenty kilometers down the road," answered one of the other men tending to the horses. The way he said it, he might have been speaking about a spot halfway around the globe.

A horn sounded, signaling that the driver was impatient to be off before the full brunt of the storm hit. With great reluctance, Sheffield climbed back into the crowded confines of the coach, consoling himself with the knowledge that the journey was near an end.

Several hours later, the horses paused before a cluster of wooden huts. "You! The fellow looking for Polyananovosk," shouted the driver from his perch. "You must get out here. And be quick about it. I haven't got all day." Already the reins were twitching in his mittened hands.

No further directions were forthcoming, and Sheffield dared not risk any questions. He grabbed his bag and stepped over his neighbors, drawing more than one tired curse. The door fell shut, the whip cracked, and the wheels creaked forward. With nary a regret, he watched the dark, lumbering shape disappear around the bend.

Then, hoisting his bag to his shoulder, he turned to make inquiries of just how he might continue on to the count's estate. The few errant flakes had become a steady fall of powdery snow. Already his toes were feeling the seep of a numbing chill through the worn leather of the secondhand boots. *Hell's teeth,* he muttered to himself. This time, his information had better be accurate or he might well end up a meal for the roving wolves of the steppes.

The gnarled old babushka, her head so heavily wrapped in a gaily patterned wool scarf that her words were barely audible, waved a scrawny finger in the direction of a faint cart path. From what he could understand, he was meant to follow it until it crossed the drive leading to the main house. When he asked how far, she merely shrugged.

Sheffield shifted his weight from one cold foot to the other, debating whether to leave the only signs of civilization for the yawing darkness of the looming forest. The sound of muffled hooves and creaking leather interrupted his thoughts. A small wagon approached, then slowed at the sight of the lone figure by the side of the cottage.

"What business have you around here?" demanded the driver, a tone of authority shading his deep growl.

"I seek the house of Count Scherbatov."

"For what reason?" The man leaned down from his seat, his narrowed eyes sweeping over Sheffield's shabby garb with undisguised suspicion.

Sheffield hesitated only a fraction. "I've been engaged as a special tutor for the young count."

The other man pursed his lips. "I have heard nothing of any new tutor. The countess did not say anything of it before she—" He stopped abruptly and fixed Sheffield with a suspicious stare. "What sort of tutor?"

"I speak English."

The man tugged at the corner of his mustache in some indecision. After lengthy consideration he finally gestured to the seat beside him. "I suppose you had better

come with me," came the gruff order. As Sheffield
scrambled up, he added, "I am Riasanov, steward to the
Scherbatov estate." He made no offer of his hand, giving
only a brisk shake of the reins as soon as Sheffield's feet
cleared the ground. Further attempts at conversation
proved futile as each simple inquiry was rebuffed with
no more than a rough grunt. Sheffield finally gave up,
and the journey continued on in an eerie silence, save
for the swirl of the wind and the whoosh of the wheels
in the drifting snow.

Turning up his collar to ward off the icy gusts, he tried
to turn his attention to the countryside and what sort of
lands his relative possessed. But even that proved impossible in the fading light and thickening flurries. It was
with great relief that he finally heard the crunch of
gravel under the lumbering cart and was able to discern
the outline of a manor house not too far ahead.

As the horses trotted into the courtyard, a groom
emerged from the barn, swathed in such layers of wool
and fur that he appeared some strange creature conjured
up from one of the fanciful wonder tales of the region.
The sound that emerged from where his mouth should
be was equally bizarre, bearing no relationship to any
words Sheffield had ever heard. His companion, however, seemed to have no difficulty in understanding the
fellow. He barked out a series of orders, then gestured
for the tutor to follow.

Stiff with cold, Sheffield managed to dismount and
trail after the steward. Any hopes of a respite from the
biting cold within the main house were dashed as the
heavy wooden front door was thrown open. It was nearly
as chilly inside. The other man stamped the snow off his
boots, leaving a shower of flakes on the stone floor. Sheffield did the same, unconsciously pulling the knitted
wool scarf tighter around his neck.

Good Lord, he thought, he hoped the fellow wouldn't
expect him to remove his coat!

His eyes darted around the dimly lit entrance hall,
taking in the heavy pine furniture, gaily painted with
bright colors and swirling motifs so very foreign to his
English eye. A shaggy bearskin was stretched out in
front of a massive sideboard, above which hung two por-

traits. With a start, he realized that the man bore a passing resemblance to his own father.

The father of young Nicholas? he wondered.

He had little chance to see much else, as the steward indicated they were to continue along a dark hallway that led off to the left. Every door they passed was shut tight, no hint of light coming from beneath them. No voices were evident either. In fact, there was no sign of life at all. Nothing but a dark, ominous silence. Sheffield could feel the knot in his stomach tighten with each step. . . .

The other man's gloved hand took hold of the thick iron latch and shouldered open the door in front of them. Sheffield tensed, half expecting some fur-clad giant to swing a cudgel at his head. Instead, it was a long-handled cooking spoon that cut through the air.

"Ah, Yevgeny! Thank the Lord. I was afraid you might be trapped in the blizzard." A short, stout woman, nearly as wide as she was tall, wiped her free hand over her patterned apron. "Warm yourself by the stove while I fetch you a cup of tea." Catching sight of Sheffield, her mouth cracked in a smile that revealed several missing teeth. "Who is this with you? By the way he is dressed, he would soon have been a carcass for the wolves if you hadn't found him."

The steward removed his fur hat and stepped over to the huge tiled stove, holding out his stiff fingers to the blast of heat. "A tutor, he says. For young Master Nicholas."

The woman tucked a wisp of graying hair up under the kerchief knotted around her head. "Tutor," she repeated, casting an appraising glance at him. "Well, best warm your bones, young man. You look as if you might like a cup of tea as well." Her glance ran over his lean form. "And a bite of supper, I imagine."

Sheffield nodded gratefully as he unwound the scarf from his neck and shook the drops of melting snow from his hat. The kitchen was blessedly warm, with the smell of fresh-baked bread and simmering borscht filling the air. He could feel the heat beginning to seep through his rough garments and wet leather of his boots. Leaving a puddle on the spotless floor, he didn't wait twice to be invited closer to the hissing stove. Afer several minutes, he finally felt able to remove his coat, though his fingers were still so wooden they let it slip to the floor in a heap.

The old woman thrust a glass of steaming tea in his hands, waving away his halting apology for creating a mess in her domain. "Sit! Sit!" she urged, motioning him to the long trestle table, still flecked with course rye flour and caraway seeds.

Sheffield obeyed. Riasanov was already settled comfortably in a chair, helping himself to a bowl of pickled beets and eggs. After a brief hesitation, the steward took one last morsel and pushed it on toward him, still without addressing a word in his direction.

"Where did you come from?" At least the woman was proving less taciturn.

"From Cheboksary," he mumbled through a mouthful of egg.

She placed a crusty loaf of dark bread on the table and began to saw off generous slabs. Sheffield could feel his mouth begin to water at the rich scent. "What were you doing there?"

His mouth crooked in a rueful smile as he accepted a piece. "I'm afraid my directions were a bit unclear. The Scherbatov family I encountered there had no person under the age of sixty-five."

"Hmmph. Bad directions, indeed." She exchanged looks with the steward. "Who hired you? The countess?" she continued, her tone growing sharp.

Sheffield paused in buttering his slice of bread. The mood in the room had become markedly chillier. "I was given the job by, er, an intermediary. I have never met the countess," he answered slowly, deciding to stick as close to the truth as possible.

"Your accent," she persisted. "You are from . . . ?"

He swallowed hard. "From outside of St. Petersburg."

Sudddenly, his head was jerked back and the bread knife pressed up against his throat. "What town, exactly?"

Sheffield didn't attempt an answer.

"As I thought," growled Riasanov, tightening his grip on Sheffield's collar. "A stupid mistake, my friend. Did you really think that we would be so stupid as to fall for such an obvious ruse? You may tell Vladimir Illich that it will not be quite so easy to steal Polyananovosk from the young master—that is, when you see him in hell!"

"Wait!" cried Sheffield as he felt the serrated blade start to move against his skin. "You are mistaken! I can prove it!"

The steward gave a harsh laugh, but the woman's face betrayed a flicker of indecision. "Yes, wait, Yevgeny. Let us hear him out." She put down the heavy iron frying pan that she had taken up from the stove. "Plenty of time to deal with him if he proves to be one of Rabatov's men."

The pressure of cold steel relaxed somewhat. "Very well. Explain yourself—and no more lies."

Sheffield took a deep breath. "It is true that I am not what I said I was, but I come as no threat to Nicholas." He gestured toward his shirt. "May I take out something that might help to convince you?"

Again the two of them exchanged glances. Riasanov growled an assent. "But slowly, and no tricks or they will be your last," he added, giving a meanful twitch of the blade.

Sheffield reached inside his shirt and removed a small oilskin packet that hung by a cord around his neck. First he unfolded several sheets of paper and pushed them to the center of the table. "I am Alexander Sheffield, an English cousin of young Nicholas's father. My grandmother and Nicholas's grandmother were sisters."

The old woman eyed the gilt crest and elegant script in confusion. It was with some concern that Sheffield realized she could not read. "Yevgeny," she said uncertainly, "Can you tell if what he says is . . . true?"

He fervently hoped that the steward could make sense of the letter of introduction from the Russian mission in London, verifying what he said.

Riasanov hesitated, then released his hold on Sheffield's coat and reached for the papers. He studied them once, then again before laying them side. "Hmmph. Such things can be forged." However, his fierce expression had tempered somewhat. "Have you any other sort of proof that you are who you say you are?"

Sheffield removed another sheet from the pouch. It was a thin parchment, much wrinkled and stained from travel. "Are you familiar with the countess's handwriting?" he asked. "This is the letter she sent to my uncle, the Earl of Chittenden, asking for our help in keeping Nicholas safe. That is why I am here. From what she said, I thought it best to be cautious and pass myself off as Russian until I could be of sure of how things stood here." He grimaced. "I pick up languages rather quickly, but I see I was not very convincing."

The steward put down the knife as well as the countess's letter. "You speak quite well, however, we would have been suspicious of anyone." He turned to the old woman. "I know the countess's hand like my own. I am sure she wrote this, so what our friend here says must be the truth." She crossed herself as Riasanov turned back to Sheffield. With an awkward bow, he essayed a few words in heavily accented English. "Welcome to Polyananovosk, my lord."

Sheffield breathed a sigh of relief at finding his neck no longer in peril. "You needn't bow as if I am the one with the title. I am merely a younger son, and it is best if you simply call me 'mister.' "

The steward shuffled his feet uncomfortably. "I hope you will forgive the rather rude welcome, Mr. Sheffield."

"Yes, and you must be starving after all your travels," added the old woman in a rush. Now that matters were cleared up, she was more than anxious to make up for the misunderstanding by plying their guest with food.

"Indeed I am, and judging by the heavenly aroma coming from your pots, I imagine I am a lucky man." A note of anticipation crept into his voice. "But first, if you please, I should very much like to meet my young cousin."

Riasanov cleared his throat. "Ah, I am afraid that is not possible, Mr. Sheffield. You see, Master Nicholas is not here."

"Is it not one of the most fantastic buildings you have ever seen, Miss Hadley?" demanded Emma, her hand nearly pulling away from Octavia's in her haste to get closer.

"Indeed," she murmured, keeping her charge from dashing away across the vast cobbled square. "Do you know an interesting story behind its creation?"

That caught the young girl's attention. She slowed her steps and looked up expectantly.

"Well, St. Basil's Cathedral was built by Ivan IV, known, I'm afraid, as Ivan the Terrible. On its completion, he was so pleased by its stunning beauty that he summoned the architect and asked the man if he could ever design anything as magnificent as the church again. Wanting to impress his czar, the man assured Ivan that of course he could, whereupon"—Octavia paused for dramatic effect—"Ivan had the man's eyes put out. To ensure that he never did."

Emma's own eyes widened, then crinkled in silent amusement. "Monarchs get to have all the fun."

Octavia repressed a smile. In her experience, most children seemed to take a ghoulish delight in such stories rather than become frightened or upset. It was clear that Emma was no different.

"Henry VIII got to cut off the head of a wife that displeased him," went on the little girl, her expression conveying a touch of longing at being able to deal with unpleasant relatives in so decisive a manner.

"Oh, I doubt you would truly enjoy making heads roll," said Octavia.

"Why not?" countered Emma.

"Too messy. I think I should make people walk the plank, like Bluebeard the Pirate."

Emma stifled a giggle. "I like being with you, Miss Hadley. You never tell me I can't think or say something because it is not the proper sentiment for a young lady. Miss Withers was forever telling me to hold my tongue. So does Aunt Renfrew."

Octavia couldn't help but be pleased with how far she had come in earning the young girl's trust. Over the past several weeks, wary suspicion had turned into a cautious acceptance. In truth, she liked Emma as well. Her charge was bright, inquisitive, and eager to learn. And beneath the sullen, willful shell she had learned to affect in the face of a series of uncaring adults, was a sensitive, vulnerable child, yearning for some real affection. "People are always telling me the same thing, you know. I'm afraid I never learned my lesson. But at least I have enjoyed the use of my brain, which is more than can be said for a vast majority of our sex."

Emma's mouth dropped slightly at hearing such mutinous thoughts expressed aloud. "Uncle Renfrew says that it is unseemly for females to think—"

"No doubt he does. What could be more threatening to a man of such little intelligence or imagination?" she said rather acidly.

The young girl's face became very thoughtful.

"But I trust you will not repeat such opinions in his presence," continued Octavia quickly.

"There is a Mrs. Wollstonecraft who believes that females are capable of rational behavior and thought, too, isn't there? I have heard my uncle lecture my aunt about how she should be thrown in Bedlam because of a book she wrote."

Octavia nodded.

"Do you have that book?"

She had to admit she did.

"Could we read a chapter of it tonight before bedtime?" asked Emma.

After her pointed words, it would have been nigh on impossible to deny the request. "Very well, but I suggest we make no mention of it to your guardians."

The young girl shot her a withering look. "What do you think I am—a child?"

Octavia gave a slight cough. "Ah, why don't we see if we might enter the cathedral and have a look at some of the icons there. Now, Andrei Tretiakov was considered the most brilliant painter of the . . ."

She launched into a detailed explanation of Russian art, while ruing her own rather precipitous tongue. She had spoken on impulse, forgetting that her listener was only twelve years old. Perhaps such views on a female's right to independent thinking were a little too complex for a child to understand, but the look of self-doubt on the young girl's face had wrenched the words out of her.

How well she knew what it was like to be told it was improper to have ideas or feelings just because of one's sex. She simply refused to let the obvious intelligence and spirit be stamped out in this young lady if she could help it.

They emerged from the candlelit cathedral some time later, their senses still reeling. The combination of the sweet, cloying incense, sonorous chanting from a group of monks clustered in one of the naves, and rich colors at every turn was a most singular experience. Octavia found herself wondering what Mr. Sheffield's opinion would have been of the exotic spectacle. From what she had overheard on the ship, she knew he had a sharp eye for observing people and a pithy sense of humor when so moved. She felt sure he would have had something interesting to say. . . .

"Miss Hadley?" Emma shook her arm, repeating her name for the third time.

"Forgive me. I fear I was woolgathering."

Her charge smiled. "What were you thinking?"

To Octavia's surprise, a faint blush of color stole to her cheeks. "Oh, nothing." Seeing the girl's face fall at the casual brush-off, she added, "Actually, it wasn't very important—I was merely wondering what one of the other passengers on the ship would have thought about St. Basil's. He . . . He knew quite a bit about Russian history, and had a certain sense of curiosity, that's all."

"*Him?*" Emma regarded her with great interest. "You hadn't mentioned a *him* before, just the odious Mrs. Phillips. Was he tall, dark, and handsome? Did you like him?"

Like Mr. Sheffield? What a ludicrous idea!

"Perhaps we should limit your reading of Mrs. Radcliffe, young lady," she replied dryly. "Come, let's buy a bag of roasted chestnuts from the vendor for the walk home."

Emma wasn't long distracted from that train of thought by the task of peeling away the hot shells. "All my other governesses have said that if I don't learn to behave properly, no man will want to marry me and then I'll end up an old maid." She made a face as she popped a piece of the sweet kernel into her mouth.

"They make it sound like a fate worse than having your head cut off by your husband." Her eyes stole a look at her companion. "Do you never wish to marry, Miss Hadley?"

Octavia took her time in answering. "I have no objection to the idea of matrimony, Emma. In fact, I should like very much to have children, a family of my own. But not at the expense of my . . . my self." She paused for a moment. "So, if I should meet a man willing to listen to my thoughts with as much attention as he pays to those of his male acquaintances, willing to discuss things rather than issue orders, willing to be a . . . friend rather than a tyrant, then I should listen quite seriously to any offer that might come my way." An ironic smile crossed her lips, and she endeavored to add a lighter note to her words. "Unfortunately, there do not seem to be an abundance of such admirable men in existence, so I am quite resigned to being, as your former governesses put it, an old maid."

Emma peeked up shyly from under the fringe of her fur hat. "Perhaps, until you meet that man, we . . . we could be friends?"

"Why, that's quite the nicest offer I have ever had!" She gave the young girl's thin shoulders a big hug. "I accept—and not just until I meet such a paragon of virtue. I should be honored if you will always consider me your friend."

Emma colored with pleasure and ducked her head to eat another chestnut.

They continued on in companionable silence for some way before Emma spoke again. "He would have to be very handsome."

Octavia's gaze jerked away from the bright gilding on one of the onion domes peeking out from behind the red brick walls of the Kremlin. "Who?"

Emma shook her head in exasperation. "Your future husband, of course. He would have to be tall as well. What color eyes do you favor?"

"Blue," she blurted out before she had a chance to think.

"A fine choice," allowed the girl. "Fair or dark haired?"

"Oh, dark, of course. What Gothic hero would dare be an insipid blond?"

Emma giggled. The rest of the walk home was spent in spelling out all the attributes needed for a man to meet their combined standards.

Ha! thought Octavia as they approached the door to the Renfrew's house. Not a bloody chance such a saint existed.

Chapter Five

"What do you mean, he is not here?" demanded Sheffield. Weariness and a wrenching sense of frustration had him perilously close to shouting. His momentary elation at having actually found his nephew made the new revelation even harder to swallow.

The steward gave an apologetic cough. "There were several incidents that might have proved fatal to the young master if we hadn't had luck on our side. Ludmilla and I decided that it would be best to send him where he would be safe from that murderous cur of an uncle until we could make contact with someone we trusted." Noting Sheffield's grim expression, he added, "Of course, we were not anticipating your arrival."

"No," allowed Sheffield. He forced a thin smile. "I do not mean to appear ungrateful—I'm afraid all the traveling and other setbacks have me rather on edge." His hand raked through his dark locks. "No doubt you have done the right thing to protect Nicholas from harm. But from whom did you seek help? We know that the countess wrote to her brother in England, but she must have been fairly certain help would not be forthcoming from there."

"Yes, she had little faith in her own family. Only desperation drove her to contact yours. But I was also asked to send off a letter to Prince Yusserov, a close friend of the late count's who has paid many a visit here to Polyananovosk. It is he who was named as the boy's guardian, not his uncle." The steward gave a helpless shrug. "But the prince, like the count, is a military man, and given the state of things, who knows when the news will reach him. After the countess's death, I also sent word to the count's man of affairs in Moscow. You see, the young master's uncle somehow contrived to cut off funds and began to turn out our servants in order to replace them with lackeys loyal to him." He gestured toward the darkened part of the house. "You no doubt noticed how deserted the house is. I refused admittance to him and his men, and he dared not try to use force— yet. But it is possible the count's man has been bribed to hold his tongue. Such a thing would not be uncommon in this country. So I have no doubt that Nicholas's uncle will be back. That is why we decided that it would be best to hide him."

Sheffield nodded, a grim expression on his tired face. "You have done well. But just where is he?"

"With his old nursemaid, in the village of Bereznik."

"And how far is that?"

Riasanov pulled a face. "Two—maybe three—days of hard travel. That is, assuming the roads are passable."

Sheffield muttered an oath, which needed no translation to convey its meaning.

So near yet so far.

Ludmilla set out three wooden bowls on the table with a deliberate clatter. "Time enough to discuss what to do in the morning," she announced in a tone that brooked no argument. "Now it is time to eat." She removed a huge copper cauldron from where it had been simmering and began to ladle out a thick stew of potatoes, onions, carrots, and chunks of wild boar, redolent with the scent of rosemary and parsley. "Things will seem better on a full stomach," she assured him.

Sheffield slumped into his chair without another word, suddenly feeling utterly drained. Exhausted from the arduous journey, depressed by this latest disappointment, he couldn't help but think that failure seemed to hang about his neck like a cursed millstone. Perhaps he should stay away from the lad—he only seemed to bring bad luck wherever he went.

With such bitter thoughts in mind, he could barely do justice to the savory meal, the first decent food he had been served in weeks. With Ludmilla clucking over him, refilling his glass with yeasty beer, pressing another slice of bread slathered with butter on his plate, he managed to swallow just enough to mollify her motherly instincts, though it might have been vinegar and chalk for all he tasted.

Riasanov guided him to a chilly bedchamber. Lighting the meager pile of split spruce did little to take the edge off the cold, but a thick eiderdown quilt promised a modicum of comfort. Shedding his travel-worn garments, he slipped between the icy sheets, giving thanks that at least they were clean. The warmth of the spirits and the hot meal gradually began to mellow his mood just a bit. At least he now knew where young Nicholas was, which was more than he could claim when the day began. That was some progress, he allowed. So perhaps Ludmilla was right and the situation was not as black as he had thought. After a good night's sleep and a much-needed bath and shave, things would no doubt look even brighter.

However, when he awoke, Sheffield found he was wrong. Oh, the situation was not black—it was white. A thick, enveloping white. The steadily falling snow of the previous night had turned into a raging blizzard that nearly obliterated all signs of life. Gazing out of the frosty window, he found he could not even discern where land left off and sky began. Tugging on his coat, he hurried to the kitchen where Ludmilla was fiddling with the brass samovar, muttering dire predictions under her breath about being trapped all winter.

Riasanov appeared moments later, shaking a shower of thick flakes from his fur cap. A layer of snow coated his legs up past the knees, telling evidence as to the state of things outside. He brushed at the tiny icicles clinging to his shaggy mustache. "It is difficult to reach even the barn, and the storm shows no sign of letting up." His lips compressed as Ludmilla pressed a glass of hot tea in his hands. "I fear that we are stuck here for some time, Mr. Sheffield."

"God's will," said Ludmilla under her breath as she cracked a dozen eggs into her frying pan and added a dollop of butter.

Sheffield also muttered the Lord's name, but in not so accepting a manner. Stifling the urge to cut the cloying sweetness of the Russian tea with a generous splash of the vodka he spied on one of the shelves, he glared out the window at the blanket of whiteness while his fingers drummed impatiently on the rough pine table. "Is there any news about the movements of the French army?" he inquired in an abrupt change of subject.

Riasanov shrugged, a gesture with which Sheffield was becoming well acquainted since his arrival in Russia. "News travels slowly here, but yesterday, while I was fetching supplies from town, the word was they have crossed the border." His gaze also went to the window, and a slight smile crossed his lips. "They will find they have to fight more than General Kutusov and his troops." He gestured at the swirling snow. "Our greatest ally—a Russian winter, though it is unusually early this year."

Sheffield grunted, and the tempo of his drumming increased.

"In Russia, we have a proverb, Mr. Sheffield. It says that patience is a virtue."

"Yes, we have a similar saying in English." Sheffield heaved a sigh of frustration. "Patience is not a quality with which I am well acquainted. However, it appears I have no choice but to wait."

Octavia closed the door of the drawing room and folded her hands primly before her.

Mrs. Renfrew looked up from her embroidery. "You seem to be handling the child without undue problems," she said.

How the woman would have any notion of how things were progressing was beyond imagination, thought Octavia waspishly, since neither she nor her husband had laid eyes on their ward for the past two weeks. Why, Emma and her governess could have set out on a trek to Siberia for all the Renfrews might have noticed! Still, she kept a rein on her tongue and merely dipped her head in silent assent.

"We are well pleased with you, Miss Hadley," continued the other woman. "I fear my nerves were quite tested by her willfulness. I mean, one has to do one's duty for family, but there is little thanks from the likes of such a child. I do hope you have no plans to . . . leave."

"Not at all. I find the situation quite to my liking."

Mrs. Renfrew seemed slightly perplexed by the answer. Her needle darted into the taut fabric, pulling the colored silk in a neat stitch. "My husband must travel to St. Petersburg for a conference with the minister there, and I plan to accompany him. We would like you to remain here with the child. I trust that presents no problems for you?"

"None at all, ma'am," replied Octavia cooly, though she was sorely tempted to remind the woman that her niece's name was Emma.

"Good." There was a small sigh of relief. "Well, then, that settles matters." The words were as good as a dismissal.

Octavia turned to leave.

"Oh, Miss Hadley, one more thing." The needle made another pass. "Naturally you are teaching the child the sorts of things she must know in order to make her way in Society? She is the daughter of a baronet, you know, and must be able to make a decent match when the time comes."

The new governess had been in the household for over a month and this was the first inquiry as to what was taking place in the schoolroom. Again, Octavia had to fight to remain civil. "Naturally," she replied.

"Good—oh dear!" Mrs. Renfrew's brows came together. "Goodness! I've put in the wrong color. I fear the design is ruined!"

It was the first sign of emotion Octavia had ever seen from the woman.

"Oh dear," repeated Mrs. Renfrew. She was so busy fretting over her spoiled handkerchief that she didn't notice the look of contempt that came to her employee's face. Octavia had to restrain the urge to go over and shake her until her teeth rattled. Instead, she took a deep breath and walked away.

Still fuming over the encounter, Octavia found herself muttering a number of unladylike words under her breath as she stalked down the hallway. It wasn't until

she was halfway up the stairs that she realized she had
forgotten to ask about borrowing the atlas from Mr.
Renfrew's library. She paused, debating whether to return to the drawing room to make the request. Given
her current mood, any further contact with her employer
was not the wisest idea. Her patience, never great to
begin with, was already stretched taut from the first
meeting. It needed only the slightest tug to snap completely. The door to the library had been ajar, revealing
that no one was there. It would only take a moment to
fetch the volume.

The oversize book was easy to spot. Taking it under
her arm, Octavia brushed past the large mahogony desk.
In her haste to be gone, her sleeve caught one of the
papers sitting on the tooled blotter, knocking it to the
carpet. She snatched it up, fully intending to place it
back where it belonged, when her eyes fell on the first
line of the elegant script.

The corners of her mouth tightened as she read on.
Duty, indeed! Why, the Renfrews were being paid hand-
somely out of Emma's trust to care for the child. Octavia
did a bit of quick calculation. The young girl's clothing
was adequate but hardly extravagant. Even adding a
more than generous amount for food and shelter, as well
as her own paltry salary, the couple was siphoning away
a handsome profit for their so-called charity.

Quickly returning the letter to the top of the pile,
she quit the room and made her way back to the stairs.
Hypocrites, she raged, her heels beating an angry tattoo
on the wooden treads. Dislike turned into loathing as
she considered the callous indifference inflicted on
young Emma by her guardians. Was there anything she
could do, she wondered, anyone she could appeal to?
Would a letter to the solicitors administering the trust
amount to anything? She paused. The word of an insig-
nificant governess against that of a respectable government functionary? Not likely! Besides, it was not as if
they were doing anything illegal, simply immoral.

It would take some thought, but she vowed she would
find a way to make the girl's situation less intolerable.

*   *   *

"You've seen this, I take it?" Viscount Alston threw the newspaper down on the center of the table, a black look on his face.

The marquess looked up from the chessboard. "Yes, I heard the news at White's this afternoon, Thomas. Unfortunately, it comes as no surprise that Boney has dealt the Russian army yet another resounding defeat. He appears to be moving ever closer to Moscow."

"Is that all you can say?" exclaimed his brother. "*Unfortunate?* Unfortunate that Alex is alone in a strange country, facing not only cutthroat Russian relatives, but about to be engulfed in the general madness of war!"

Their uncle fingered one of the carved ivory pieces already removed from the game. "It is unfair to ring a peal over William's head. If anyone is to be blamed, Thomas, it is me. I did not think Bonaparte would be able to advance so quickly against as canny a general as Kutusov."

Alston took a deep breath. "Forgive me," he muttered. "I fear I'm feeling a bit overset at the moment."

"And with good reason. We are all concerned for Alex. I've managed to send a letter along with the latest government dispatches to our St. Petersburg mission asking for whatever help they can provide in locating him—"

The viscount gave an exasperated snort. "Oh come, you know as well as I that they won't be able to do a thing! Not with the whole damn French army advancing on Moscow."

Chittenden gave a sigh. "Nonetheless, it is the best we can do."

His younger nephew stalked to the sideboard and poured himself a stiff brandy. "Perhaps not."

The earl's head came up. "What do you mean, Thomas?"

"What I mean is, I don't intend to sit by and watch another brother perish if there is aught I can do about it."

"Good Lord! You can't intend to—"

"To set off for Russia myself? That's *exactly* what I intend, William."

"And what of Olivia? And Ranleigh Hall?"

"Olivia is in full agreement with me, and my steward is perfectly capable of running the estate until my return." He cleared his throat. "A dispatch ship leaves from Gravesend in three days' time. The admiral has made room for my passage."

There was silence in the library, save for the crackling of the logs in the fireplace.

"Dash it all," growled the marquess after some moments. "You had best make sure there are *two* berths in that cabin."

"Now, William, you know you cannot leave all your responsibilities—"

"Perhaps my responsibility as head of this family is the most important one right now," answered the marquess softly. "It's high time we reach out a hand to Alex."

"You are sure Augusta shall not kick up a dust?"

He made a wry grimace. "The females of this family have always had a tender spot for Alex, you know. More likely she would rake me over the coals if I *didn't* go."

"Well, then, we have much to do before—"

"I daresay the admiral can be convinced to allow a third party to join in."

Both of the younger gentlemen nearly spilled their drinks. "Uncle Ivor," sputtered the marquess. "Don't you think the, er, rigors of a sea voyage and a Russian winter would be . . . rather uncomfortable for—"

"If you say for a man of my age, you young pup, I'll show I am not so deep in my dotage that I can't still take a birch to your backside! I set all of this in motion, so of course I shall join in seeing it set to rights." There was a slight twinkle in his eyes as he went on. "Besides, I have wanted to visit St. Petersburg ever since I was a young boy and saw Czar Peter himself striding along the streets of London in those magnificent tall boots of his."

His nephews knew the futility of arguing with their uncle when his mind was set.

"Ah, well, in for a penny, in for a pound," said the marquess with a sigh.

The earl grinned. "Good, then it's settled." He turned toward the paneled oak door and raised his voice. "You ladies may as well come in now. No doubt you will have a number of suggestions to add as we begin to make plans."

The brass knob turned very slowly. Both Augusta and Olivia looked slightly abashed as they sought to smooth the telltale creases caused by kneeling from their skirts. "We . . . We were just passing by, Uncle Ivor."

"Yes, I know, and the keyhole jumped up and took hold of that lovely ear of yours."

Augusta directed an indignant look at her uncle while Olivia contrived to look injured. "Well, we wouldn't have to stoop to such measures if you would admit that we are just as capable of rational thought as you are. It's not fair that you men skulk off and lock yourself in the library to discuss all the interesting matters. If you mean to make important decisions about the family, we should be included, too," she retorted. "After all," she added sharply, with a pointed glare at her husband, "we *do* play rather a large role in ensuring that there will be a Sheffield line in the future."

"An excellent point, my dear," said the earl with a chuckle, ignoring the baleful expressions of his two nephews. "I have long since realized that my nieces are blessed with brains as well as beauty. Of course you should be included. Come take a seat on the sofa and let us start to make plans."

The two ladies settled themselves on the plump cushions with a deliberate flounce.

"Now, William," he continued, "kindly take up a pen so that we may keep a list of all the things that we are going to need. . . ."

The young man who opened the door scowled at the sight of the elegant gentleman. "He ain't here. He's left town for a time, so if it's some debt you've come to collect, you'll have to wait."

Alston's hand shot out to keep the door from slamming shut in his face. "I've not come about a loan, Squid—it *is* Squid, isn't it?"

The young man's scowl turned to a look of wariness. "How did ye know me name?" he asked, surprise causing a lapse into cant. "And who are ye, then? Don't recall having seen yer mug around here before."

"I'm Alston." At the blank look that greeted the announcement, he was forced to add, "Sheffield's brother."

Squid fell back in consternation as the viscount stepped into the modest set of rooms. "N-nothing has happened to Mr. Alex, has it?" he asked quickly.

"As far as I know, my brother hasn't stuck his spoon in the wall yet." The viscount glanced at the battered desk and the stacks of books and papers piled haphazardly on its nicked surface. "I mean to see that it stays that way. So I've come to check whether he might have left a Russian lexicon lying around, and perhaps a more detailed atlas than the one I was able to purchase."

The valet eyed him with some suspicion. "Here now, why should I let you go through his things?"

The viscount was already thumbing through one of the thick leather-bound volumes on the top of one stack. "Because if I am to be of any help to him, I need to know all I can about Russia."

Squid took a moment to mull over the words. "You are going to Russia?" he asked very slowly, disbelief evident on his face.

Alston nodded as he picked up another book.

"But . . . But Mr. Alex says his family don't give a dam—deuce about him. Says you all wish him to the devil."

"Yes, I know. And that is exactly where he has been driving himself these past years, with a vengeance. However, like the rest of us, my brother can be very wrong about certain things."

Squid regarded the viscount with a cagey look that belied the youthful innocence of his features. "Yer serious," he said after a bit. "Ye really mean to go after him?"

"Yes."

"Then I mean to come, too."

Alston had to repress a laugh. At the rate things were going, they would need a troop transport to convey the veritable army that was volunteering on his brother's behalf. "My thanks for your concern, but I don't think that will be necessary. My other brother and my uncle are to accompany me as well. The three of us shall manage adequately."

"Ha!" Squid pulled a face. "A marquess, an earl, and

a viscount. How are the likes of you fine gentlemen gonna know how to ferret out information from the locals? Or do some of the squirmy things that need be done in certain situations, like? Me, I got experience in such things. I could be . . . useful. Mr. Alex has said so on any number of occasions."

Alston's brows drew together in thought.

"I can brush a coat and press a cravat tolerably well," went on Squid in a dogged voice. "And I'm handy with me fives or a shiv or barking iron. Surely the three of you could do with a valet of my skills, rather than one of the useless slow tops that blacken yer boots."

"Well—"

"Mr. Alex even taught me a bit of the lingo. *Das vedanya*. That means 'good day' in Russian."

The viscount stroked his jaw. "Hmmm. I suppose you might prove helpful."

"I know Mr. Alex better 'n anyone. Wherever he is in that snow and ice, I'll track him down. I swear I will."

Surprised by the intensity of the young man's loyalty, Alston took a moment to answer. "I shall discuss the matter with the rest of the family. If you care to bring around these books to Grosvenor Square this afternoon at four, we shall inform you of what we mean to do."

Squid grinned. "Yes, milord."

"It is number—"

"Oh, I know where Killingworth House is, milord. Mr. Alex may think I don't notice, but when he passes anywhere near, he can't help but stare up at those fancy steps and marble pillars with . . ." His voice trailed off and he swallowed uncomfortably.

Alston's lips compressed. He spent some minutes in silence, perusing the rest of the papers and books, then arranged a neat pile of the things he had chosen. "At four, then?"

The valet moved to open the door. "I'll be there, sir."

Octavia pushed the sheet of foolscap back across the desk. "You must check your figures once more, Emma. I fear you have still not mastered the rudiments of geometry."

The young girl made a face. "I don't see why I have to fuss with all those numbers. It's not as if I will ever be a post captain in need of shooting the sun and figuring out my latitudes and longitudes."

"That may be so, but mathematics are part of a sound education. They challenge the mind, and you never know, geometry may come in very useful on some occasion."

Emma's lower lip jutted out. "Name one."

Octavia was forced to resort to a reply found effective by generations of governesses. "I'll not argue with you over this. Whether it pleases you or not, you will finish your lessons before we read another chapter of Miss Austen."

"Oh, very well." An exaggerated sigh filled the air as she reluctantly took up her pen and set back to work.

Octavia made a show of studying the book in her lap in order to hide her smile. Her young charge was proving to be both a challenge and a delight. The girl showed intelligence and spirit, which spoke volumes about her character, considering what she had been through. And even though the wall she had erected around herself had not completely crumbled, the touching need for real affection was more and more evident through the chinks. There were still times of rebellion and childish sulks, but a genuine rapport was growing between them with each passing day. The smiles were beginning to match the scowls, and the eagerness for learning usually overcame any fit of pique.

The scratching of the quill suddenly stopped and there was a giggle.

Octavia's brow raised in question.

"I have just figured it out."

"I am glad to hear it, since you have been dawdling over this particular problem for—"

"Not just the answer. The occasion."

Octavia's expression remained one of puzzlement.

"When I might need geometry," explained Emma. She gave a mischievous grin. "Why, if I were to build a structure as magnificent as St. Basil's Cathedral, I imagine it would be useful in figuring out the diameter of the onion domes and the height of the spires."

"Quite right." Octavia's lips twitched upward. "If you become a famous architect, you would certainly have to have a knowledge of geometry."

"But of course, I wouldn't admit it, so Czar Alexander could not put out my eyes." She pushed the paper back to Octavia with a triumphant flourish. "There, it's done."

"And done correctly this time. I'm quite proud of you. It was a difficult problem."

Emma flushed with pleasure at the praise. "If I can see a reason for doing something, then the task always becomes easier."

It was a perceptive comment, especially from a child, and one with which she most heartily agreed. It was, however, time for another lesson. "Well, unfortunately, we all must at times do things that we do not see the reason for."

Emma scrunched up her face. "Even adults?"

"Most definitely adults. Especially female adults."

The girl's face took on a mulish expression. "I thought you believed many of the strictures unfair and unreasonable."

"Some of them," admitted Octavia. "But that doesn't mean I don't accept that I must live with them. I do. Why, look at the characters in Miss Austen's book. They all must conform to certain rules, though they may not like it. In truth, they sometimes discover it was their own misconceptions that make things look unreasonable. However, in the end, her heroines usually manage to satisfy both the conventions of Society and their own sense of what is right." She gave a slight smile. "You see, we females just need to be a bit . . . creative within the boundaries set for us."

Emma looked thoughtful as she brushed the tip of her quill against her cheek.

"Come, shall we see how Elinor and Mr. Ferrars are going to resolve their problems?"

The girl's eyes lit up. "Oh, yes." She jumped up from her chair to fetch the book. "Perhaps she will finally shake some sense into Marianne."

Chapter Six

Sheffield pulled the fur blanket up a bit higher. His feet felt like blocks of ice and his cheeks were so stiff with cold he could barely speak. "How much farther? Or are we meant to turn into snow statues, like some cursed characters in one of your wonder tales?" At least the interminable hours of travel had allowed him to improve his command of the language to the point where he was conversing quite easily in the foreign tongue.

Riasanov grinned, crackling the tiny icicles on his mustache and beard. "Russian winter, Mr. Sheffield. Suffering! Hardship! Is good for the soul." He thumped his chest as he slapped the reins against the traces. Bells jangled as the sleigh crept through the drifts of snow. "It makes us poets."

"It makes you madmen," grumbled Sheffield. He slapped his mittens together and thought longingly of the crackling fires in his favorite haunts in London, bottles of brandy, and the willing warmth of some voluptuous beauty. Hell's teeth, what had he been thinking! He was as mad as any Russian to have set out on such a harebrained adventure.

"Another few miles and there is an inn. We shall stop for the night."

Recalling the last two nights, with the abysmal food and flea-ridden bedchambers, he was not sure the news would serve to improve his dark mood. As if to further dampen his spirits, the wind picked up and snow began to fall once again. With a muffled oath, he buried his chin deeper into the upturned collar of his coat, and watched the ghostly white fir trees drift by.

The inn was even worse than he had imagined. It was

a wretched affair of rough logs and loose shingles, the common room nearly as frigid as the outdoors, despite the fire. Sheffield pushed aside the rancid stew after several bites. Even the vodka was nearly unpalatable, harsh and greasy as it burned down his gullet. At least it created a semblance of warmth in his insides. Lapsing into a brooding silence, he poured another glass for himself, ignoring the sidelong glances from his companion. He drained it with a grimace, then picked up the bottle and bade Riasanov a curt good night.

With nary a thought to removing more than his overcoat and boots, Sheffield slipped under the dirty blankets. Repressing a shiver, he took a long pull at the bottle for good measure. Slowly the vodka began to dull the worst of the cold. It could not, however, dull the feeling of emptiness inside him. Good Lord, was this what his life was coming to—day after day of nothing to look forward to but an endless night, with naught but a bottle of spirits to drown his loneliness and despair?

His eyes pressed closed. Of late, he had begun to realize that the copious amounts of brandy, the reckless gambling, the blatant risks, and the frequent bedding of virtual strangers were no longer allowing him to hide from himself. Quite simply, he was getting tired of such behavior. If he wanted to put a period to his existence, mayhap he should put a pistol to his head. It would be faster, and, in some ways, cleaner.

Is that what he truly wanted?

He thought for some time, staring up at the cobwebbed ceiling. He used to have hopes and dreams, though it was so long ago he could hardly remember what they were. Silly ones, no doubt, for he had been nothing but a raw youth. Still, perhaps it wasn't too late to have new ones.

A rueful smile stole to his lips. Perhaps he had a touch of Russian temperament, for the winter seemed to be affecting his own soul as well. He wasn't usually given to such introspection. In the past he had always managed to keep such disturbing thoughts at bay with whatever excess happened to be at hand. Sheffield regarded the bottle in his fist with a grimace of disgust, then slowly let it drop to the floor.

Jack was gone, irrevocably gone, drowned in the ocean. Perhaps it was time for him to stop drowning in self-pity.

The next morning he arose, his head for once not quite so fuzzed with drink, and his spirits a bit brighter than they had been in some time. Riasanov's bushy brow rose at the sight of Sheffield's light step and sunny countenance. "Not feeling like a black bear this morning? I had feared you were on the verge of abandoning the journey and leaving the young master to his fate." He gestured toward the drafty windows. "But look, the snows have stopped, and the temperature is rising. We should reach Bereznik by this afternoon."

"Oh, you'll find I'm a rather stubborn fellow. I don't give up so easily."

Riasanov lowered his voice. "You may need that resolve, Mr. Sheffield. The word is that the French have moved much more rapidly than expected. It is said they may even threaten Moscow." He stopped to cross himself. "Though I pray the rumors are wrong."

"What of Kutusov and his army?" asked Sheffield in some surprise.

The other man lifted his shoulders.

Sheffield bit back an oath. "Well then, let us be off at once."

"Without my tea?"

"Suffering. Is good for the soul, remember?" he muttered, taking up his coat and heading for the door.

The journey proceeded with little conversation, both men preoccupied with their own thoughts. Less snow had fallen in these parts and the way became easier going. After a bit, it thinned to a mere dusting, and the sun broke through the clouds. Riasanov gave a shake of his head at the sudden change. "Russian winter," was all he murmured.

Rather than feeling buoyed by the passing miles, Sheffield couldn't shake a sense of unease. In the past hour, several conveyances piled high with household belongings had passed them, going in the opposite direction. Even more ominous was the fact that the last small village they had passed through looked to be nigh on deserted, no smoke coming from the chimneys, no sign of life in the yards.

Riasanov muttered darkly under his breath. The whip cracked in the air, urging the horses to greater speed.

His lips thinning to a tight line, Sheffield shifted in impatience under the heavy blanket. *Hell and damnation!* He certainly hadn't anticipated that the French would advance as quickly as signs indicated. With a start, he realized that if Moscow was indeed the target, then poor Miss Hadley was in even more danger than he was. He found himself hoping that she would come out of the panic and chaos of war unscathed. Then he forced such thoughts aside. He had enough of his own problems to worry about, and there was precious little he could do for her.

Besides, he thought with a wry smile, she seemed rather good at taking care of herself.

It seemed like an age before his companion slowed the team to a walk and pointed ahead. A number of dwellings, weathered a silvery gray from the elements, came into view, nearly dwarfed by a stand of towering spruce and fir behind them. The steward grunted something unintelligible, then guided the sleigh toward a simple cottage at some distance from the rest of the houses. He slowly dismounted and thumped his mittened fist on the door.

Sheffield held his breath. There was no sign of a reply. Riasanov was just raising his hand to knock again when it opened a crack.

"Yevgeny! Thank God you have come." The little old woman threw her arms around Riasanov's neck, a feat made more difficult by the fact that her kerchiefed head came barely level with his chest.

"Of course I have, Natasha. And I have brought . . . a friend."

She stole a glance at the figure in the sleigh, then turned her attention back to the steward, tugging on his arm. "Come inside, both of you. The stove is warm and the samovar is hot. We have much to talk about."

Sheffield climbed down from his perch, stiff with cold, and followed the others into the cozy kitchen. A boy was curled up in a chair by the large tiled stove, reading a book. At the sound of voices, his head jerked up. He looked to be rather small for his age, with rather delicate features and a thin nose apt to be termed aquiline as he grew older. A shock of hair the color of a raven's wing nearly obscured the large hazel eyes. He broke into a smile at the sight of Riasanov; then his expression turned wary as he took notice of the tall stranger behind the steward.

Sheffield noted that the boy's fingers tightened on the spine of the book, and his gaze darted toward a small door hidden in the shadows behind a large pantry. A welling of sympathy caught in his throat as he remembered that within the space of several months, his young relative had not only lost both parents but had found his very life threatened by the only other family he knew.

Good Lord. And he had the nerve to feel sorry for himself!

Before anyone else could speak, Sheffield stepped forward and stamped the snow from his boots, a tentative smile on his lips. "I have been looking forward to making your acquaintance, Nicholas," he said in English as he extended his hand. "I am your cousin Alex, and I have come at your mama's request to take you back to England."

The boy stared at him, as if uncomprehending what had been said.

Behind them, a gasp of surprise came as Riasanov whispered a translation to the boy's old nurse.

Just as Sheffield began to phrase his greeting in Russian, the boy put aside his book and stood up. He took a few steps forward, then bowed with a formality that nearly brought a smile to Sheffield's face. "I am most pleased to make your acquaintance, too, sir," he replied in the same language his cousin had used. "My mother—" His voice caught in his throat for a moment. "My mother and father used to speak often of our English relatives, as did my grandmother." He took a deep breath, struggling manfully to control his emotions. "So her letter reached you?"

Sheffield nodded.

"I . . . I didn't think you would come." His toe kicked

at the fringe of the thick rag rug. "And now I fear it is for nothing," he added in a wavering tone. "The French army is fast approaching. You will be trapped here as well."

Sheffield moved to where the boy stood and placed an arm around his shoulders. "I have managed, against all odds, to find you here. I daresay I shall figure out a way to get us safely to St. Petersburg."

Nicholas looked up, hope kindling in his eyes. "You . . . really think so, sir?"

"Indeed I do. Oh, and I would take it kindly if you will dispense with 'sir' and call me Cousin Alex."

The old woman could no longer restrain herself, and began to speak in a rush. Riasanov stooped to whisper something in her ear. A rush of color came to her broad cheeks and she set to preparing tea and a platter of thick-sliced rye, radishes, and smoked fish. Above the clinking of the glasses and the rattle of cutlery, the steward gestured for the three of them to be seated at the table. Natasha joined them shortly, with profuse apologies for her lack of hospitality. She placed the food in front of Sheffield and clucked at him until he had piled enough onto his plate that not a bit of the brightly painted pattern showed.

Satisfied that he would not expire from hunger in the next few minutes, she took a seat herself and began where she had left off. ". . . And Radischev says that our troops have retreated from Borodino, which means the French cannot be far from here. What are we to do?" She looked first to Riasanov, then to Sheffield.

The steward scratched at his beard. "You will return with me to Polyananovosk, of course. I don't believe they will push that far east." He slanted a look at Sheffield. "But as for the young master and Mr. Sheffield . . ."

"I will need horses and a sleigh."

Riasanov pulled a face. "It will not be easy, especially now."

"I can pay very well."

The old woman thought for a moment, then thumped her glass down on the table. "My nephew Igor may be persuaded. If not, I will take a broom to his backside."

*   *   *

Some time later, as Sheffield surveyed the two mismatched nags and the ancient vehicle, he couldn't refrain from thinking that not only had he paid very generously, he had paid through the nose. At least the animals looked to have some stamina despite their ugly appearance, and the sleigh, on further inspection, did not seem in imminent danger of falling apart at the first bump. And no doubt the other two were right—he had precious little choice.

He handed over the exorbitant sum and climbed into the creaky seat. Though accounted a dab hand with the ribbons, he soon found that handling a vehicle on runners over slick ice and snow was an entirely new experience. *Well,* he thought wryly, *he would undoubtedly have plenty of practice at it before he reached St. Petersburg.* Somehow, he arrived back at the cottage without serious mishap. After he and Riasanov had put the horses away, they returned to the kitchen where Natasha had laid out yet another meal.

Sheffield stared for a moment at the tumbler of vodka that the steward offered him, then waved it away. "We will need warm clothing and extra blankets." His fingers drummed on the table. "I suppose it would also be wise to take a supply of provisions, in case we must avoid the main roads."

"Or in case the villages have been looted and burned," added Riasanov in a grim voice. "You will also need to take a pistol."

A ghost of a smile came to Sheffield's lips. "You may be sure I have already thought of that. A brace of Manton's best have been in my satchel since I stepped off the ship."

Though he had no idea of who Manton was, the steward understood the gist of the reply and nodded in approval.

"I have plenty of spare blankets, and a thick fur robe that will serve well to protect you as you drive, sir," piped up the old woman. Her face screwed up in thought as she slanted a glance at her pantry. "I shall fix an ample supply of food—"

"Just remember, we do not need to feed an army—at least, we hope not," interrupted Sheffield with a short laugh. "The horses must be able to pull the sleigh."

Natasha cast an aggrieved look at the grins around her. "You must be able to keep up your strength. It is a long journey, and who knows what awful dangers will be lurking behind every tree."

"Let's have no talk of Baba Yagar sweeping down to carry off the young master and his English cousin in her mortar and pestle," admonished the steward. "We have enough real concerns without you frightening the boy with your lurid folk tales of ravenous wolves and evil witches."

She fell silent, but the expression on her lined face showed that she considered such threats very real indeed. With a warning waggle of her finger, she stood up and shuffled off to get the supplies ready.

"I have been thinking," said Riasanov as he listened to the dark muttering coming from the pantry with an amused shake of his head. "It makes more sense for me to take the horses and sleigh that you purchased today, while you and the young master take ones from Polyananovosk."

Sheffield made to protest, but the steward held up his hand. "No arguments, Mr. Sheffield. You have a much greater distance to travel. Besides, they belong to Master Nicholas."

The sense of such reasoning made further discussion unnecessary. "Very well." He turned to the boy seated by his side, who looked to be a bit dazed by all that was going on. "Perhaps you might see if you can locate an extra lantern or two, then help Natasha gather the blankets while I have a word with Nicholas."

The steward nodded in understanding and left the room.

Sheffield took a deep breath, trying to figure out how to begin. He had little experience in speaking to children—with a prick of conscience, he realized he had never even met William's two boys, who must be at least seven and five by now, or Thomas's brood of three toddlers. How did one avoid sounding pompous, or worse, condescending?

The luminous dark eyes that looked up at him in expectation settled things quickly. He would just have to say what he honestly felt, and hope it was good enough.

"I won't insult you by claiming I know how terrible things have been for you these past months," he said gently. "Nobody but you can truly fathom the depths of your hurt. But I, too, know what it is like to lose someone very close to you. My oldest brother died in a boating accident and I . . . I still miss him very much. My family and I can never replace the one you have lost, but we should like to offer you our love and a home where you may be safe." He bent lower, so that his eyes came level with those of the boy's. "You may count on me as a friend, Nicholas. We have a difficult journey ahead of us, if you choose to make it. One that may even be dangerous at times, but I'll do my best to see us through it unscathed. What say you? Shall we make a go of it together?"

Nicholas blinked several times. "When do you wish to leave, Cousin Alex?"

He ruffled the boy's dark hair. "You're top of the trees, lad. We should be off at first light."

"Top of the trees?" asked Nicholas in confusion. "Must we also climb trees?"

Sheffield laughed. "It's an expression. It means you are a great fellow."

"Oh, I see." The boy appeared to be making a mental note of it. "I imagine there will be many peculiar English sayings I will not understand."

"Don't worry. I'll be able to teach you more than a few before we reach St. Petersburg." He grinned. "I shall try not to introduce too many unacceptable words into your vocabulary. No doubt my sisters-in-law will be boxing both our ears if I don't watch my tongue."

Nicholas gave the first hint of a smile. "Like what?"

Sheffield lowered his voice to a conspiratorial whisper. "Well, to begin with, you are on no account to say 'bloody bastard' in proper company, especially if a lady is present."

"What is 'bloody bastard?' "

"The worst sort of evil fellow you can imagine."

"Ah." The boy fiddled with his knife. "Like Uncle Vladimir?"

"*Exactly* like Uncle Vladimir." He pushed his chair back from the table. "Now, I think both of us had better get some rest if we are to leave at dawn."

Nicholas got up as well.

Sheffield extended his hand, but the boy ignored it, gesturing instead for him to lean down. He did as he was bade and suddenly found himself enveloped in a hug. "Good night, Cousin Alex."

Sheffield felt his throat constrict as he gave an awkward squeeze to the boy's thin shoulders. "Good night, Nicholas."

Octavia undid the strings to her fur hat and laid the thick muff on the table. "The snow is starting again," she said to the butler, who, aside from Mrs. Renfrew's lady's maid was the only other English servant in the house. "There appears to be an unusual amount of activity in the streets, and from what I can gather, a number of disturbing rumors going around as well. Have you heard any further news from the embassy?"

He shook his head. "No, but when I was out this morning, I also noticed a number of carriages leaving by the northern route. Perhaps I should go and make some inquiries?"

"I think that might be wise." She paused for a moment. "I had thought that Kutusov was accorded to be a competant general. Even though he had to fall back from Smolensk, it was said he inflicted severe casualties on the French army. Do you really think he has allowed the French to march on his country's capital unopposed?"

The butler's expression didn't hide his opinion of foreigners in general. "Who knows what sort of cowardice these barbarians are capable of? Now, if Wellington was in command, he would drive those Frogs—"

"No doubt, but he is not. So let us try to discover exactly what is happening."

He fetched his overcoat, still grumbling under his breath, and stepped out into the frigid air. Octavia's brow furrowed in concern as she watched the door fall shut. She had not liked the mood of fear she had sensed in the streets. A number of people had brushed past her, arms loaded with staples like flour and potatoes, as though preparing for the worst. Certainly, the news from the front had not been good. Each skirmish or battle had ended with a retreat by the Russian forces. If it was true that the French were moving slowly, inexorably, to within striking distance of Moscow, there was good reason for her to be worried.

Not for a moment did she think the Renfrews would give a thought to their being trapped in the capital. For all she knew, they might stand to come into Emma's inheritance if anything happened to the child, and so would welcome any attack by the enemy. No, if anyone was to look out for their safety, it would have to be her.

She quickly climbed the stairs to Emma's attic quarters. The girl was reading a book in the schoolroom, but immediately laid it aside on seeing Octavia's grave expression.

"Is something amiss, Miss Hadley?"

"I am not quite sure, Emma, but it appears that the French army may be closer to the city that any of us thought."

The girl remained silent for several moments, then asked in a tentative voice, "What will happen to us?"

Octavia had no idea. But she was sure she did not want to find out. Though she had no firsthand experience with the ravages of war, she had read enough of both past and present conflicts to know that there would be terrible destruction and chaos if the enemy forces marched on Moscow. Perhaps it would be possible to take refuge at the embassy, but as England was also at war with the French, it seemed likely that would offer little real protection.

Emma was still looking at her, eyes clouded with apprehension.

"I'm not sure," she admitted frankly. "However, I think it best to be prepared for any emergency. I would like you to pack a small bag and have your warmest garments ready in case we must leave in a hurry. Can you do that, Emma, while I make some inquiries downstairs?"

A slight smile came to the girl's lips. "I'll not throw a fit of vapors, if that is what you mean."

"Good girl."

Octavia hurried toward the kitchen. The Russian cook had taken a liking to her on account of her interest in learning the language. As he had spoke some English as well, they had enjoyed a number of pleasant conversations over steaming cups of tea. With friends and family in the city, surely he would have some idea of what was going on.

Her hand flew to her throat as she regarded an empty room, pots in disarray, the stove nearly cold. "Mr. Shishkov?" she ventured.

A grunt came from the pantry. He emerged a moment later, dragging a sack filled with turnips and onions. He added it to a growing pile of staples near the scullery door, then turned and wiped the sweat from his brow.

"Is the news that dire, then?" she asked.

"Miss Hadley, rumors are swirling everywhere, but from the best I can make out, our troops have suffered a grievous defeat at the village of Borodino. If that is true, the French may enter the city in a day's time, if not sooner."

She went very pale.

"Already there are fires breaking out in parts of the city, whether by chance or by Count Rostopchin's orders, I don't know, but it's a very dangerous situation. There was a near riot at the market near the Kremlin when bread ran out. If I were you, I would not stay here in Moscow."

Her jaw tightened. "Where might one have a chance of catching a coach for the north?"

The cook's face betrayed his surprise. "The master has made no provisions for you and the little one to leave?"

She shook her head.

He muttered something in Russian she didn't understand, which was probably just as well. "I suppose it should not surprise me. He and his lady are as cold as our Siberian steppes." He hesitated as he placed several sharp cooking knives on top of the other items he had gathered. "My son will come around with our wagon in an hour. We are leaving the city to stay with my wife's family in Gzhatsk. If you wish, you may travel with us for a way. It will be easier to find transportation to St. Petersburg once you are away from Moscow."

Octavia took only a second to make her decision. "That is most kind of you. Emma and I will be ready."

There was little time to lose. Her first stop was Mr. Renfrew's study. Heading immediately to his heavy pine desk, she began a careful search of the drawers. On finding one of them locked, she grabbed up the heavy iron poker by the fireplace and, without hesitation, smashed the brass fixture. As she had hoped, there was a leather purse hidden under a sheaf of documents. It was not quite as heavy as she might have wished, but at least the coins were all gold imperials.

Tucking it into one of her pockets, she continued to go through the rest of the contents, in case there was anything else that might be useful. Her hand came across a thin wooden case at the very bottom of the drawer. Opening it, she found a pistol, along with a supply of powder and bullets. She relatched the case and took it under her arm. After a quick look in the rest of the compartments, which turned up a small brass compass as the only other item of interest, she penned a quick note of explanation to the butler, then hurried back up to her own room to collect a few extra garments and personal things.

Emma was seated on the edge of her bed, a small valise at her feet. Her face looked serious, but Octavia was glad to note there was no trace of panic.

"Mr. Shishkov has offered to take us out of Moscow, to a place where we might more easily catch a coach to St. Petersburg. But we must leave immediately." Octavia crouched down so her eyes were level with those of the girl. "I think it the best decision, Emma. There will be chaos when the French march in, and I don't think we can trust that the Renfrews will give a thought to our being trapped here."

Emma's lips curled slightly at Octavia's frank assessment of her aunt's and uncle's character. "I imagine you are right."

"It may be a difficult journey, and mayhap even frightening or dangerous at times, but I truly believe it is our only choice."

"If you think it is the right decision, Miss Hadley, then you may count on me to do as you say." The girl's eyes took on a decided gleam. "Why, it sounds like we are embarking on some adventure just like out of Mrs. Radcliffe's novels. All we need is a tall, handsome hero to come to our assistance."

Octavia was secretly relieved that the girl was excited rather than terrified at the idea of setting off alone and unprotected into a strange country. However, she sought to put a damper on such fanciful notions. "Pray, do not count on that, Emma. Real life is rarely as romantic as the tales in those horrid novels. I'm afraid that I am all you have got."

Chapter Seven

*T*he wagon was piled so high with furniture and household goods that there was scarely room for Octavia and Emma to squeeze in. Shishkov's wife made no comment at the sight of the two foreigners, but the slight narrowing of her eyes as they climbed aboard betrayed what she thought of the additional burden. The son helped his father load the foodstuffs into the back, then went to take up the reins. With an apologetic shrug of his shoulders, Shishkov handed them their meager luggage before joining his family on the high planked seat.

Despite being wedged between a painted chest and several chairs, Octavia felt nothing but relief as the wheels rolled forward. She shifted a large sack of grain to serve as a seat, and arranged several blankets to create a passably comfortable nook for Emma and herself. Her arm came around the girl's shoulders, and she gave her a reassuring smile, which was returned without hesitation.

The situation in the streets had become noticeably more tense since morning. Crowds had gathered on a number of street corners, shouting frantic questions at the detachment of Hussars that passed by at a hurried trot. As church bells began to peal, there were signs of incipient panic—the breaking of glass as a stone smashed through a shop window, the clatter of hooves as an elegant carriage raced by, its team galloping at a breakneck speed, heedless of the milling people.

Despite the confusion, Shishkov's wagon managed to make its way to the outskirts of the city without mishap, and though the road leading north, away from the approaching enemy was filled with other fleeing vehicles, progress was steady enough. However, even though the sack of grain provided a measure of padding, the constant heaves and jolts were beginning to take their toll. Emma's excited observations had slowly ebbed away, and her lids began to droop. By the time the gilt domes of the Novedivichey Monastery had disappeared from view, she had fallen into a fitful doze, slumped against Octavia's shoulder.

Though she was exhausted as well by the dizzying turn of events, Octavia found her mind was in too much of a whirl to allow any sleep. She couldn't help but wonder whether her decision, made on the spur of the moment, would prove to be a rash mistake. What if the threat had been nothing but exaggerated rumor, and the Renfrews were to return to the capital to find their governess had gone haring off with their young ward? She grimaced. It didn't do to think about it, especially considering the purse of gold coins tucked inside the bodice of her gown. No doubt she could be charged with robbery as well as kidnapping.

A glance around served to calm such anxieties. It was clear that the danger was hardly imagined. Conveyances of every description jostled past the plodding wagon, haggard expressions on the faces of the drivers and their passengers. On more than one occasion, a mud-spattered officer, his once resplendent uniform in tatters, his horse lathered with sweat, galloped past, shouting curses at the slow-moving vehicles to move aside. Even now, far back in the distance, she thought she detected a thin haze of smoke rising from the direction of the city.

The wagon stopped long enough for Shishkov to dismount and come around to hand up a wedge of sour rye and a jug of cider. "I'm sorry, but there is no time to step down and stretch your legs. We had best keep going until nightfall," he murmured, trying to ignore the disapproving glare of his wife.

Octavia nodded as she gratefully accepted the food. "Of course. Do not give it a second thought. You have been more than kind already."

Emma stirred and looked up, blinking sleepily as the wagon started up again. "Are we there yet?"

Octavia couldn't help but smile, despite her own gnawing worries. "My little lamb, I'm afraid it will be many more stops and starts before we are there."

The girl sat up and rubbed her eyes. "Oh—of course. What a silly goose I am." She looked around at the dense forest of larch and spruce, nearly black in the fading light of late afternoon, with great interest. "It's very unlike England, is it not, Miss Hadley?"

"Very." Octavia passed her a piece of the bread.

Emma wrinkled her nose at the sight of the plain crust. "I'm not that hungry. I shall wait for teatime."

"Emma," counseled Octavia in a low voice, "there will be no such thing as teatime or the sort of meals you are used to at home while we are on this journey. In fact, there may be times when we have little or no food at all. You must get used to accepting what there is."

"But it's dry. Is there not some butter or jam?"

"There is not." At the sight of Emma's mouth turning downward into a pout, Octavia tried a different tack. "If the hardships seem too great, we can always turn back and wait meekly for what fate has in store for us in Moscow. I would certainly understand such a decision— adventure and danger are not the thing for most young ladies."

Emma reached for the bread and ate it without further complaint.

It was past dark when the wagon finally pulled into a clearing by the side of the road where the snow was only a dusting on the stubbled grass. Shishkov and his son began to unharness the horses while his wife set down several iron pots, taking care to make her displeasure with the situation known through a series of loud bangs. She stalked off to gather wood, leaving Octavia to help Emma down by herself.

"Come, let us try to be of some help," whispered Octavia as she led the girl toward the edge of the woods. "Pick up whatever small branches you can manage."

They both returned with an armful, earning a brief smile from their erstwhile cook.

"I think it best that you leave us off at the first place

where we might catch a coach going in the direction of
St. Petersburg," said Octavia in a low voice as she
dropped the wood by his side. "We do not wish to be
any more of a burden on you and your family than
necessary."

Shishkov pulled a face. "You must excuse my wife. It
is the shock of being uprooted from her—"

"Of course. She has good reason to be upset. All the
more reason why we should not impose on your hospitality past tomorrow."

He flashed her a look of gratitude, though it was
quickly replaced by one of concern. "How will you manage the . . . expense?"

"I have funds enough," she assured him. Her lips
quirked upward. "You were not the only one to, er,
explore for what items might be of use."

He nodded in approval. "Well, I see I shall not have
to worry overly for you, Miss Hadley."

His wife was slightly mollified on hearing that the unwanted guests would soon be leaving them. She unbent
enough to offer a thin smile as she passed a bowl of
bean soup to Octavia, and even went so far as to pat
Emma on the cheek. "You and the child may sleep in
the back of the wagon for tonight." The family's bedding
had already been spread out on top of a thick felt pad
by the fire, leaving a small sliver of space by the high
wooden sides.

Octavia made to protest, knowing it was where the
woman would normally have slept herself, but was
waved to silence. "Take it and be happy," she said in a
doleful voice. "It will likely be the best spot you have
for some time to come."

The next morning Octavia couldn't help but think that
if such a prediction were true, she might indeed wish
that she had stayed in the city and suffered whatever
the French had to throw at her. Her back ached from
the hard planks and every joint seemed stiff with cold.
With movements as jerky as those of a marionette, she
tried to tidy her gown, then bring some semblance of
order to her unruly hair. Shishkov had fetched a pot of
water from a nearby stream and offered her what was
left from brewing a kettle of tea to wash up. It was only

lukewarm, but a quick splash at least took away the dust of yesterday's travel, leaving her feeling somewhat better.

Emma peeked out from under her blankets. Displaying no adverse effects from a night on the hard boards, she scrambled up and bounced to the ground. "Did you see the stars, Miss Hadley? Every time I opened my eyes, the sky was aglitter with countless points of light!"

In truth, Octavia had been too tired to notice much of anything, but she nodded anyway. "Yes, quite magnificent, wasn't it?"

"I like sleeping outside," she announced. "I hope we can do it every night."

Octavia shuddered at the thought.

Breakfast was a quick affair, but the plate of hot bacon and cup of steaming tea did much to restore her flagging spirits even though a light but steady snow had begun to fall. By the time the fire had been put out and the wagon repacked, she was feeling more herself again. After traveling several versts down the main road, Shishkov turned off to the west.

The steady stream of carts and carriages all but disappeared, bringing a frown of concern to Octavia's face. Seeming to sense her dismay, the cook turned around. "Though we are now heading for Gzhatsk, in a few hour's time we intersect another road leading north. My wife's family knows the innkeeper there. There it will be easier to arrange for your passage to St. Petersburg."

Octavia was not unhappy to finally climb down from their perch on the sack of grain. Much as she appreciated the cook's kindness, every bone in her body ached from the rough jarring of the lumbering wagon. Surely even the worst-sprung coach must be a vast improvement over such a means of travel. She stamped her feet on the snowy ground, trying to restore some circulation, then reached up to help Emma over the jumble of crates and boxes. While Shishkov went to speak with the innkeeper, his son tossed down the two small valises.

The thought that soon they would be truly alone, without any friend, however casual, to turn to, made Octavia swallow hard. Her fingers crept of their own accord to touch the reticule looped on one wrist. During the morning, while Emma napped, she had taken the precaution of removing the loaded pistol from its case and placing it within easy access. She was not unaware of what sorts of dire things might befall a lone woman traveling with only a child for a companion. It didn't do to dwell on them, but at least she was not totally unprepared for whatever might happen.

The cook appeared at the door of the inn and motioned for her to approach. "Miss Hadley," he said in a low voice before taking her inside, "there is a fellow here willing to hire himself to you for the entire journey. It would be vastly more comfortable than traveling by public conveyance." He paused before adding, "And no doubt safer for you and the child. However, it will cost you."

"How much?"

He named the price.

Octavia took a moment to consider. The sum was high, but not outrageously so. She should still have enough left for their passage to London, if need be. And as her friend suggested, it offered a number of advantages. "That is acceptable."

"Good. Let us go make the deal." His voice dropped even more. "I will haggle, of course. You do not want him to see you as an easy mark. I have also not mentioned you are English. Just mutter an occasional answer in Russian, and you should be able to manage. He won't expect any more from a woman."

She nodded her understanding.

"Another thing, he will want an advance. Take it out now, so you do not show him your entire purse."

She had already thought to transfer several of the gold coins into her pocket and gave them a jingle. The sound elicited a thin smile of approval. "As I said, you have a good head on your shoulders."

He pushed the door open, and they went inside. It reeked of stale beer, and the air was thick with the smoke from the iron woodstove and a number of Turkish cheroots. Three rough-looking men drinking kvass at one of the small tables fell silent as she walked by. One of them made a lewd comment, and the others snickered, adding their own coarse remarks. She ignored them.

Shishkov led her to where a heavy fellow with greasy blond hair and a spiky beard to match was sitting with his hands outstretched to the stove. Though his person could have done with a bit of soap and water, he had a cheerful countenance and clear blue eyes that crinkled in good humor as he got to his feet. Octavia found herself warming to him already.

"This is my . . . relative, who wishes to join her husband in St. Petersburg," began Shishkov. "While she is interested in your services, only a drunken donkey would be foolish enough to consider such a price. . . ."

A heated negotiation followed, accompanied by dark mutterings, expressions of outrage, and injured shrugs. A price was finally arrived at, with each party assuring the other that he had gotten the best of the deal. On Shishkov's signal, Octavia passed several gold imperials to the newly hired driver.

"I wish to leave as soon as possible," she said.

He smiled, revealing a wide gap between his front teeth. "I shall see to having the horses harnessed. Best have a bite to eat here, ma'am. There's no telling what we may find ahead."

"Well, he seems a decent enough fellow," she whispered, once he had left the room.

Shishkov nodded. "The innkeeper says he is trustworthy, so I think you will not regret engaging his services."

They went back outside. Emma left off tossing pebbles into the brook that skirted the stableyard and came running to Octavia's side. The cook crouched down and touched her cheek. "Take care of yourself, Miss Emma," he said. "I wish you Godspeed on your journey."

She gave him a big hug. "Thank you, Mr. Shishkov. I shall miss your apple tarts and your blini with sour cream."

He got to his feet and held out his hand to Octavia. "And Godspeed to you, Miss Hadley. You are a good woman, to look after the child. And a brave one."

She felt a sudden constriction in her throat as she made her own thanks. It was not easy to part with the only acquaintance she had in this part of the world. Still, she kept on a brave face as he mounted the seat of his wagon, then turned for a final wave, as it lurched around a stand of silvery birches and towering Sitka spruce.

Emma's hand tightened in Octavia's. "What are we going to do now, Miss Hadley?" she inquired in a small voice.

"We are going to have a nice hot meal," she answered with a rather forced gaiety. "And then we will set off in grand style, in our own private carriage, traveling just as any grand heroine would."

The little girl's eyes lit up. "We are?"

"Yes. Mr. Fetisov is going to drive us all the way to St. Petersburg, so we will not have to sleep on a sack of grain again. Or spend the night under the stars. No matter how much you enjoyed it, I, for one, do not fancy being out in the open when the snows begin." She looked up as another flake fell on her cheek. "For it seems that a Russian winter is fast approaching."

Though loath to go back into the fetid public room, Octavia forced aside any lingering hesitation. They would have to get used to rude remarks and bold stares from now on. It was best to get it over with. Taking Emma's arm, she walked purposefully through the creaking door and chose a little table in the far corner of the room. The trio of men fell silent when she reappeared, but their attention soon returned to their tumblers of kvass, and their conversation slowly picked up again, to her considerable relief.

The innkeeper quickly brought over two bowls of thick borscht, along with a wedge of dark pumpernickel bread liberally studded with caraway seeds. Chiding herself for being so apprehensive, Octavia let their two valises and her reticule settle to the floor, then slid her coat off onto the back of her chair. They began to eat, Emma peppering her with all manner of questions about the coming journey around mouthfuls of soup. More than once, Octavia had to remind the girl to keep her voice to a low whisper, for to announce that they were foreigners on top of being women traveling unescorted could only bring even more unwanted attention. Still, the hot food and the warm room were a welcome respite from the rigors of the journey so far. . . .

A slurred shout suddenly interrupted their meal.

"Is that man speaking to us?" asked Emma, twisting in her chair to stare across the room.

"Ignore him," ordered Octavia in a low hiss. "And turn around this instant."

Startled by the sharp rebuke, the girl did as she was told. "But why is he yelling?" she persisted.

"Pay it no mind. He is saying something . . . improper."

"Why?"

"Not now, Emma. I will explain some other time. Put on your coat. We are going to leave."

"But I haven't finished—" She stopped in midsentence on catching the look on Octavia's face.

Octavia dropped a coin on the table, not caring that it was considerably more than necessary. "Stay close by my side, Emma," she said, reaching for their bags. "And pray, do not stop or say a word as we pass by them."

"You're a flashy bit of brass, aren't you?" came another loud taunt. "Coming in here passing out a handful of gold. Care to share your favors with us as well?"

Octavia's cheeks flushed crimson as she made for the door.

Emboldened by drink, one of them stood up to block her retreat. "Hear now, you hussy, we are talking to you!"

"I am a respectable woman. Kindly let me leave with my daughter."

"Respectable!" jeered one of the others. "No respectable woman travels alone." He lurched to his feet as well. "Is the girl included in the fun? She's a pretty little thing, ain't she, Dimitri?"

The third one smacked his lips. "A tasty morsel, Ilya. Both of them. And the purse will be even sweeter."

Laughter echoed through the dark space. The innkeeper, on hearing the drunken exchange, slowly backed toward his kitchen and crept behind the door. The bolt slid home with a distinct click.

Octavia swallowed her rising fear. "Stand aside, sir."

The one called Ilya narrowed his eyes, an ugly leer twisting his face. "Shut up! You ain't giving the orders here."

Behind the men, the door pushed open to admit her hired coachman. "Ma'am, the horses are ready—" He bit off his words, and his jovial face paled as he regarded the scene before him.

A knife flashed out from the pocket of one of the ruffians. "Be off, if you know what's good for you," he snarled. "You've got your share of that fat purse. We mean to have ours—and more."

"Mr. Fetisov . . ." Octavia tried to keep her voice level. "Perhaps you might assist us to your carriage."

He bit his lip. "I—I have a wife and child, ma'am," he stammered. "I'm—I'm sorry."

She fell back a step as the door slowly swung shut. Pushing Emma behind her so that she might serve to shield the girl, Octavia reached into her reticule and withdrew the pistol. "I shan't repeat it again—stand aside!" she said, with considerably more bravado than she felt.

A look of disbelief swept over Ilya's face, quickly replaced by a surge of anger at the prospect that their plans might be thwarted. "Pay the wench no heed," he snarled to his cohorts. Turning back to Octavia, he added, "You probably ain't never aimed one of those in your life."

"Perhaps not, but at this distance, I am bound to hit one of you," she said levelly as she cocked the hammer.

Ilya swore under his breath while the two behind him exchanged uneasy glances. They edged back toward their table.

"We are going to leave now. Any of you who trys to stop us will get a bullet for his troubles." Octavia whispered for Emma to follow close behind and started forward.

"Don't be idiots!" cried Ilya as the two others stumbled back another several paces. "She's only one bullet and there are three of us!"

Octavia paused and drew a bead on each of the men in turn. "So who wishes to be the lucky one? You? You? Or you?"

Ilya snarled a curse at her, then waved his hand at his comrades. "Split up, fools! Come at her from three directions."

Fear gripped at her heart. The man was right—there seemed to be no way out of this coil. Her mind raced, trying desperately to come up with some plan that might hold them at bay. Fortunately, the two men behind the leader still hesitated in obeying his command, allowing her a few extra seconds to think.

Then Ilya slowly took a nasty-looking knife from his own pocket and spat on the floor. "Afraid of a damn woman? I'll show you how to deal with the bitch." The blade cut through the air in a menacing swipe. "You are going to pay for this!"

Just as he was about to lunge forward, the front door swung open once again. Ilya's head jerked around. "I told you, coachman, get out of here or you shall have your gut carved up when we've finished with these two."

The figure silhouetted in the door was not, however, that of the driver Fetisov, but rather a much taller, leaner man. Glancing quickly from the group of men brandishing knives to Octavia with her pistol outstretched in a slightly trembling arm, a faint smile stole to the newcomer's lips.

"Why, Miss Hadley, I am glad to see that in the face of three assailants you have the good sense not to count on your knee."

Chapter Eight

"*M*r. Sheffield! What on earth are *you* doing here?"

His lips quirked. "Come, Miss Hadley, I should have expected something a good deal more dramatic than that. You might say, 'Oh, thank the Lord my daring rescuer has arrived!' Or you might at least swoon."

She glared at him. "That's *not* funny. This is no time for joking."

"No, I can see that." His expression immediately turned serious. "You have done extremely well for yourself, but now, perhaps you would allow me to take that pistol from you. I fancy I have a good deal more experience with such things than you."

She started to turn.

"Pray, do not alter your aim, Miss Hadley," he said calmly as he stepped inside the inn. "I am going to move to your side, but I suggest neither of us take our eyes off of these fellows."

Ilya flung a particularly obscene curse at Sheffield, then kicked a chair over to punctuate his mounting frustration. "Who is this son of a whore? What in the name of the devil are they saying?" he demanded in a querulous voice, for the last little exchange had taken place entirely in English.

"What we have been saying is that if you and those other two mangy curs don't take yourselves off instantly, I shall be forced to ram what few teeth you possess down your throat," answered Sheffield in Russian. "Which I may still do if you utter one more rude word in front of the ladies."

With a roar of fury, Ilya launched himself at the new

arrival, blade flashing in his outstretched hand. At the last moment, Sheffield twisted neatly aside. As he did so, his boot dealt a solid blow to the back of the other man's knee, drawing a scream of pain as the Russian sprawled to the floor. With uncanny quickness, however, Ilya rolled on his shoulder and sprang back to his feet. The knife was still in his hand, and with another angry curse he came at Sheffield again, this time a bit more warily.

Octavia bit her lip. The man was too close to Sheffield for her to risk a shot.

"What are you standing there for, like pigs stuck in mud?" he snarled at his companions as he feinted a slash at Sheffield's ribs. "He has no weapon. Grab him!" The knife darted forward again. "You miserable bastard, I'll roast your liver over the coals for interfering with me."

The two men glanced nervously at the pistol that quickly jerked around to point at them.

"One step and I assure you I shall pull the trigger!" warned Octavia. Her tone left little doubt as to her resolve. The two men melted back into the shadows, drawing a jeer from their leader.

"Cowards," grunted Ilya. "Running away like old women. I'll show you how to deal with these two." With a series of wild jabs of the blade, he forced Sheffield to retreat in the direction of the heavy pine bar. Despite his stocky build and a surfeit of alcohol, he moved with a cagey quickness. It was clear that this sort of situation was one he was well used to. A sneer curled on his thick lips as another flick of the knife caused Sheffield to back up again. In another few steps he would be trapped up against the long expanse of rough-hewn wood.

"Mr. Sheffield, have a care! The bar is close behind you!" called Octavia. Her attention was riveted on Ilya's flashing blade. Things seemed quite dire for her would-be rescuer, but he appeared unruffled by the danger.

"Thank you, Miss Hadley. I am aware of it." He flicked a chair in his attacker's way, causing him to stumble slightly. Spinning deftly around a second chair, Sheffield edged to one side, gaining a bit more space between the two of them.

Octavia squinted through the smoky haze. "I believe I have a shot, Mr. Sheffield. Shall I pull the trigger?"

He ducked around a small table. "Pray, not quite yet. I think I should rather risk a knife than your aim."

"Really! I am only trying to—"

"Miss Hadley! Watch out!" Emma tugged at Octavia's coat, just as an arm lunged at the pistol in her hand. She fell back with a cry of surprise, narrowly averting the man's grasp. As she did so, the weapon slipped from her hands and clattered to the floor. In an instant, her assailant dropped to his knees and began pawing around under a table for where it had fallen. Furious with herself for allowing such a thing to happen, Octavia was determined not to allow him to gain the upper hand. Her eyes fell on a nearby bottle, still half full with vodka. She grabbed hold of it, and when the man's head came up with a cry of triumph on his lips, her hand came down.

There was a sickening thud. The gloat quickly turned into a groan as the man sank to the floor in a lifeless heap.

"Miss Hadley! Over there!"

Octavia jerked around to where Emma was pointing. The third man, knife also in hand, had blocked Sheffield's line of retreat, and they now appeared to have him trapped. Ilya faked a move to his left, then whirled suddenly in the opposite direction, his blade snaking out in a lightning strike that cut dangerously close to Sheffield's arm.

With a gasp of dismay, Octavia finally managed to pry the pistol out of the fallen man's fingers. Taking as best aim as she could, she closed her eyes, said a silent prayer, and squeezed off a shot.

A resounding bang echoed through the dimly lit room.

Both Ilya and his cohort ducked instinctively, giving Sheffield just enough time to make his escape. Vaulting over one of the upturned tables, he hit the floor and, keeping low, slithered to where Octavia and Emma were crouching.

"I think it is time to make our exit," he drawled. "Kindly run to the door! *Now!*" he added as Octavia made to open her mouth.

Eschewing further argument, she took Emma's hand

and did as she was told, the smoking pistol still in her hand. Sheffield grabbed up their bags and followed close on their heels. While the other man was still cowering behind a cluster of chairs, Ilya recovered his feet and came in pursuit, angling his attack to cut off Octavia.

This time it was Emma who made use of a handy bottle. Ilya was forced to duck as the wildly spinning object came flying through the air. Sheffield pushed ahead, then let go of one of the bags long enough to land a jarring left to the other man's jaw. He toppled backward, onto the top of a round table, momentarily stunned.

"Go!" yelled Sheffield. Out of the corner of his eye, he could see that fellow Octavia had hit was slowly getting his wits back while the third one was finally creeping out from his hiding place.

Octavia flung open the door and the three of them stumbled into the bracing fresh air.

"Over there!" Sheffield indicated the sturdy black sleigh pulled to one side of the yard. Under the startled gaze of the two ostlers, they crossed the rutted snow at a dead run. On reaching the vehicle, Sheffield tossed the bags up on the seat, then followed by taking first Emma, then Octavia by the waist and depositing them unceremoniously on top of them. Leaping up beside the ladies, he gave a slap of the reins, sending the horses hurtling off at a gallop just as the three men emerged from the inn, brandishing a musket they had wrenched from the terrified owner.

A bullet whistled over their heads, spurring the horses to even greater speed. The vehicle bounced over the narrow road, then disappeared into a copse of silvery birch trees. It continued on for a mile or two at a breakneck pace before Sheffield pulled the horses to a leisurely walk.

He turned to face Octavia, one brow raised in question. "Are you all right, Miss Hadley?"

She nodded.

"And your redoubtable companion?"

Emma was staring at him, eyes wide with admiration.

"Yes, we are both fine," answered Octavia slowly.

"Thanks to your help, sir—even though it was a most foolhardy thing to do, facing off against three men with nary a means to defend yourself."

There was a flash of humor in his eyes. "Ah, but with you and that look of steely resolve on your face, I felt the odds were decidedly in our favor. I know *I* was quaking in my boots at the thought of that pistol being pointed at me."

She caught her breath. "Oh, do you think . . . that my bullet . . ."

"I believe the lantern on the far wall may have suffered a mortal wound, but no doubt the innkeeper will give it a hero's burial."

Despite herself, Octavia found she could not repress a laugh. "Do you never cease teasing, Mr. Sheffield—"

Emma's eyes grew even wider. "Is this the Mr. Sheffield who accompanied you on the journey from England?"

"Indeed it is." He grinned. "How heartening to know I have been the subject of Miss Hadley's conversation. I had feared I had not made much of an impression upon her—at least not one she might wish to recall."

A faint tinge rose to Octavia's cheeks. "Mr. Sheffield," she warned.

"Aren't you going to introduce me to your charming companion, Miss Hadley?" he continued smoothly. "I should be honored to make the acquaintance of such a stalwart young female. Indeed, she appears to be well on her way to matching the spirit you display in a pinch."

"Oh!" Octavia's color deepened on being reminded of her lapse in courtesy. "This is Emma Renfrew, sir. The young lady whom I was engaged to care for."

The girl blushed to her roots as Sheffield brought her gloved hand to his lips with a gallant flourish. "How do you do, Miss Renfrew? Alexander Sheffield at your service—though I doubt that either of you were really in need of much help back there."

The girl stammered some incoherent reply.

Sheffield's words caused Octavia to shudder. Until now, her emotions had still been too much in a whirl to reflect on how narrowly they had escaped an unthinkable fate, thanks to his aid. She lowered her eyes, her hands clenching together in her lap. "That is hardly true, sir. Without your timely intervention, I don't know what would have . . ." She trailed off, not wanting Emma to know just how dire their situation had been. "I . . . I certainly owe you a debt of gratitude."

"Not at all," he said quietly. "I seem to remember that when I was in need of assistance, you did not turn your back on me."

Octavia was saved from having to make a reply by a series of loud bangings from inside the sleigh. "Alex, Alex! Is something wrong?" called a muffled voice. "What happened to our tea?"

"Good Lord," muttered Sheffield under his breath. "I forgot all about Nicholas." At Octavia's questioning look, his mouth crooked in a rueful smile. "You are not the only one traveling with a child." He jumped down from his perch and went to unlatch the door.

"I am *not* a child," piped up Emma in an injured voice. "I'll have you know I am thirteen. Well, almost."

His hand slapped up against his forehead. "Child? Did I say child? My English has become sadly rusty these past few weeks. I can only plead that all the commotion has sadly addled my faculties. I pray you will forgive me."

Emma's look of dismay disappeared. "Oh, of course, Mr. Sheffield. It is entirely understandable—" Her nose wrinkled at the sight of the touseled dark head that poked out of the darkened interior. "Who is . . . that?"

"That, Miss Renfrew, is the young man whom I was . . . engaged to care for. Allow me to present Count Nicholas Alexander Scherbatov."

The two young people stared at each other.

Sheffield cleared his throat. "Nicholas, this is Miss Hadley and Miss Renfrew, our new traveling companions."

There was a prolonged silence before the boy spoke. "But, Alex, I thought you said it would be best if there were only the two of us." He slanted another look at the newcomers, Emma in particular. "Can't we leave them off at the next coaching stop?"

"That would hardly be a gentlemanly thing to do," answered Sheffield. His voice dropped a notch. "And speaking of gentlemanly behavior, that is hardly the proper way to acknowledge an introduction, as I'm sure you have been taught."

The boy flushed slightly at the mild rebuke. "How do you do, Miss Hadley"—there was a slight pause—"and Miss Renfrew?" The words were hardly more than a mumble, and the boy's eyes steadfastly refused to raise above ground level, but Sheffield chose to let it pass.

Octavia also ignored the less than perfect deportment, nodding politely at the young man. "It is a pleasure to make your acquaintance, Count Scherbatov."

Sheffield cleared his throat. "Just Nicholas, if you please, Miss Hadley. There are, er, reasons we do not wish to call attention to my young friend's identity."

The smile disappeared from Octavia's face. Good Lord, she thought. Had she escaped one set of criminals only to fall in with another? Had the impecunious tutor taken it into his head to do something rash—like make off with his young charge in order to demand a fat ransom? Or worse?

Her face must have betrayed the drift of her thoughts, for Sheffield gave a low chuckle. "I am aware that you have no great opinion of my character, but you needn't fear I am engaged in any nefarious schemes regarding the count, Miss Hadley. Perhaps if Miss Renfrew would consent to ride inside with Nicholas, and you would not mind enduring a bit more chill up on the box, I could explain things to you more fully."

Emma's lower lips jutted out. "I don't mind the cold, either."

"That may be so, but Mr. Sheffield wishes to discuss something with me. In private," chided Octavia gently.

The scowl became more pronounced. "Why can't *I* hear what Mr. Sheffield has to say, too?"

"Emma . . ."

The girl looked to speak again when Sheffield reached up and took her firmly by the waist. Her mouth froze in an "O" of surprise as he swung her down into his arms. Before she could recover her voice, he seated her beside an equally shocked Nicholas, then firmly shut the door in their mutinous faces.

"I imagine we shall hear some warning noises before

blood is actually spilled," quipped Sheffield as he took up the reins once more.

Octavia couldn't help but return his grin. "I assure you, Emma is not normally so ill-mannered."

"Nor is Nicholas."

"It is strange." She shook her head. "For some odd reason, they seem to be bringing out the worst in each other—"

"Hmmm. Rather like us."

Her face twisted in some confusion. "I . . . I . . ."

There was a decided twinkle in his eye. "Well, you have to admit it is true. I do not normally behave in such an ungentlemanly manner to innocent females, and you, I am sure, are not usually so rude as to deliberately avoid engaging in conversation with a fellow passenger for an entire voyage, no matter that the two of us were the only ones with anything of interest to say."

Octavia felt the heat rise to her face. "I . . ."

He saved her from having to go on by continuing himself. "But that is a matter for some other discussion. At present, you wish to know what in the deuce I am doing racketing across the country with young Count Scherbatov in tow, is that not so?"

Octavia had recovered enough of her composure to match his dry humor. "It *does* call to mind a number of questions."

"Yes, almost as many as why you are traveling unescorted with young Miss Renfrew."

"There is a very reasonable explanation to my predicament," she said quickly. "But I prefer to hear you out first."

"Very well." He paused as if to consider how to begin. "Nicholas has lost both of his parents in the last six months. His father, an officer on Kutusov's staff, was killed in Austria, while his mother died during an outbreak of influenza—"

"The poor lad," she interrupted. "But how is it that his English is so good? You cannot have spent more than a few weeks with him."

The faint smile reappeared. "No, I am not *that* good of a teacher. His mother was English, as was his grandmother." Then his expression sobered once again. "To put it simply, it appears Nicholas is now in grave danger from his Russian relatives. If the boy were to meet with an untimely accident, his father's considerable fortune, as well as the title, would pass to his uncle."

"I see." There was a slight hesitation. "I take it there has already been a questionable incident."

"Several, actually."

Octavia didn't speak for several minutes. The sleigh ghosted past several fields of stubbled wheat, then entered another thick stand of fir and larch. It was considerably darker underneath the thick boughs, and she pulled her heavy coat tighter to ward off the accompanying chill. A shiver ran down her spine, but somehow she sensed it was not entirely caused by the weather. Stealing a sideways glance at Sheffield's face, she noted the fine lines etched around his mouth and the dark shadows under his eyes. Despite his penchant for making light of things, he looked to be under a good deal of strain.

"Is this uncle pursuing you?"

He drew in a deep breath. "I am not sure," he admitted. "However, it would not be surprising. He is desperate for both the money and the title, and I do not doubt he will use every resource at his command to track us down."

"Just where are you going, that you believe the boy will be safe?"

"St. Petersburg."

Octavia started. "St. Petersburg! Why, that is where—" She bit her lip. "What makes you think he will be safe there? Has he relatives in the city who can be trusted?"

"Not exactly. But there are ships there heading for England."

There was another bit of silence before Octavia turned a penetrating gaze on him. "How is it you, a recently arrived tutor, have come to be involved in all of this?"

Sheffield kept his eyes leveled on the road ahead, though his mouth twitched in a reluctant smile. "I'll not waste time trying to fob you off with some made-up taradiddle. I have not been entirely forthcoming with you, Miss Hadley. I have been . . . engaged by Nicholas's

English relatives not merely to teach the lad history and geography, but to see him safely to London."

"It seems a rather dangerous assignment. Why you?"

"I imagine that, based on my past, they assumed I might be willing to take the risk."

"I hope the reward is worth it."

His jaw set. "Oh, it is."

Ah, so he was doing this for money. He must be getting quite a lot of it to venture losing his life. Her hands clasped even tighter in her lap. And just what did he mean by his comment about the past? No doubt there were any number of unsavory incidents that didn't bear asking about. She already knew he was prone to becoming thoroughly cupshot and had a penchant for chasing skirts. And he had handled the recent encounter with knives and fists with a cool aplomb that made it evident he was no stranger to back-alley brawls—or worse.

Sheffield slanted a faintly amused look at her. "Debating whether you have jumped out of the frying pan and into the fire?"

How was it that he seemed able to read her thoughts? A flush stole over her face as she fumbled to turn the collar of her coat up to cover her cheeks. "I imagine I am better off being roasted with you than being burned by that lot back there."

He laughed. "I shall take that as a compliment, for it will no doubt be the closest to one that I shall ever wrest from your lips."

There was a slow intake of breath. "Mr. Sheffield, I have no illusions as to your faults—and I am sure they are many—"

"Too numerous to recite," he murmured in interruption.

"—but I hope I should not be so churlish as to fail to convey my gratitude for your actions at the inn. Without your bravery, our fate would have been . . . unspeakable."

"Well, it didn't come to that, so let us put the matter behind us," he said quickly. Then, to keep her from dwelling on such disturbing thoughts, he sought to change the subject. "Now that you know of my travails, it's time you explain to me just how you have come to be wandering with Miss Renfrew in the wilds of the countryside."

She told him briefly what had happened, sticking to the barest of facts, but when she finished, his brow was furrowed in anger as well as concern.

"The greedy louts," he muttered. "They should be horsewhipped at the very least, for abandoning the two of you."

Octavia's jaw tightened. "Indeed. And you may be sure that I shall see to it that Emma never again has to endure the prospect of life with relatives who offer no warmth or affection but care only to wrest some sort of advantage for themselves from someone else's vulnerability."

He didn't answer, but a thoughtful expression came over his features as he guided the horses around a fallen spruce. It was only after the sleigh had brushed through a small drift of snow that he spoke again. "You mean to see the girl back to England, I take it?"

She nodded.

"And so you go to St. Petersburg as well." It was a statement rather than a question. "Just how do you expect to manage that?"

Octavia's spine stiffened. "That's hardly any of your concern. You may leave us off at the next coaching stop. I have sufficient funds and am perfectly capable of"— her voice caught for a fraction as she recalled what had just happened—"of managing a simple journey for the two of us." Even to her own ears, her bravado rang rather hollow, given the circumstances.

Sheffield gave a snort. "How long to you think it will take to have that scene at the inn repeated, Miss Hadley?"

Her chin jutted out.

"You may be as stubborn as a mule, but you are not a fool. You were very lucky that I happened along, but Lady Luck is a fickle companion—I wouldn't count on her company. A female traveling alone and unprotected is a tempting target for all manner of rapacious men, especially in this country." When she still didn't speak, he added, "If I leave you off as you wish, I don't doubt you will be robbed and raped by morning."

She sucked in her breath. "I certainly appreciate your tact and delicacy, Mr. Sheffield." The edge of sarcasm in her voice was honed by the fact that she knew he was probably right. "But you are forgetting I have a pistol with which to defend myself."

"It might make a difference if you could hit more than the damn wall," he retorted. "And perhaps *you* are forgetting that the sort of cur we are talking about usually runs in a pack."

Octavia refused to let her shoulders sag under the weighty truth of his words. "Well, I have no choice," she snapped. "So I will just have to cope as best I can and hope that Luck, if she is truly a lady, will not desert a fellow female."

"You have a choice, Miss Hadley, though I fear I cannot promise it will be any less perilous than the other alternative." His lips twitched. "Only your life may be at stake, not your virtue."

Despite everything, she couldn't keep her own mouth from quirking upward as well. "How very reassuring." Her expression then turned serious again. "You have enough troubles of your own without being burdened with mine. Your offer is very kind, but I find I must decline."

Sheffield's eyes narrowed. "Actually, I was wrong. You do *not* have a choice. You and the child are coming with us, and that is all there is to it."

"Oh come, you needn't feel compelled by some absurd notion of gentlemanly honor to put yourself in such an awkward position."

He stared straight ahead, a rigid set to his lean features. "Because, of course, I am no gentleman?"

She looked taken aback, then a soft laugh escaped her lips. "Mr. Sheffield, if you were a gentleman, you would not be stuck in such a coil as this, so far away from home. Outcasts and misfits such as us must do what we must to survive."

He grinned. "There, you see? You have just admitted we make a matched pair. Surely you cannot—"

A shriek from inside the sleigh interrupted the discussion.

Sheffield pulled the horses to a stop and jumped down from his perch, Octavia close on his heels. The sight that confronted the two of them when he yanked open the door was enough to draw a gasp of surprise from both adults.

Emma's fur hat was sadly askew, and her face was already stained with tears. Nicholas's cheek bore the angry red imprint of a slap, and though he refrained from any such unmanly display of emotion, his lower lip was quivering quite perceptibly.

"Good Lord," muttered Sheffield under his breath. "At least the two of us have not yet found it necessary to come to blows."

"At least not yet," murmured Octavia. In a louder voice she sought to sort out the trouble. "Emma—" she began.

"He pulled my braid!" wailed the girl.

"She called me a bad name!" cried the boy at the same time.

"I did not!"

"Yes, you did. You called me ass." He turned to Sheffield. "What is 'ass'?"

"It's a donkey, stupid."

"Emma!" said Octavia sternly. "It is most unfair to call someone stupid for not understanding—"

"*She* is the stupid one," jeered Nicholas. "She—"

"That is quite enough!" roared Sheffield.

An instant silence descended on the little group.

"Now, perhaps we may deal with this in a more civilized fashion." He regarded the two young people with a quelling gaze. "Miss Renfrew, kindly tell me what happened."

A squeak of protest from Nicholas was quickly cut off by another stern look. "You will have your turn as well," said Sheffield. He crossed his arms over his chest. "Miss Renfrew? Miss Hadley and I are waiting."

Emma's eyes dropped to the carriage floor. "He pulled my hair. Hard. So I slapped him."

"And why did he pull your hair?"

Her mouth scrunched up in a rather guilty expression. "Boys are odious," was all she muttered.

Sheffield turned to Nicholas.

"She called me a bad name, Alex," he said with a pout. "I do not like her at all. I want her to leave—the sooner the better."

Sheffield's countenance began to glaze over. Armed assailants he could deal with, but two brangling children . . .

"He started it, Mr. Sheffield. Truly, I did not even speak to him until it became clear he was out to provoke me."

The boy howled in outrage. "That's not true!"

Octavia took one look at Sheffield's confused expression and took matters into her own hands. "I've heard quite enough from both of you. Emma, you will apologize this instant to the count for your unladylike behavior."

"But—" One look at her guardian's face caused the girl to reconsider her protest. A barely audible mumble followed, delivered with a decided lack of grace, but Octavia let it pass.

The boy's smug expression was quickly wiped from his face by her next words. "And you, Master Nicholas, will apologize to Miss Renfrew for your own shabby conduct."

The look of mute appeal thrown Sheffield's way was studiously ignored. The boy swallowed hard, then forced out the required response.

"Now the two of you will shake on it."

With great reluctance, the two small hands barely grazed each other before being jerked back as if scorched by a flame.

"Consider any debt you feel you might owe me paid in full," murmured Sheffield as his fingers sought to loosen the scarf at his neck.

A ghost of a smile appeared on her face as she stepped several paces away from the carriage. "Perhaps now you would care to reconsider your offer?"

"Surely it can't get any worse than that."

Her brow arched. "Did you not have any sisters, Mr. Sheffield?"

He shook his head.

"Well that explains such a sanguine outlook." She

pulled her coat closer and stamped her feet on the frozen ground. "Should we not be off before the horses take a chill? We could argue until doomsday without coming to any accord, but it can wait until later." Her gaze darted back toward the door that was still ajar. "I suppose I had best ride inside to forestall any further fireworks."

"You have my eternal gratitude."

"I would rather have your best efforts at the ribbons. I have a feeling the sooner we get to St. Petersburg, the better."

Chapter Nine

Sheffield settled the fur blanket around his legs and set the horses in motion, grateful for a bit of solitude in which to order his thoughts. He should be cursing the heavens for the trick of fate that had landed yet more responsibilities in his lap, but oddly enough the only sound coming from his throat was a burble of rueful laughter. Well, it certainly could not be said that their encounters with each other lacked for a touch of the dramatic. Good Lord, it was *he* who had nearly swooned, rather than the intrepid Miss Hadley, on seeing her confronted by those three armed ruffians.

The sight of her brandishing a pistol at them had stirred a number of strange sensations in his breast. He wasn't sure whether he wanted to ring a peal over her head for having put herself in the way of such danger or pull her to his chest and melt the steely resolve on her lips with his kisses. What he was sure of was that he would have launched himself bare-handed at any number of assailants who posed a threat to her.

He shook his head. Chivalry had not exactly been his strong suit since longer than he cared to remember. It made no sense. She was not by any stretch the most beautiful woman he had ever encountered, nor were her charms such as to twine a man in a net of silky infatuation. At that thought, another laugh nearly burst forth. *Seek to charm him?* By God, she could barely tolerate his presence! But somehow, she affected him like no other woman he had ever met.

Sheffield's brow furrowed. Over the past ten years he had met quite a few others, and each had provided a certain diversion. Yes, women had always served as a welcome distraction. The curve of a breast, the throaty trill of a laugh, the sensuous smile as flagrant as a written invitation to dally—at one time or another they had all heated his blood enough to make him feel . . . alive. But the passion was always fleeting, the transient pleasure unable to keep at bay the dull ache that inevitably crept back to suffuse his very being.

What was it about the prim Miss Hadley that seemed . . . different? When he looked in her eyes, he saw no trace of artifice, only a keen intelligence that cared not a whit who perceived it. Her words, as well, were unadorned with fripperies. None of the banal observations usually mouthed by those of her sex for Miss Octavia Hadley! Why, he realized with a start, she was the only female of his acquaintance with whom he felt he could have an interesting conversation, save perhaps his sisters-in law.

There was no denying that she had spirit and courage as well, qualities he was more used to attributing to his friends than his bedmates. Nothing seemed to quell her spark. Eyes blazing, she kept her chin up, as proud as her namesake in the face of adversity. He had only to recall their first encounter to be reminded of that. Most other females would have screamed or fainted, but she had relied on her own resources—quite credibly he might add. A certain part of his anatomy had ached for some time after that.

With a rueful grimace, he realized that their first meeting had also revealed that she possessed other, more conventional female attributes beneath that high-necked wool gown. And despite her cold dismissal, he had caught the stirrings of a hot passion lurking beneath the icy shell. He found himself wondering what it would be like to fan its fire again, to have its flames lick over him and . . .

The runners of the sleigh hit a frozen rut, jarring his thoughts back to frigid reality. The cold had dropped even more, forming his breath into ethereal white puffs, which the biting wind quickly swirled away. Sheffield watched as they were dispersed, then tightened his grip on the reins. Wishes and dreams were as chimerical as such clouds. He had learned that long ago. Just as he had learned not to probe too deeply into his feelings, for the pain was too searing. It was best not to begin now. No matter how intriguing he found Miss Hadley, the attraction would soon die away, just like everything else that had mattered in his life.

It was after dark before they approached a low split-log structure set off from the thick forest by a field of wheat. Smoke curling up from the single chimney was the only sign of life, for the shutters were pulled so tightly closed that nary a shaft of light could escape. The stable, barely larger than a hen coop, also appeared deserted, but the sound of the runners crunching over frozen puddles brought a figure swathed in a grimy assortment of wool shuffling from inside, his muttered curses exploding in small puffs of vapor like so many artillery shells.

Sheffield stumbled down from his seat, his feet so numb with cold that he might as well have been walking on blocks of wood. Somehow he managed to undo the door latch and hand the three occupants out from inside the inky interior.

"It hardly looks to be the most appealing of places, but I fear we have little choice. At least there is a fire and, with any luck, a hot meal." The act of speaking proved so difficult that the words came out in little more than a labored slur.

Octavia's lips pursed as she regarded the dusting of ice crystals on his cheeks, but she merely nodded and set to follow the children toward the inn. Behind her, Sheffield's steps faltered again, as he fought to regain some feeling in his lower limbs. She paused, then turned back and slipped her arm under his elbow

"You've only to manage a few more paces, Mr. Sheffield."

Inside, the room was not nearly so bad as expected. The dim oil lamps revealed that the place was moderately clean, and the tall tiled stove set in the corner cast enough warmth to make it almost cozy. Without a word, Octavia guided Sheffield close to its hissing bulk and slowly unwound the scarf from his neck. He started to fumble with the buttons of his coat, but somehow his fingers refused to cooperate in the normal manner. She pushed them gently aside and undid the fastenings herself, letting the garment slide off his shoulders and to the floor.

"Emma, bring a chair for Mr. Sheffield."

The girl obeyed with alacrity, dragging the heavy wooden legs across the uneven planks and nearly knocking over Nicholas in the process. He made a face, but the little kick he lashed out wasn't quick enough to find its mark. Though the action didn't escape her notice, Octavia chose to ignore it. She reached up to take the thick wool hat from Sheffield's head. "Sit down, sir."

"I c-c-can—" To his chagrin he found his teeth were chattering uncontrollably.

"You will sit down like a sensible person so I can help you remove those boots, or do you intend to be stubborn enough to compel me to use force?" Her eyes strayed to the floor. "The leather looks as stiff as a board."

He sat down without further argument, for she looked perfectly capable of carrying out her threat.

The proprietor approached, eyeing their modest attire with an ill-disguised frown.

"Tea. Right away, please," said Octavia. "And something hot to eat."

The man didn't move.

Her head came up. "We are cold, and hungry. You do have food and drink here?" she demanded.

A rather rude grunt followed. "For those who can pay."

"Be assured, you will be well rewarded for your trouble." She withdrew several coins from her pocket and tossed them at the man's feet.

The change in the fellow's demeanor was instantaneous. "Yes, ma'am," he said as he bent to retrieve the money. "Right away."

"Do you always find a way to make someone jump at your command?" murmured Sheffield, his face sufficiently thawed to manage coherent speech. "Perhaps you should have remained in Moscow to direct Kutusov in fending off the Frogs."

"I have enough on my hands trying to deal with two young people intent on doing each other bodily harm and a tutor who seems to lack for common sense, if not for sarcasm," she retorted.

He couldn't repress a chuckle. "It was that bad inside the carriage?"

"Don't ask." Her tone softened considerably as she eased off the first boot and felt his foot. "But not as bad as what you have endured during the journey. Your feet are nearly frozen, Mr. Sheffield. And your cheeks are only now beginning to lose their coating of frost."

He cleared his throat as he leaned over to tug off the remaining boot. "Well, I daresay I'll survive." The boot slipped through his fingers and clattered to the floor. A sigh of relief followed, though he sought to mask it with a cough.

"It's hardly a joke. I'll not have you forced to drive hour after hour without relief. You'll catch your death of cold."

It had been so long since someone had voiced concern over his welfare that he was left speechless for a moment. Then a slight smile came to his face. "I appreciate the sentiment, Miss Hadley, but there is little choice if we are to reach St. Petersburg."

Her chin jutted forward. "I shall just have to learn to handle the ribbons too. That way we may spell each other. I have quite a lot of experience in driving my father's gig. It cannot be that much more difficult to handle a team and sleigh."

Sheffield nearly spilled the steaming cup of tea the proprietor had handed to him. But the urge to tell her she was utterly mad died on his lips on catching the glint of determination in her eye. He suddenly found himself thinking on how many of the soft, voluptuous ladies who had shared his bed would make such an offer to share the hardships of driving a lumbering sleigh through the beginnings of a Russian winter.

"Stop kicking me!"

"I'm not kicking you. I'm swinging my foot and you are in the way."

Octavia turned quickly. "Emma, Nicholas, you must remember not to speak English in a public place," she warned in a low voice. "We do not wish to call attention to ourselves."

The girl lowered her head and gave a sniff. "Then tell him to leave me alone," she whispered.

Nicholas crossed his arms and glowered.

The arrival of four bowls of an indeterminable stew, along with a stale loaf of black bread, forestalled the latest skirmish. The two young people were too tired to bicker and eat at the same time, so they applied themselves to the meal without further ado. Octavia ate in silence too, but noted with some concern that Sheffield hardly took a bite. Instead he ordered a bottle of spirits to go with his tea. Despite his earlier attempts at dry humor, he looked unusually serious as he poured a glass and drained it with one gulp.

She couldn't help but wonder whether he was roundly cursing the fates that had thrust her and Emma in his path as he quickly measured out a refill. He could hardly be blamed if he was, she admitted. His task had become infinitely more difficult with the addition of two more people to look after. And if he failed to convey the young count to St. Petersburg, it wasn't likely he would be paid a farthing for all his risks. She could well imagine what that would mean for an impecunious tutor—or whatever he was. Perhaps he would not be forced to the street, as she would be, because men had other options. But the future would no doubt be grim.

She stole another glance at his shadowed profile. Judging by the lines around his tired eyes and compressed mouth, the past had not been terribly kind either. On rare occasions the mask of nonchalance slipped, revealing quite another face, one that showed the scars of pain and doubt. What sort of life had he lived that had left such marks? What sort of perceived failures? The signs of dissolution were evident. That he drank too much she knew. That he looked to women for amusement she guessed. His other vices she could only imagine.

Yet, with a curse of her own, she vowed she would not be the cause of his failure in this endeavor. In spite of their obvious differences, she felt a strange sort of kinship bound them together. After all, they were both friendless, penniless souls depending solely on their own wits and fortitude to survive in the world. So regardless of his considerable faults, she was determined to be a help rather than a hindrance.

The sound of a knife falling to the floor disturbed her

reverie. Sheffield's chin had sunk to his chest and a low rumble emitted from his chest. Octavia laid aside her spoon and rose. It took little time to arrange for two rooms once another few coins had changed hands.

She returned and laid a hand on his shoulder. "Mr. Sheffield."

His eyes fluttered open, and he stared at her in some consternation before he seemed to recall where he was. He grimaced as he shifted against the hard back of the chair.

"I've taken rooms for us," she said. "I daresay you will be a bit more comfortable sleeping there, though not much. I imagine we'll all be flea-bitten by morning."

"Ah, but when you are jug bitten, you tend not to notice." He signaled to the proprietor and called for the whole bottle of vodka to take with him.

"Surely you don't mean to drink that, not with the boy with you." Even though she spoke softly her voice was full of reproach.

He gave her a mocking smile. "Don't worry. I don't mean to share it."

She found it difficult to believe she had ever felt in charity with the rogue. "You should be ashamed of yourself, setting such a bad example."

His eyes narrowed. "Well, if it bothers you so much, put the children in together and share my room instead. After all, you are no stranger to my habits. I daresay you might even unbend enought to admit that you rather enjoyed your brief taste."

"I see it was a mistake to get your blood heated," she said coldly. "Apparently in such a state you become so desperate you will grab at anything in a skirt, even a middle-aged spinster."

His brows drew together.

"Now kindly remove your hand from my elbow and try not to make an unseemly spectacle in front of innocent eyes."

His arm fell away, and he took up the bottle. "Come along, Nicholas, let us find our beds. Good night, Miss Hadley and Miss Renfrew." After a moment he added, "Sweet dreams."

Hardly, thought Octavia sourly.

*   *   *

Gregori Bechusky, head steward to Vladimir Illich Rabatov, regarded the deserted cottage with a snarl of frustration and stalked back to a copse of trees. The young count's uncle had entrusted him with tracking down the boy, and given the fat purse that was promised for completion of the job, his mood took an evil swing on finding his quarry had somehow slipped through his fingers. Mounting his horse, he threaded his way through the needled boughs to rejoin the three other men hidden in the forest.

"They've left. Let us split up and make inquiries." He tossed several gold imperials to each of his cohorts. "Someone must have seen or heard something that will be of use to us. And be quick about it. We'll meet back at the tavern in several hours."

The others spurred off, while the steward sat for a moment in deep thought. It had been a fortuitous break, to overhear the idle comment about the young count's nurse having recently retired to her old village. His instincts had told him the boy would be here, so the ensuing disappointment at finding the place empty was only the more galling. *But he hadn't been wrong.* A careful inspection of the old woman's dwelling had revealed traces of the boy's presence, so a starting point had now been established. A trail, however well disguised, would lead from it. And he did not doubt for an instant that he would be able to suss it out.

His confidence was soon proved justified by the nugget of information one of his men pried out of the old woman's nephew. A sleigh had been purchased only two days ago, along with two shambling nags. Bechusky gave a grim smile as he drained his flagon of kvass. His task was going to be that much easier with the young count on the run rather than holed up at Polyananovosk.

As his fingers drummed on the rough pine, he considered where his quarry might be headed. The advance of the French army made Moscow, or points west, an unlikely choice. Routes south, too, were fraught with danger. East or north seemed more likely. It should not be difficult to pick up the trail.

Only one nagging question remained unanswered. He had determined that the old nurse had left with Riasanov, heading back in the direction of the Scherbatov estate. *So who was with the boy?* The description of the tall, broad-shouldered driver of the young count's vehicle matched up with none of the household servants his spies had reported were still loyal to the boy's family.

After a few more minutes, Bechusky slid his chair back and slapped a coin onto the table, signaling to the others it was time to be on their way. As he checked the pistol tucked inside the folds of his coat, he decided it was not worth worrying about the stranger. After all, it hardly mattered who the fellow was—he was not going to be alive much longer.

Sheffield woke with an aching head and a wooly mouth, an all-too-familiar condition that left him longing for Squid's sympathetic ministrations and the soothing draughts the resourceful valet could always be counted on to deliver to his bedside. There was, however, no magic elixir waiting to wash away the sour taste of the previous night. He winced as he shifted under the ragged blanket, not only from the stab of pain at his temples but on recalling his behavior. Lord, he had acted badly.

No, he had acted worse than badly.

Damnation! How was it that a prim, sharp-tongued governess had him in such a pelter? He had barely been able to touch his dinner, so disquieted had he been by her unexpected actions. He was well aware of her intellect, her pluck, and even her prickly pride. It was her quiet kindness and compassion that had thrown him into such a state of confusion. Why, she had made it quite clear that she didn't even like him, and yet she had noticed his stumbling steps, and it had mattered to her that he had been cold and tired. Just as during that first night aboard the ship she had somehow sensed his desperate need not to be abandoned and hadn't walked away, though it was what he richly deserved. He couldn't remember the last person who had ever bothered to see in him aught but the studied nonchalance of a hardened libertine.

He swallowed hard. There had been care in her voice, gentleness in her fingers as they removed his boots. And when her ungloved hand had grazed his cheek while unwinding the scarf from his neck, its touch had sparked embers inside him he had thought long since burned out. If truth be told, the heat frightened him more than he cared to admit. He had grown so used to the cold, the thought of rekindling any flame was too threatening. Fire crackled, danced, licked, and roared. It was something one couldn't control. Badly singed so long ago, he had vowed he would never let it happen again.

But despite all such resolve, he found himself being drawn to the odd figure of Miss Hadley like a moth to a candle. The attraction was thoroughly puzzling. Over the past ten years, he had fallen into bed with any number of willing ladies, always careful to let them touch nothing of him but the lithe planes of his flesh. Why was it now that he appeared in danger of letting a rather prim, outspoken female get beneath his skin? A low groan caught in his throat. He wasn't sure he wanted to face the answer and so he had done his best to push her away. To keep his own fears at bay he had deliberately sought to give her a disgust of him.

Well, he had certainly succeeded in doing that. In spades.

He rolled onto his side, causing the empty vodka bottle to fall to the floor.

"Cousin Alex?" ventured a small voice. "Are you . . . awake?"

A wave of guilt washed over him. Good Lord, he had nearly forgotten about Nicholas! "Yes, lad." He propped himself up on one elbow and ran a hand through his tangled hair. It was still quite dark outside, but by the faint stirrings below in the taproom, he figured it must be morning.

"Are you going to want to stay in bed all day?" asked Nicholas, the light from the single candle illuminating his pinched face.

"Why would you think that?"

There was a long pause. "Mr. Bolotnikov, my old tutor, kept spirits hidden in his desk. Whenever he claimed he was too ill to rise for my lessons, I could be sure of finding an empty bottle stashed somewhere in the schoolroom. It started to happen often enough that Mama found him out. She was very angry and sent him off." His eyes strayed to the floor. "She said it was a . . . a bad habit."

"She was right."

"Then why do *you* do it?"

Sheffield would never have imagined that a twelve-year-old was capable of making him blush, yet the simple question left him feeling more exposed than if he'd been caught running stark naked down Rotten Row. He turned his head to find the boy was looking at him expectantly, which only served to increase his discomfiture. Indeed, he had to fight down the urge to throw the covers up over his head and, like the unfortunate tutor, claim he was too indisposed to face the day. Instead, he forced himself to a sitting position and cleared his throat—but the words remained stuck there. Answers were proving elusive this morning.

"We had best hurry in dressing," he finally mumbled. "It would not do to keep Miss Hadley and Miss Renfew waiting too long."

To his relief, that managed to deflect the boy's attention to another touchy subject. Nicholas's lower lip slowly jutted out. "I don't want to travel with them any longer. I hate girls. They are silly and helpless, and do nothing but whine and carry on in the most annoying manner."

"I should be careful about voicing such an opinion within earshot of Miss Hadley," replied Sheffield dryly. "And as for taking them along, I'm afraid we have no choice—I've already explained that as gentlemen, we simply cannot abandon them. Besides, Miss Renfrew has already proved herself to be a most brave and resourceful companion."

Nicholas shot him a look of disbelief. "Ha! Miss Hadley told me how it was *you* who saved them from a band of ruffians."

"Did she also tell you how it was *she* who was holding three of them at bay with a pistol when I arrived?"

The boy's eyes gew wide.

"Or how Miss Renfrew took up a bottle and flung it

at the leader, just as he was about to stick his knife in
my ribs? With quite credible aim I might add."

"She did?" he said in a faint voice.

Sheffield nodded. "Yes, and she doesn't appear to be
making a whine or a squeak about being abandoned in
a strange country by selfish relatives, with nary a soul to
turn to if not for the kindness of Miss Hadley. Both her
parents are deceased, you see."

Nicholas was silent for several moments. Then, without further argument, he pushed back his covers and
began to pull on his jacket.

"I hate boys. They are brainless and loud, and do nothing but think of stupid pranks to annoy those who are
around them." Emma pulled the blanket up to her chin,
a black expression on her scrunched features. "Can't we
hire some other coach to take us to St. Petersburg?"

"We have tried that, without a great deal of success,"
reminded Octavia. "And even if we wished to try such
a risky thing again, I doubt we could find a vehicle or
driver willing to undertake such a journey. No, I fear we
have no choice but to continue on with Mr. Sheffield."

"Well, at least *he* is not in the least odious."

Ha! thought Octavia, running a brush through her hair
with a bit more force than necessary. She left her private
feelings on that score unsaid, however, as she searched
for some means to lessen the girl's pique. Suddenly, an
idea occured.

"Emma, perhaps you would have a little more charity
for the poor lad if you knew the real story." She lowered
her voice to a conspiratorial whisper. "I am sure Mr.
Sheffield would agree that you are old enough to trust
with the secret. . . ."

Emma waited with bated breath.

"Did you know that Nicholas has recently lost both
his parents?"

The girl bit her lip and shook her head.

"That is not the worst of it. His wicked uncle covets
his title and fortune, and is determined, so it seems, to
see that some 'accident' befalls Nicholas. So Mr. Shef-

field has been engaged by the boy's English relatives to bring him safely to London."

Emma's eyes took on a decided shine. "Why, this is even more exciting than one of Mrs. Radcliffe's novels."

Octavia repressed a smile. "I think it would be less than honorable if we were to abandon the two of them. There is a real chance that Nicholas may be in danger during this journey. And knowing men and the stupid things they are wont to do, he and Mr. Sheffield are bound to need our help along the way."

The girl was out of bed and dressed before Octavia had stuck the last hairpin into the prim bun at the back of her neck.

They descended the stairs before the men. Octavia wheedled the promise of a decent breakfast out of the proprietor, then took him aside by the elbow for a huddled conference. After a moment, he bobbed his head, a mercenary smile revealing a set of crooked yellow teeth, and moved off, leaving her to take a seat with a rather satisfied expression on her face.

It was not long before Sheffield appeared, trailed by Nicholas. Awkward greetings were exchanged; then the arrival of the tea and a platter of cold meats and bread made further words unnecessary. Sheffield took up his glass and walked to the window where he stood gazing out at the pale morning light, smudged gray with the threat of storm. As he passed her, Octavia did not fail to note the haggard hollows of his cheeks or the dark circles under his eyes. Her lips thinned, but whether in concern or in censure even she wasn't sure.

Truly, he was the most exasperating person she had ever encountered—cool and courageous one moment, obnoxious and odious the next. He had wit and intelligence, which he took pains to hide behind a mask of bored indifference. *Which was the true Mr. Sheffield?* She thought for a moment, deciding the answer was much more complex than she had first imagined. Why, for a fleeting instant, she had the oddest notion—perhaps he wasn't sure either.

Oh, it was clear he wished the world to think him a cynical rake, caring for naught but his own pleasures.

But she had heard the pain in his voice that night on the ship, a cry of longing no amount of spirits could slur. She had no notion of what lay behind such feelings, but what she did know was that he was not as hardened as he pretended. Even his blatant attempts at seduction were softened by the look she had detected in his eyes. Rather than a calculating coldness, there was something more akin to regret.

Octavia swallowed the last of her tea. Whether he was an unprincipled rogue or a stalwart champion, he was who they were all depending on to get them safely to St. Petersburg. And judging by his current appearance, they had better get moving.

Chapter Ten

Sheffield swirled the dregs of his brew. He could hardly blame her for the look of disgust that spasmed over her features as he had passed. His actions had, after all, been deliberately insulting. Yet for some reason it bothered him to think she found him less than admirable. His jaw tightened. It should hardly matter since he had become well used to disappointing those around him.

With a muttered oath he drank off the rest of the thick, sweet tea, vowing to put all such disquieting reflections aside. In their current state, his fuzzed wits had enough to deal with in trying to get all of them safely north, without becoming sidetracked in such wayward meanderings. He must marshal his mismatched troops and get them on the road, despite the fact that the rapidly dropping temperature was already tracing a pattern of ice crystals acrosss the windowpanes.

It would be bitterly cold on the driver's box, and nearly as uncomfortable inside the small sleigh, for the few blankets he had managed to procure would be woefully inadequate to stave off the brewing storm. But there was little choice in the matter. They must keep moving north. At least, he thought with a rueful grimace, there was little chance that he would have to endure the frosty demeanor of his new traveling companion during the journey. Under the circumstances, it was quite unlikely she would renew her absurd offer to handle the ribbons.

He turned from the window, only to catch a glance of Octavia rising in response to a gesture from the proprietor. It was with some surprise that he watched her follow the fellow into a small storage room, then emerge a short time later with a heavy blanket in her hands, twisted together to form a makeshift sack.

"Are the two of you ready to leave?" he inquired, on coming up to her side. His brows couldn't help but arch at the sight of the bundle in her arms.

She ignored his questioning look. "Yes. As the weather looks to be worsening, we should at least try to cover some of the miles between us and our goal." Her manner was cool, but no more than he expected.

Sheffield's head inclined a fraction. "Then I shall give notice that the horses are to be readied." Though he was only outdoors for a brief time, his cheeks were ruddy with cold when he came stomping back in.

Octavia laid a hand on his sleeve as he bent to pick up her small valise and that of Emma's. "A moment, Mr. Sheffield." She withdrew a sturdy pair of felt boots and a thick fur hat from the recesses of the blanket. "I believe you may be a bit more comfortable in these."

His face betrayed his utter surprise. *"What?"*

"You will catch your death of cold if you try to drive wearing what you have on."

He was speechless for a moment. "How did you manage to come by these?"

"I purchased them, of course." She gestured to the blanket. "And several more blankets and other things that may come in useful."

"You bought those for me?" he asked, unable to keep the note of incredulousness out of his voice.

A ghost of a smile crossed her lips. "You needn't make a fuss about it. They are hardly tokens of endearment, Mr. Sheffield. It is in my best interest to see to it that you do not expire before we reach St. Petersburg."

His lips quirked upward too. "Even though what you really wish is to take a poker to my skull for my behavior of last night."

"Or some other part of your anatomy."

He gave a bark of laughter. "I shall have a care in your proximity, knowing full well you are quite capable of putting me in my place."

There was a brief pause. "Then let me start now. If

we are to rub along together without constant sparks, you will kindly cease such crude attentions. Your amorous games may be amusing to you, but I do not find them so. Not in the least."

"Games?"

"Oh come now, don't play the fool. I have seen you are no such thing. And as I have told you before, you are much more interesting to be with when you do not feel impelled to play the hardened wastrel." Her voice lowered. "And it is not setting a good example for the children."

With a start, he realized her words, though couched as a set down, only had the effect of lightening his dark mood. It was a long time since anyone had spoken to him as if he were capable of doing the right thing. Indeed, she seemed to be implying that she did not consider him completely beyond the pale.

"So, do we have an agreement?" she went on.

He regarded her with an inscrutable expression. "Very well, Miss Hadley. No games."

The sleigh veered precariously to one side. "Steady! You must try not to jerk the reins, but rather use a steady presssure." Sheffield's mittened hands came over hers. "Like so." In an instant, the horses had steadied their gait and swung back to the center of the narrow road.

Octavia muttered an oath under her breath as she sought to manage the tangle of leather.

"You are doing a very credible job," he added.

She had indeed insisted on learning to handle the team, and no amount of argument had blunted her determination. He had finally relented, trusting that a few minutes on the box would serve better than words to convince her of her folly. However, she had surprised him once again, showing her mettle in yet another way.

She grimaced but was able to control a sway to the left on her own. "Actually, I do believe I am getting the hang of it. Perhaps you would like to go inside and rest for a bit. I promise I shall not drive us into a ditch or shatter a runner."

"Are not you cold and tired yourself?"

She shot him a quick glance. "You appear to need it more than I."

Sheffield looked away for a moment. "Don't worry," he answered in a clipped voice. "I am well able to function, no matter what it may appear."

Octavia made no reply but kept her eyes leveled on the road ahead. It was only after several miles had passed that she spoke up again.

"Why?"

Sheffield's head came up with a start. "Why what?"

"Why do you feel compelled to submerge your talents in such superficial behavior?"

This question, of all the ones raised that morning, was perhaps the most blunt. Yet it cut more deeply than the others. "Have a care for that rock," he snapped. "And my actions are none of your deuced business."

She guided the horses around the obstacle. "You are quite right. They are not."

An awkward silence descended over them, broken only by the rustle of the heavy pine boughs and the creaking of the old sled.

"Sorry," he finally muttered. "I expect I owe you an apology, both for now and for last night."

Octavia's features remained impassive. "You owe me nothing, Mr. Sheffield. As you have so rightly reminded me, your personal matters are none of my concern. I am quite aware that neither of us would have chosen the current situation, since we are exact opposites."

Sheffield seemed to remember from his scientific studies that opposites could attract.

"But we can at least try not to raise each other's hackles," she continued. "Now, don't you wish to retire inside for a short while?"

He found himself breaking into a grin. "No doubt it will be more peaceful up here, despite our differences." He cocked his ear. "Though, as of yet, I've not heard anything that might indicate things have escalated into a full-scale war."

"I must admit, I have resorted to a bit of underhanded manipulation in order to defuse the situation."

"Oh?"

"Well, knowing Emma's penchant for the melodramatic, I fear I rather exaggerated the danger that Nicholas may be in. She is now in alt at finding herself in the midst of an adventure suitable for Mrs. Radcliffe's pages, so I would not be surprised if her attitude toward the lad has undergone a distinct change."

Sheffield laughed. "My tack was to inform Nicholas, in great detail, of how Emma had saved me from imminent harm with her bravery. He was suitably impressed." His eyes glinted with amusement. "Really though, I should not have expected you to allow such frivolous readings as Mrs. Radcliffe into your course of studies."

"We all need a bit of escape from the everyday. Besides she is an excellent writer."

"I should have expected no less of you than to defend a female author, however prone to descriptive excess."

Her own eyes took on a decided twinkle. "Why, Mr. Sheffield, one would almost imagine that you had read such works yourself." As his chuckle subsided she added, "As for female authors, Jane Austen is also among our favorites."

"Ah, Miss Austen. Now that is another matter . . ."

The conversation turned into a spirited sojourn through English literature of the past fifty years. Though Sheffield insisted on taking over the reins when the road narrowed into a particularly steep and winding incline, the change in drivers did nothing to slow the pace of their opinions. Ideas galloped back and forth, engendering both shared laughter and heated argument over nuances of meaning and intent. Sheffield realized he hadn't enjoyed himself so much in years. He had nearly forgotten how stimulating an intelligent conversation was—even more so than the usual activities he was accustomed to with females. But then, this was a most unusual female.

It was with a real twinge of regret that he broke off a debate on the merits of the Lake Poets just as it was heating up, for he suddenly noticed that Octavia's lips had turned a rather ghastly shade of blue and her cheeks had gone from red to white. His mitten came up to brush the tip of her frozen nose. "Into the sleigh with you now. I'll not have my tiger turning into a block of ice."

"You speak as if you are familiar with such luxuries.

I did not think penniless tutors could afford anything like a tiger," she said lightly, reluctant herself to end the discussion.

"No, of course not," he replied quicky. "I meant the other sort."

A spasm of emotion flickered across her face. "You think me all fangs and claws?"

He eyed her for a moment. "Tigers have a silky softness to them as well. And the strength that lurks beneath their lithe curves only adds to the fascination."

The color returned to her cheeks. "Mr. Sheffield," she warned. "I thought you promised not to indulge in such blatant nonsense."

"Hmmm." He pulled the horses to a halt and got down from his perch. "Though we may argue over the finer points of rhyming couplets until the Neva freezes over, I'll brook no resistance from you about going inside for a time."

Though Octavia had taken the precaution of securing a pair of warm felt boots and a flapped fur hat for herself, she found the cold had still penetrated every muscle, making even the slightest movement a chore. Grateful for his outstretched arms, she allowed him to help her to the ground. "Very well. But only if you join us for a brief respite. Surely you must be hungry by now. I had the proprietor make up a parcel of bread, cheese, and something I assume is pickled cabbage. Perhaps we might even kindle a fire for some hot tea."

His hands seemed to remain around her waist a touch longer than was necessary. "I suppose it would do no harm to rest for a while." He let go of her and started toward the door. "Still no sounds of battle," he said in a low voice. "Either peace has been declared or the casualties have been heavy."

Though she smiled, his words also brought a guilty expression to her face. "We *have* left them to their own devices for an inordinate amount of time. I don't know how the hours could have passed so quickly. . . ."

Sheffield opened the carriage door. At first there was no movement inside, only the soft murmur of a voice, a female voice, from the far corner. ". . . It was a still moonlight night, and the music, which yet sounded on the air, directed her steps from the high road, up a shadowy lane, that led to the woods. . . ." Then slowly Emma looked up from the book in her lap as she became aware of the two adults peering in.

From beside her came a strangled gasp. "Don't stop now, Miss Emma! What is going to happen to her in the woods?"

Octavia fought to keep a straight face. "I believe you will survive the suspense until after a bit of luncheon, Nicholas. Emma, kindly hand me the parcel at your feet."

The girl reluctantly laid aside the leather-bound volume. "Oh, very well."

"Alex," exclaimed his young cousin. "We are reading a most enjoyable tale in which—"

"Yes, I am familiar with *The Mysteries of Udolpho*. You have yet to come to the really good parts, with dungeons and fainting heroines."

The boy's eyes lit up.

"Why does the heroine always have to faint? *I* wouldn't faint," groused Emma as she passed the bulky oilskin package to Octavia. "Why can't the hero faint sometimes?"

"Men don't faint," scoffed the boy. "Only—"

"It does seem shockingly unfair," murmured Sheffield quickly before the truce between the two young people could be broken. "Apparently Mrs. Radcliffe did not have the good fortune to meet such fomidable females as our present company, else her tale would be a great deal more . . . interesting. Don't you agree, Miss Hadley?"

Octavia tried to ignore the dancing blue eyes and teasing smile, but a little shiver coursed down her spine that had nothing to do with the weather. "Come along, all of you," she said briskly. "We should not linger overly long if we wish to reach the next inn before nightfall."

It was, however, well past dark by the time the little party pulled to a halt before a timbered structure even more ramshackle than the previous stop. Sheffield helped the others down from the interior of the sleigh, having insisted that Octavia go inside with the young people for the last few hours of the journey. For some reason, she had not argued.

Smoke from a leaky stove swirled around the small public room, but it was at least warm, and the few other travelers hunched in their seats paid them little heed. After choosing a table in the far corner, Sheffield went to inquire about supper and lodging for the night.

"Cabbage soup," he announced with a grimace on his return. "I vow, I shall shortly grow long ears and a fluffy white tail if this keeps up. It is almost enough to make one long for the execrable meals at White's—"

Octavia looked at him oddly.

"—The White Swan, that is," he went on hastily. "In Whitechapel. The food is terrible, but it is a pleasant enough place to meet one's friends."

Emma and Nicholas had brought the book with them. Heads bent low over the open pages, they were soon engrossed in finishing off another chapter. Their excited whispers rose and fell with the rhythms of the Gothic prose.

"I see that Montoni and company have not yet lost their appeal," remarked Sheffield.

Octavia heaved a mock sigh. "I may be forced to reconsider your remark on a certain author being prone to excess sensibilities, especially when forced to endure several hours of such work read aloud by two enthusiastic twelve-year-olds." She shook her head. "Whose performance, I might add, would no doubt match anything seen on the boards in London."

Sheffield chuckled. "Good Lord, what a day you have had of it. A fine choice—faced with either the exuberance of the innocent or the cynicism of the jaded."

She took a sip of her soup. "Is that how you see yourself?"

There was a slight pause. "That is how others see me."

"That is not what I asked."

He looked away, toward where the innkeeper had set down the bottle of vodka he had ordered along with the meal. Instinctively his hand reached out and filled the glass sitting next to it. As he brought it to his lips, he caught sight of her expression. Had it been one of simple disapproval, he would have drained the contents and poured another. But it was more a mixture of concern, tinged with . . . disappointment?

Suddenly the clear liquid felt like hot coals in his mouth. After a small swallow, he placed aside the glass. "Emma?" said Octavia softly.

The girl's head had sunk perilously close to her half-finished bowl of soup. At the sound of her name, she started in her chair, nearly sending the book and the rest of her supper crashing to the floor.

Sheffield pushed one of the stubby tallow candles across the table to Nicholas. "Perhaps you migh take Miss Emma's bag and see her to her room while I assist Miss Hadley with the rest of our things."

No grimace or yelp of protest followed the request. Rather, the lad jumped to attention and tucked the small valise under one arm as he reached out with the other to take the open book from Emma's lap. He closed it carefully and offered it back to her.

Emma hesitated. "You may keep it for tonight, if you like. But only if you promise not to peek ahead!"

Nicholas looked suitably awed with the treasure being entrusted to him. "I promise."

The two young people made their way through the shadows to a set of narrow stairs as Octavia and Sheffield gathered the rest of their meager belongings. "Isn't is amazing how quickly sworn enemies can become allies?" she remarked, watching the lad stop to free the hem of Emma's dress from where it had caught on a rusty nail.

"Yes, isn't it?" murmured Sheffield. He took up the remaining candle. For an instant, his gaze lingered on the nearly full bottle of spirits, but then he wrenched it away and forced his steps in the opposite direction. Octavia followed several paces behind.

The hallway at the top of the stairs was nearly pitch-black, save for a faint sliver of moonlight coming through a tiny window. He paused by the door to her room and moved the light to shine on the flimsy iron latch.

"Good night, Mr. Sheffield. At this rate it appears we shall soon be in St. Petersburg without further incident."

The shadows cast by the taper danced and flickered,

hiding a good part of his face. "Yes, it seems the danger was exaggerated."

Octavia's pulse quickened. He was very wrong, she thought. The journey was proving more dangerous than she had ever imagined. Attacks on her person, the threat of poverty, the callous indifference of the outside world—these were all assaults she could stand up to without flinching. But suddenly the carefully constructed wall around her feelings, one that she had thought quite impenetrable, was in dire peril of crumbling in the face of a charming rogue. Those quixotic slate blue eyes, hardened one moment, vulnerable the next, were threatening to leave her utterly defenseless.

What a fool! Why, he would hardly notice her existence if there were anything else in a skirt to chase, she reminded herself.

She raised her eyes enough to catch a glimpse of the dark and light playing over his lean features. His character, too, was a study in contrasts. Wit and intelligence warred with the forces of reckless abandon. A keen sense of honor sought to keep jaded cynicism at bay.

But enough! It was ridiculous that she, a mature female, was mooning on as if she was an impressionable miss still in the schoolroom. Or even worse, a flighty heroine in a Radcliffe novel!

His hand came over hers as she fumbled with the door. "Take the candle with you." He opened her palm to receive the holder, bending slightly so that his face was mere inches from hers. "Good night, Miss Hadley. It has been a most interesting afternoon. I look forward to exploring . . . other subjects with you."

Octavia swallowed hard. "Mr. Sheffield, need I remind you about—"

"Playing games? No, you do not."

There was a slight movement, and her heart skipped a beat as she thought he might attempt to kiss her. When he simply straightened and stepped away into the darkness, she wasn't sure whether she was relieved or disappointed.

Chapter Eleven

*A*nother wave slapped against the side of the hull, sending an icy spray of saltwater over the hunched shoulders hanging over the leeward rail.

"The captain expects the weather to moderate by dawn," announced the cloaked figure who was picking his way through the web of clew lines and sheets. He stopped to regain his footing, then grimaced as another pelter of hail rattled against the canvas sails.

The man at the rail responded by casting up his accounts into the churning waters.

"Come below, William. Surely you will feel better if you lie down."

"And be flung arse over tea kettle against an oak beam? I'm not sure which is bloody worse," cursed the marquess. "If Alex wished some revenge for my past actions, he may count himself well on the way to extracting his pound of flesh."

His brother regarded the leaden waves. "And perhaps a few more ounces on top of that," he said dryly.

The ship plunged down into a trough, causing another heave of the marquess's stomach. He groaned. "Remind me to avoid all future endeavors that require even so much as a rowboat."

"If it is any consolation, Uncle Ivor is feeling just as poorly. However, the indefatigable Squid claims he has a cure for this as well, so let me assist you to our cabin."

Down below in the cramped quarters, Sheffield's valet was indeed administering a draught to the recumbent earl, accompanied by a dose of cheerful chatter, which had the older man turning even greener about the gills. "Oh, I've become quite a dab hand at remedying any sort of queasy stomach, like one caused by a bellyful of champagne, or brandy, or claret—"

The marquess put a hand to his mouth.

"—especially when followed by several cigars, and—"

"Ah, I think we need not go into the gruesome details, Squid," said Thomas, as he dropped his elder brother onto one of the narrow berths.

"What—oh, er, sorry." He poured another tumbler of a greenish liquid from the pewter pitcher at his side and passed it to the viscount. "Here now, have his lordship swill a bit of this. It'll have him feeling top of the trees in no time."

The marquess croaked a feeble protest, but his brother would have none of it. "If Squid says it will be effective, than you had best down the stuff, no matter how vile it looks. He has certainly proved to be a fellow of most interesting skills."

Squid grinned at the compliment. "I daresay I've kept Mr. Alex out of trouble. More times than I can count on me fingers or toes."

"Well, I hope you have another digit saved, for I have a feeling my younger brother may need it." The viscount wedged himself into the third berth, using his long legs and shoulders to keep from being tossed about.

The young valet seemed to have no trouble keeping his feet, rolling effortlessly with the pitched rhythm of the ship's motion while straightening up the small cabin. "Has the captain any notion of when we may arrive, sir?" he asked as he folded a rumpled linen shirt and put it away.

"Another two days, at least. Apparently we must be on guard for a squadron of French frigates newly arrived in the Baltic, so our course may have us veer more to the north than we might wish."

At that, the marquess gave a low groan, though it was not clear whether it was due to this latest bit of news or his queasy stomach.

"Come now, William. At least you are not alone in your misery, while Alex is no doubt having to cope with even worse surroundings." That is, he added to himself, assuming his brother was still alive.

"I am happy to say that Alex's usual behavior gives

me cause—for once—to feel sanguine about his situation. For to tell the truth, I think it unlikely that he ever left St. Petersburg. Why, he probably encountered some attractive little bit of muslin, found a snug set of rooms along with a copious supply of the local spirits, and is, as we speak, a good deal more comfortable than we are." There was not a trace of rancor in his tone. "And I, for one, shall be more than delighted if all we have to do is pry him, dead drunk, from between the sheets."

"If he's there," piped up Squid, "I'll suss him out in a flash, sir. Don't you worry about that."

The marquess propped himself up on one elbow, revealing that his face had regained some semblance of its natural color. "I have complete faith in your odd but useful abilities, my man. Already I am feeling more the thing," he murmured. "Would you by any chance consider a change of employment on return to England— that is, if you can tie a cravat and polish a boot as well."

The valet laughed. "Oh no, sir. Ye'd find me sadly disappointing in them sort of boring details. Besides, who would keep Mr. Alex out of trouble?"

Alston regarded his brother and the other man with a troubled mien. "I think we may find that you are mistaken about Alex, William. Even as a boy, he was all that was honorable, never cowardly or craven. Neither Uncle Ivor nor I believe he is so lost to his true self that he would abandon someone in need once committed to the task." He heaved a heavy sigh. "No, I fear our brother is not enjoying the company of any female at the moment."

Octavia pulled her hair back into a more severe style than usual. It only accentuated the dark circles under her eyes, but that hardly mattered, she thought, as she peered into the cracked mirror. It was best she saw things for what they really were—she was an aging spinster with no family, no dowry, and no prospects. Another hairpin jabbed into place. She was being more foolish than the children to let a sugary tale of heroes and happy endings have any effect on her own normally rational thoughts. Determined to keep all such mutinous fantasies at bay, she thrust her brush into her reticule and marched downstairs. This morning *she* would drive and Mr. Sheffield could sit inside and endure the trials and tribulations of Emily and Valancourt.

Mr. Sheffield had other ideas on the matter. His brows arched at her announcement. "Start off the journey inside with the child—er, young people while you take the ribbons? Not likely."

"Well, I don't believe I can tolerate another melodramatic chapter at this hour in the morning," she said under her breath.

"What? I thought you a true romantic at heart."

She colored, much to her dismay. "Hardly," she snapped. "You know very well I am no such thing."

"Hmmm." He took up her bag, along with his own. "The sleigh and horses are ready. We can continue what promises to be an interesting discussion on the driver's box, if you truly do not wish to avail yourself of the inside comforts." His faint smile seemed no less than a challenge.

Octavia wasn't sure which was more unsettling—submitting to the breathless narrative of Emma and Nicholas or sitting disturbingly close to Sheffield. However, her chin rose a fraction as she followed him through the door. After all, she now had full rein of her emotions. She could certainly manage to converse with him without any more girlish flutters.

Emma and Nicholas took up their places without the least bit of protest. The book was immediately opened to the marked place and their heads craned forward. A discussion arose as to who would read first, which Octavia interrupted in order to pile in several of the extra blankets as well as the rest of their belongings. Leaving them to settle the matter themselves, she shut the door and climbed up beside Sheffield.

"You are quite sure you want to miss the description of the castle dungeons?"

She rolled her eyes.

"Very well. But tie the flaps of your hat a bit tighter. It is getting even colder." With that, he gave a flick of the reins and the two horses plodded off.

Much to her relief, he steered the conversation back

to literature rather than forcing any scrutiny of her personal views. His sly sense of humor had not completely deserted him, however, for he inquired whether she had ever read Cleland's *Memoirs of a Woman of Pleasure*.

Once again she felt a blush steal to her cheeks. "Certainly not."

"Ah, but I think you would appreciate *Fanny Hill*." He was in the midst of an entertaining description of the plot, which elicited a reluctant smile or two from Octavia despite her resolve to be cool.

"I see I shall have to expand my horizons in books," she said as he finished. "It sounds a most interesting work."

"Yes, why not take a chance in venturing beyond what you are familiar with? It can be . . . exhilarating."

"It can also be dangerous."

He regarded her with a veiled expression. "You do not appear to be intimidated by the threat of danger, Miss Hadley."

"How can you say so? You do not know me very well."

"Well enough." Before she could reply, he pulled the sled to the side of the road. "And now, judging by the color of your cheeks, I think it is time you went inside for a while. If it is too much to bear, you might simply toss the book out the window."

"You may think I do not fear danger, but neither do I seek out my imminent demise." Secretly relieved that he took the redness of her face as reaction to the cold, she kept her tone as dry as his.

He laughed. "Then perhaps you might insist on a break for other lessons. A long mathematical equation would silence them for a few hours."

"I shall survive." She shook out her skirts in readiness to descend. "But I shall expect you to come inside yourself in a short while, and let me handle the reins."

Sheffield took up his station and set the sleigh at a leisurely trot. His smile remained as he recounted her reactions to his bawdy account of the story. He couldn't resist sparking the flash in her lovely geen eyes with his teasings, just as he couldn't resist wondering what other actions of his could bring such fire to her face. Last night, it had almost seemed as she would have welcomed . . . A sudden movement caused his head to jerk up, then a low oath escaped his lips.

Four horsemen had materialized from out of the thick pine forest fringing the road and drew abreast to block the way.

Sheffield started for the pistol in his pocket, but thought better of it. The odds were simply too great, for each of the men ahead already had a gun pointed straight at his breast. His jaw set, but his arm fell away from his coat and he drew the sled to a sharp stop.

"What is it you want?" he called loudly, hoping that those inside would have some warning of the trouble brewing outside. "If you seek money, you have made a poor choice of victims. I have little to offer."

The riders approached. One of them, a wiry Cossack with a drooping mustache nearly as greasy as his thick sheepskin coat, edged ahead. "We want Count Scherbatov," he growled. The pistol in his hand didn't waver. "Any trouble and you will be feeding the ravens."

Sheffield stared at him blankly for a moment, then gave a rough guffaw. "A count? Oh, aye, he's in the back, along with Czar Alexander and Prince Golitsyn."

The other man looked slightly taken aback and shifted in his saddle. "Take a look," he ordered curtly, motioning to the two on his left.

Sheffield sought desperately to think of some way of escape, but the leader was no slow top. The fellow had stationed the fouth man at the head of the horses, while keeping a close eye on him. There was nothing to do at the moment but sit by helplessly and pray that an opportunity would present itself.

"Who is inside?" demanded the leader as the two men circled around to the door.

"My family," he said sullenly. Perhaps he could bluff his way out of this.

The door was yanked open and one of the swarthy men leaned inside.

Octavia shrunk back against the squabs and made a show of pulling Emma closer. "Leave my daughter alone, you ruffians!" she cried shrilly. "Alexei, make them go away!"

As if on cue, Emma let go with a piercing wail and buried her face in Octavia's shoulder. Another loud sob followed, and another.

The man's head jerked back instinctively, a harried expression on his face.

"What do you see?"

The man scratched at his beard. "A woman and a girl."

The shrieks increased in volume.

"No one else?"

The shake of his head was confirmed by his companion, who took a quick peek inside. "Just the two of them."

At that, Octavia began to cry as well, loud teary sobs that threatened to dissolve into outright hysteria.

The door slammed shut and the two men backed away.

"Please, like most women, my wife and daughter are easily frightened by strangers," said Sheffield, still in a loud voice. He couldn't resist adding, "My wife is also in a most delicate condition, which makes her even more prone to an attack of nerves. No doubt she will have a headache for days."

The leader chewed on the edge of his mustache in some confusion. "Who are you? Where have you come from, and where are you going?"

"Alexei Menshikov. A baker. From Moscow. We are fleeing the fighting and go to relatives in Novgorod."

With his weapon still pointed at Sheffield's chest, the leader gathered his men around for a hurried conference. After a few minutes, he broke away from the others and slowly circled the sleigh, stopping to examine the small storage boot at the rear of the sled and sweep his gaze over the roof. He even darted a quick look of his own into the interior, setting off yet another round of shrieks and tears.

Grudgingly satisfied, he tucked his pistol in his belt and motioned Sheffield on his way. "Be off with you, then. But breathe a word of this to anyone and you shall not survive to see your second born." He shot a look at the closed door of the sled and muttered, "You should pray to the Almighty that he blesses you with a son."

Sheffield needed no further encouragement. A shake of the reins sent the horses into a lurching trot, which he quickly whipped into as hard a gallop as he dared over the icy road. Several miles flew by before he dared stop to let the tired animals recover their wind. He leaped to the ground and flung open the door.

Octavia and Emma were still sitting side by side, skirts covered by a layering of blankets. There was no sign of Nicholas. Sheffield's brows drew together until he noticed a slight twitch of the heavy wool at their feet. His face relaxed into a broad smile. "Well done, ladies. A ruse worthy of any of your Gothic stories."

A dark shock of hair poked out from under the edge of the coverings. "May I come out yet?" came a muffled voice. "It's damned uncomfortable under here."

"You can't say 'damned' in mixed company, Nicholas. You must say 'deuced.'" cautioned Emma in a low voice.

"Alex says damned. I heard him. Twice."

"Grown-ups get away with more than we do."

Sheffield repressed a laugh. "Yes, come on out." To Octavia he added, "That was damned quick thinking, Miss Hadley. We are indebted to you."

"I fear the trick would not have worked had Emma not thought to fall into a fit of vapors."

"Yes, we men may meet pistols at dawn with nary a blink, but even the most hardened scoundrels quail before a female's tears."

"So it seems. I shall make note of that."

"Pray, do not. I cannot imagine you turning truly missish under any conditions." His expression sobered considerably as Nicholas extracted himself from the tangle of blankets.

"They are gone, but not for long. As soon as they reach the inn, they will learn of their mistake and will be back with a vengeance."

"What do you suggest we do?" asked Octavia softly.

Sheffield looked grim. "These nags will never outdistance their mounts. And there are few other roads to turn off on, so trying to elude them seems impossible."

"Why, we can't just sit here and wait for them to return."

"Of course not." He paused for a moment. "We must abandon the sleigh and try to lose ourselves in the forest. If we each take up one of the children along with our supplies, I think we might be able to manage. You can ride, can you not?"

She nodded. "And if I did not, I should quickly learn."

"That's the spirit. Now, all of you, pack up as quickly as you can—and leave behind anything that is not truly necessary. I am going to lead the horses off the road to somewhere we can conceal the sleigh, at least for a bit. If we can delay pursuit for even a short while, it will help our chances."

He found a small clearing and unharnessed the pair, cutting down the long reins to leave a makeshift arrangement for riding. After hacking off a number of pine boughs to help disguise the sleigh's presence, he tossed a folded blanket over each horse to serve as a saddle and split up their supplies. Emma was put on his mount, while Nicholas went up with Octavia. Sheffield's hand lingered on her knee after helping her arrange her skirts for riding astride.

"You show a pretty ankle," he murmured.

"My ankle, Mr. Sheffield, is encased in a felt boot the size of a small, furry animal."

"Well, I have no doubt it would be a very pretty ankle if it were not."

Was it her imagination, or did he have the nerve to wink at her? "We are wasting precious time, sir. Let us be off," she said, trying to sound stern.

"An excellent idea—" He stopped abruptly as a snow-flake drifted down onto his cheek. Looking up at the ominous gray sky his lips compressed in a tight line.

"Damn!"

It was only a dusting, but the powdery flakes had been accompanied by a decided drop in temperature. The towering trees had, at least, provided a measure of protection from the gusting winds, though it was hard going through the slap of branches and tangle of undergrowth. It was difficult to see as well, the thick canopy of needles blocking out much of the pale light. Finally, when it was too dark to continue, Sheffield chose a spot by a large fallen tree to stop for the night.

Emma and Nicholas were sent to collect firewood while Octavia searched for a source of fresh water. In the meantime, Sheffield set to making some sort of shelter from the elements. A number of large pine boughs angled across the downed trunk created a tentlike structure that was actually quite snug inside, once a goodly pile of dead needles had been spread over the frozen ground.

A blazing fire at the narrow entrance also added a measure of warmth, enough that the blue tinge to Emma's mouth slowly disappeared and she was able to move her lips. The lad had also been suffering from the cold, though he had tried manfully to suppress his chattering teeth. But they refrained from any complaints as they sat huddled under the extra blankets, even when supper turned out to be no more than a cup of weak tea and a meager portion of cold meat and bread. Nor did they argue when Octavia insisted that they take their blankets and retreat into the depths of the shelter. In fact, they appeared too exhausted to do much else than crawl inside and wrap themselves tightly in their coverings as bidden.

"You must lie close together," called Sheffield. On catching the look on Octavia's face, he dropped his voice. "Highly improper, I know, but shared bodily warmth will help stave off the cold."

"Well, I suppose you know a thing or two about that," she murmured under her breath.

His lips twitched. "I am glad to see the hardships of the day haven't dulled your sharp claws, my tiger. The time you cease your cutting set downs is the time I shall be truly worried that the strain has been too much."

She leaned back against the rough bark and swirled the dregs of her cup. "I imagine my choice of words is the least of our worries. We are not in a terribly good position, are we, Sheffield?"

His amused expression quickly disappeared. "No, we are not." He added another branch to the fire and stared at the leaping flames. "We have only enough food for another day or two, our horses are nags and I doubt the children can endure too much exposure to the elements. And if it begins to snow in earnest . . ." He let his words trail off. After a moment he cleared his throat. "I'm sorry to have involved you and Emma in this."

She essayed a tight smile. "What? And deprive Emma of matching the exploits of her favorite heroine?"

That drew a low chuckle.

"And besides, the alternative was hardly more appealing. So don't rake yourself over the coals. You have handled things quite credibly up to now, and I'm sure you will find a way to bring us all through to safety."

Sheffield's jaw tightened. "You may find yourself sadly disappointed. I should warn you, not many people have any faith in my abilities."

"The only important opinion is your own, sir." She drew a deep breath. "Now, perhaps we should—"

He looked at her in some amazement. "You are truly remarkable, Miss Hadley. I know of no other female who could sit calmly in the middle of the wilds and discuss how to save her neck, with nary a sob or shriek of remonstrance."

"I am used to adversity. And if my neck is to be saved, I have long ago learned that I had better figure out how to do it. Sobs and shrieks are all very well for fine ladies who can afford such delicate sensibilities. I cannot."

He poked at the glowing coals, suddenly filled with a desire to know more about her life. "Why?"

"Why what?"

"Why are you so used to adversity? Tell me something of your family, your circumstances."

Octavia's hands tightened around her cup. "It's hardly an interesting story. Or a unique one. In fact, my situation is most likely not a great deal different than yours—parents poor as church mice, no inheritance, no influential relatives, that sort of thing."

"Nevertheless, I should like to hear it."

She had never spoken about growing up an only child alone with a scholarly father who had little connection with the realities of the outside world, who was blithely unaware that butchers and candle makers expected payment, that thatched roofs leaked, that housekeepers required a salary. But for some reason—she wasn't quite sure how—he managed to coax a brief account of her history, ending with the little contretemps that had precipitated her journey to Russia.

When he had finished laughing over that, she rearranged the blanket around her shoulders and composed her own twitching lips. To her surprise, she felt better for talking about things that had seemed too painful to ever share. "And now you, sir."

He looked a bit startled. "Me?"

"It's only fair. I have subjected myself to your scrutiny, and your laughter. You can hardly refuse to do the same."

The blue of his eyes hardened into a stormy gray. "My story is not one that should sully the ears of a gently born female. Best leave it at that."

"Oh no, that won't fadge, sir. You won't escape quite so easily. As you have seen, I am not so easily sent into a fit of vapors," she said in her best governess tone.

Indeed, he did look a bit like a recalcitrant schoolboy as he tried to duck her question. "We have a long day ahead of us. I suggest you get some sleep."

"Later."

Seeing that she would not be put off, he let out a harried sigh. "Very well. My father was perhaps not as . . . poor as yours. I received a decent education, was sent to Oxford, where I made the first few missteps on my road to ruin." A sardonic twist pulled at his lips. "One of those youthful slips resulted in my being sent down in disgrace. It caused an . . . estrangement from my family, and I have been on my own since then. There, now that should satisfy your curiosity."

In fact, it was only piqued. "It is my turn to ask why," she said softly.

His jaw went rigid. "Why I was sent down? For seducing the wife of a don," he said roughly.

If he expected her to recoil in shock, he was wrong. She regarded him with a thoughtful expression, not one of scorn, and drew her knees up to her chest. "What makes a man do such a thing?" she mused aloud. "Was it just another game, or was she so beautiful and alluring that you were beyond all reason?" Her voice dropped to a near whisper. "I wonder, what would it be like to inspire such passion?" A resigned sigh followed. "Not that I shall ever know, of course."

Her response, like so much else about her, knocked him off-kilter. He wasn't at all sure how to answer the complex questions she had raised, but what he did know at that instant was that she had been wrong earlier—it was *her* opinion of him that was most important. He suddenly cared very much whether she thought him an unprincipled cad.

"I didn't," he blurted out. It was the first time he had ever told anyone the truth. "Didn't seduce her, that is. I am guilty of many sins, but not of that one."

Octavia took in his pale features and bit her lip. "I'm sorry. I shouldn't have pressed you. You don't have to talk about it . . . that is, unless you wish to."

Surprisingly, he found he did. "The outraged husband had caught only a distant glimpse of the tall dark fellow dallying in the field with his wife. My friend was a brilliant student, with a promising future. He was, however, quite unschooled in the ways of the world. When the lady—a lady well experienced in the subject—encouraged his advances, he was too naive to realize the consequences." Sheffield paused to jab a stick at the burning coals. "My friend's family had no money or influence. His life would have been ruined had he been expelled from university, while I . . . I had already earned a reputation for reckless behavior." His lip curled in self-mockery. "The lady was happy enough to go along when the blame was shifted to a rakehell scoundrel. And no one else found it difficult to think me the guilty party— after all, what else could be expected from someone who had killed his brother."

She gasped, but then her chin tilted up. "I don't believe you capable of such a thing. Not for an instant."

"Oh, not intentionally." He ducked his head to hide how much her simple statement affected him. "But it is true all the same."

Slowly, haltingly, the story came out—Jack's invitation to join in a lark, the bottles of brandy, the exhilaration of the wind and waves. And then the storm. "If Jack hadn't had so much to drink . . . if *I* hadn't been foxed as well," finished Sheffield in a near whisper, "we might have been able to handle the sails. Or at least, when our sloop capsized, he might have been able to keep a grip on my hand. I should have been able to hold on. But I couldn't." He turned away to toss another piece of wood on the fire, but the flare of light caught the anguish in his eyes.

Octavia said nothing, but reached out and touched his arm. He looked for a moment as if to brush away her hand, but then, as she slowly pulled him close, his head came, unresisting, onto her breast. She simply held him tight.

He lay very still, except for a slight heaving of his shoulders. When he finally looked up, his emotions were once more under rigid control, save for a note of uncertainty in his voice. "It is a good thing Emma is not awake to witness such a craven display of spirit. What a pitiful hero I should appear in her book."

"Valancourt is fashioned out of paper and ink while you, sir, are cut from real cloth. It is easy to be perfect when you are no more substantial than a dribble of ink from someone's pen. You have been way too hard on yourself. We would not be human if we didn't make mistakes. Or have regrets." She paused for a fraction. "You have nothing to be ashamed of, Mr. Sheffield. Though you may consign my opinion to the devil, I counsel you to talk with your father and make him see the truth. Both of you would feel infinitely better for it."

"It is too late for that. He's gone."

"What of the rest of your family? Have you siblings?"

"Two older brothers. We are also estranged."

"Don't be a fool. You must settle things with them. Promise me you will."

"What you ask is—"

"Please."

He drew in a sharp breath. "Very well. I promise I will try."

Octavia made a show of shaking out the blanket that had been draped around her shoulders. "Well, perhaps we should get some sleep ourselves. I'm sure in the morning things will not appear quite so dark, and we can devise a plan worthy of our favorite author."

His lips twitched upward.

She moved to settle herself just inside the small shelter. "Why, Mr. Sheffield, you have no blanket of your own," she said.

"I shall manage."

"Indeed, you will not! I insist you come share this one with me."

She was happy to see the hurt in his eye was quickly replaced by the mischievous twinkle she had become accustomed to. "Now that is the most tempting offer I have had in quite some time. But I should not wish to cause you any discomfort."

"Well, it would not be the first time we have ended up twined together—perhaps I am getting rather used to it."

A strange expression flitted over his features as he slid his weary frame down next to hers.

"Good night, Mr. Sheffield," she nurmured.

He gave a soft chuckle. "You might at least call me Alex, seeing we have come to be on such intimate terms."

"Good night, then . . . Alex."

"Good night, Octavia."

Chapter Twelve

Morning—it if could be called that—gave rise to no more than a gloomy half-light that barely penetrated the canopy of pine needles. It was hardly something to inspire a brighter outlook on their predicament, thought Sheffield as he shifted slightly on the frozen ground. The movement caused his thigh to brush against the sleeping form beside him, and a faint smile stole to his lips. The situation may be grave, but for now, all he could think of was the reassuring warmth stealing through the rough wool of his clothing, a warmth more penetrating than any he could remember experiencing. He closed his eyes, and his arm stole around her waist, drawing her even closer.

Her words from the night before still echoed in his ears. They had offered a measure of comfort and support that he had given up on ever hearing, even from those closest to him. Once again, she had not shied away in disgust at his weaknesses or his pain, but had embraced him—faults and all.

The faint smile crooked into a rueful grimace. It wouldn't do to read too much into her actions, he reminded himself. She was also capable of verbally boxing his ears with the bruising power of Gentleman Jackson himself, and she had made it quite clear on any number of occasions that she held him in little regard. No doubt it was only her innate championing of the underdog, the same sentiment that made her jump to the defense of helpless children—and stray animals, he imagined—that inspired such kindness. *Yes, Miss Hadley was truly an extraordinary—and complex—female.*

His breath came out in a sigh that stirred the loose

tendrils of hair at the nape of her neck. She was a lovely one as well, despite her assertions to the contrary. He wondered why it was she thought herself unattractive. Had none of the country louts she had grown up with ever noticed those intriguing green eyes and flowing curves? Even now he tried to keep his thoughts from wondering what her firm, rounded breasts would feel like in his hand, whether those long legs were as shapely as he imagined—

Octavia's eyes fluttered open. For an instant she snuggled even closer to him; then, as everything came into focus, she pulled away with a little start. "Oh!"

"Good morning, Octavia," he said softly.

A flush of color rose to her cheeks. "Er, good morning." She sought to extract herself from his arm.

"Alex," he reminded her, not quite letting go. "After all, we *have* spent the night together."

The blush deepened. "Do stop teasing. As if—" Her words cut off.

"As if what?"

She swallowed hard. "As if . . . as if we have time to waste." She struggled to a sitting position. "We had better start thinking of a way to extricate ourselves from this coil."

Sheffield reluctantly let his hand fall away from her hip. "Mmmmm. Right." It was most difficult to turn his attention from the cascade of honey-colored tresses that tumbled down her back to more practical matters.

With a stick, he prodded a few of the embers into flame, then added an armful of fresh wood to the fire. His eyes glanced upward, only to narrow in concern at the ominous gray clouds rolling in from the east. "I think we have no choice but to continue with the horses and try to find a way out of this damned forest." He pulled a rough map from inside his coat. "If we head west, we must come out somewhere here." His finger traced along a sketchy road and stopped higher up, where several village names were scrawled. "At least we may find some food and shelter, and perhaps a conveyance to purchase or a public coach heading north."

Octavia regarded the wrinkled piece of paper. "We were there?" She pointed to a spot.

He nodded.

"And now we are here?" Her gesture indicated a wide, empty patch between the inked lines.

"Yes."

"Well, that should mean that it will take some time for our pursuers to make their way around to where we intend to come out."

His voice had a hard edge to it. "Yes—assuming they go by the road."

Octavia hung the battered kettle, still half full with water, over the coals. "I had better rouse the children."

That proved no easy task. Both of them were loath to leave what little warmth their blankets provided, and a bit of petulant whining reached Sheffield's ear. Emma, it appeared, was in a testy mood.

"I'm hungry, Miss Hadley," she complained. "And cold. And I want to sleep in a bed, not this pile of dirt and leaves."

"None of us are terribly comfortable, Emma, but we must make the best of it." Sheffield watched with some admiration as Octavia managed to coax the girl out of her cocoon with a few more encouraging words. "Now please help Nicholas gather some wood for the fire while I make some tea."

Emma's lower lip thrust out, but she rose to her feet and stumbled off after the boy without further complaint.

"Well done," he murmured when Octavia returned to begin fixing their last bit of gruel. "You have a deft touch with . . . difficult people."

She ducked her head to hide her smile. "Indeed, I find that all it takes is—"

Her reply was cut short by a loud cry. Both Sheffield and Octavia jumped to their feet, but he was the first to sprint through the tangle of thorns and dead branches to reach the prostate child. Emma had lost her balance atop a fallen tree and tumbled to the ground below. There was a tear in her coat where a broken branch had snagged the material, and her face had several nasty scratches across her left cheek, now thoroughly awash in a stream of tears.

"I want to go home," she sobbed. "I want—"

Sheffield knelt down and gathered her in his arms. "Of course you do, sweeting, and that is where I mean to take you." Her head burrowed deeper against his shoulder, and he was amazed at the surge of protectiveness that coursed through him as the child's arms came around his neck. He, who had thought precious little of anything but his own amusements for more time than he cared to remember, was suddenly aware that he would commit murder with his bare hands if any man dared lay a finger on Emma, or the others.

His hand stroked her quivering shoulders. "Look at me, Emma," he urged softly.

The tearstained face slowly rose a fraction.

"Now, I thought you said you wanted the heroes to cry, not the heroines."

She tried to stop sobbing. "I-I'm frightened, Mr. Sheffield."

"I may not be as chivalrous as Valancourt," he continued in a low voice, "but I promise you that no harm will come to you."

"You are ever so much better than that nodcock, Mr. Sheffield," she said through her sniffling. "You are the nicest hero I could ever imagine."

"Why don't you call me Alex. It seems we have become a family of sorts, at least for a time, so we might dispense with the formalities."

A tentative smile came to her face. "Oh, I should like that very much—Alex."

The sound of snapping branches caused all of them to start. "Is Emma all right?" cried Nicholas, sliding to a halt with a stout length of wood clutched in his hand.

"She is just fine," answered Sheffield. "Are you recovered enough to go back?" he asked of her.

Emma brushed away her tears and nodded.

"That's my brave girl." He pressed a light kiss on her cheek.

Her mouth dropped in confused wonder; then she began to giggle. "You are all prickly, Alex."

He ran a hand over his dark stubble. "Yes, well, my valet must have overslept this morning. I shall have to speak to him about such a regrettable lapse."

She giggled even louder.

"I should be happy to take her now," offered Octavia, who had come up close behind them.

Sheffield turned to find her regarding him with an expression that caused his stomach to give a little lurch. "I don't mind," he replied rather shakily. "I shall take her back to the camp."

The look of gratitude she gave him sent another sort of emotion coursing through him. *Damnation*, he thought. It was getting cursed difficult to ignore the growing attraction he was feeling. *But he must.* There were too many other things to concern him at the moment than the state of his heart.

Like the state of their necks.

They hurried through the simple meal and began to ready their things for the journey. As Emma lugged her small bag out of the shelter and handed it over to Sheffield, a heavy item fell to the ground. Her face took on a guilty look. "I . . . I know you said we must only bring essentials, but—"

He gave her a surreptitious wink and slipped it back in with her other belongings. "But of course *The Mysteries of Udolpho* is essential for this trip. I, for one, could not forgo seeing who overcomes the greatest of perils— us or them."

Octavia chose to walk rather than ride the plodding mount. Though the brambles and underbrush made progress difficult, it was better than being bounced like a sack of grain by the animal's uneven gait. The sky had become even darker, forcing her to keep an eye glued on the horse ahead so as not to get lost. Sheffield, too, had opted to go on foot, though his arm remained curled around Emma's waist to steady her seat. The girl seemed quite recovered from her mishap. From what snatches of conversation drifted back to her, it appeared that Emma was deep into explaining the latest threat from the dastardly Montoni.

That Sheffield tolerated such childish chatter without complaint caused her lips to quirk upward. He was providing no end of surprises. To think that only a few days ago she had thought him a rather shallow rake. A

charming one to be sure, but not a man given to much
of any thoughts save his own desires. *How wrong she
had been!* Beneath the devil-may-care manner, he was
not nearly as hardened as he wished the world to think.
Last night he had shown himself capable of pain, of remorse and, perhaps most touching of all, of a fear of
being alone in the world. In that, she mused, he was not
so very different than Emma—or herself.

Then, just now, he had revealed a gentle, compassionate side of his character. She would not have guessed he
would be so good with children, but the flash in his eyes
as Emma had wound her thin arms around his neck had
been unfeigned. Why, she had almost felt jealous of the
child! If a man had looked at *her* in such a manner, she
would have found her insides melting into mush. Perhaps
it was best that such a thing was nigh on impossible.
Even if she hadn't warned him off in no uncertain terms,
his mild flirtations were merely that—a game that men
and women played, where both knew the rules, as well
as the boundaries.

*So why did her mind keep straying beyond those
confines?*

That he was devilishly attractive was undeniable. But
it was more than his broad shoulders and chiseled features that had her emotions in a state of turmoil. Rather,
it was the unexpected sensitivity, which along with a
keen intelligence and quick wit had her . . . well, had
her gushing like some flighty chit in a horrid novel. Her
gaze couldn't help but linger on the tall figure up ahead.
Even cloaked in the heavy coat and shaggy fur hat, he
exuded a rampant strength and masculinity that caused
her pulse to quicken.

Good Lord, she chided herself, she was in danger of
waxing even more sentimental than the worst of that
sort of prose. Her cheeks tinged with color at the absur-
dity of entertaining such improper thoughts. Forcing a
deep breath, she vowed to put them aside and concen-
trate on the problems at hand. It was well she did, for
a hidden outcropping of rock nearly sent her sprawling.

Sheffield whipped around at the sound of her stumble,
his expression of concern softening into a smile of encouragement on seeing she was still on her feet. In fact,

she thought she detected a wink before he turned back to guiding the tired horse through yet another thicket of densely knit boughs.

Despite her resolve, she couldn't quite help wondering what it was he saw when he looked at her. An aging governess with the pinched features of a disapproving harridan? No, it was a tiger that he had compared her with. The thought of it made her feel rather low. *Was she really all roar and sharp claws?* For once in her life she found herself wishing she were somehow more like a kitten—softer, cuddlier, sweeter. In other words, all the things she abhorred in those of her sex. She might judge such qualities ridiculous, but men seemed to find them . . . irresistible.

It would be nice to be found irresistible—

A loud crack, like the snapping of a branch, jarred her back to her senses. She looked up, just in time to feel the whoosh of air on her cheek as a bullet whistled by not a foot from her head. Sheffield screamed a warning to get down as he grabbed Emma from atop her mount and thrust her into the cover of some underbrush. Heedless of her own safety, Octavia reached for Nicholas and jerked him from the makeshift saddle. Another shot rang out, causing the boy to cry out in terror.

The gnarled roots of an old Sitka spruce offered some small measure of protection. She dragged him down behind their shelter, pausing a moment to catch her breath. There was no sound, save for the pounding of her heart, but she had no illusions that the danger was past. She eyed their old horse, which was still standing where she had left him, flanks quivering, too tired to bolt. *Her reticule!* she thought. She needed her reticule! Inside it was the pistol, their only chance at fighting back.

"For God's sake, Octavia, stay where you are," cried Sheffield as she slithered away from the spruce and scrambled to her feet.

A dark shape exploded from shadows, coming straight for her. Even in the faint light, she caught the glint of steel as the raised pistol of the rider arced up to take dead aim.

"Damnation!" came the muffled shout. A smaller shape was moving with even greater speed toward her.

Sheffield caught the shaggy stallion by its bridle and yanked its head to one side.

The spooked animal tried to rear, throwing the man in the saddle off balance. Another curse, this one in Russian, pierced the air. Their assailant tried to spur forward, even though the effort caused him to drop his own weapon, but Sheffield hung on and lunged for the man's hand. The shot aimed at Octavia went just wide. With a roar of anger, the man twisted and lashed out a vicious blow at Sheffield's head with the butt of his pistol.

He ducked and with a hard flick of his wrist sent the weapon flying in the air. At the same time, he grabbed hold of the other man's sleeve and started to drag him off his mount. A flailing boot caught him square in the midriff, knocking him to his knees. Still, his grip never loosened and the two of them ended up locked in a furious struggle amid a churning of snow and pine needles.

A second rider appeared among the trees. Octavia managed to shout a warning before she had to duck for cover. She saw, however, that Sheffield had gained the upper hand in his battle. In a flash, his fist drew back and landed a hard shot to the other man's jaw. The fellow's head snapped back and he fell backward, unconscious. Then, mindful of the new danger, Sheffield rolled quickly to his right, just as the impact of a bullet sent a spray of frozen dirt into the air.

The new assailant, recognizable as the leader of the band by his distinctive drooping mustache, brought his skittish mount under control in the tight space and maneuvered with practiced skill for a better angle of attack on the unarmed Sheffield.

Octavia spotted something jutting out from the fallen man's waistband. "Alex! In his belt! A second pistol!"

Sheffield dodged to one side, then flung himself at the prostrate body. In one motion he drew the weapon, rolled, and squeezed off a shot.

The horse, suddenly riderless, whinnied in fright. Octavia took two steps forward; then her knees nearly buckled at the sight of the bloodied face, the top of his skull nearly blown clean away.

Somewhere close by there was an agitated shout, then the snapping of branches and the dull thud of hoofbeats receding.

"Don't look," snapped Sheffield as his arm came around her waist and spun her roughly away. "Catch hold of those horses. We shall need them." He took one glance at her wan face and gave her shoulders a shake. "Come, don't turn missish on me now! The other two have taken themselves off, but it's best to be away from here as quickly as possible."

In a near daze, she obeyed his curt order while he made a quick search of the dead man's pockets. He stuffed several items into his pockets, then gathered up the pistols and came back to her side. Octavia swallowed hard and tried to control the trembling of her hands. He looked furious, and with good reason, she supposed. Once again he had been forced to risk his neck for her—he must be getting heartily tired of it.

"I . . ." she began

Ignoring her halting words, he shoved all but one of the weapons into the saddlebags of one of the horses. "Stay here while I get the children," he barked.

He quickly returned with Emma in his arms and Nicholas clinging to his arm. She was whimpering softly. The lad, too, had streaks of tears on his dirty cheeks, though he made no sound. Sheffield smoothed the tangle of hair off the girl's pale brow and whispered something in her ear before placing her in the saddle. He took Nicholas around to the other mount, but before lifting him in place, squatted down so that their faces were only inches apart. A short exchange followed, ending with Nicholas nodding solemnly and essaying a brave smile. Then he, too, was made ready for the ride.

Sheffield made one more trip to strip their belongings from the tired pack animals. When everything was fastened securely on their new mounts, he finally turned his attention back to Octavia. His eyes were narrowed, and she noted they were flooded not with the gentle compassion he had just displayed with the children but some other emotion—something, she imagined, between anger and exasperation.

"Hell's teeth! What did you think you were doing?" he demanded through gritted teeth.

"My reticule," she stammered. "My pistol was in my reticule."

"Good Lord, what did you think you were going to do with it? With your aim, only the trees would have been in danger."

Her chin came up a fraction. "Well, you had dropped your weapon. I had to do *something*."

"You did quite enough by braving those bullets to drag Nicholas to safety." His tone had softened somewhat. "In the future, kindly leave any sort dealings with firearms to me."

She turned visibly paler at his words.

Sheffield took hold of her shoulders, none too gently. "Are you are all right?"

She nodded, averting her eyes from his. "What of . . . him?" she whispered, catching sight of the unconscious assailant.

"He'll have a long walk back to the road during which to reflect whether to choose a new line of work." His breath came out in a harried sigh. "The children have had quite a shock. They need to recover with a rest and perhaps something hot. But not here. Are you sure you can manage?"

She could have used a hug or murmured words of encouragement herself, but she merely set her jaw and nodded an assent.

"Then up you go." He boosted her up behind Nicholas. "And Octavia," he added softly.

She looked at him expectantly. Perhaps now he might say something kind. After all, she thought, she had received just as big a shock as the children.

"Don't *ever* do anything as damn foolish as that again," he growled.

So much for being cuddly and irresistible.

Hell's teeth, repeated Sheffield to himself as he watched Octavia's head duck to avoid another drooping pine bough. His heart had nearly stopped on seeing the pistol aimed at her breast. Good Lord, she had nearly been killed because of her gritty courage! Why couldn't she be like other females and faint, or at least collapse in a fit of vapors, so he could protect her without having to resort to such melodramatic efforts?

He gave a slight shake of his head. Really, this was beginning to outdo even the worst sort of horrid novel. His lips twitched at the notion that mayhap he should take up pen and paper himself—the tale would have the ladies of the *ton* swooning in droves, allowing him to supplement his quarterly allowance quite nicely. The only trouble was, any sensible person would dismiss the plot as ridiculous beyond belief.

The ghost of a smile quickly disappeared as his thoughts turned back to what had just occurred. The children and Octavia were depending on him, and he had nearly brought them all to grief because he hadn't sensed the danger. He tried to take a deep breath, but suddenly his chest felt as if it were encircled by an iron band, slowly, inexorably twisting tighter and tighter.

What if he had failed once again to save those he cared about?

His eyes pressed closed and the realization washed over him that if such a thing had happened, he might well go ahead and blow out his own brains because he wouldn't be able to live with himself. He stifled a groan as a wave of black despair threatened to engulf him, like it had so many other times—

"Alex?" A small voice cut through the darkness.

He forced his lids open. Emma had turned to regard him, her eyes wide in awestruck admiration. "That was the bravest thing I have ever seen, the way you knocked that horrible man down before he could hurt Miss Hadley."

His jaw dropped slightly.

"And then, how you laid him out without so much as a blink of your eye," she went on, in a reverent tone. "So you could blast that other villain to the devil. Why, you are quite the best hero in the whole world."

Octavia had reined in her horse at the crest of a small ridge so that the last of Emma's words drifted up to her and Nicholas. The boy was quick to add his own effusive praise.

Sheffield looked rather dazed. Of their own accord, his eyes sought Octavia.

"Hmmm," she murmured, her voice rich with a sly humor. "Yes, I suppose we must give him the edge over Valancourt."

A rumble of a chuckle started in his throat as he found he could suddenly breathe again.

"You were, you know," she added softly, her voice no longer teasing.

When his brow rose in question, she went on. "Wonderful, that is. Quite wonderful."

He swallowed hard as one bedraggled governess and two dirt-streaked twelve-year-olds, leaves and pine needles clinging to their garments, regarded him with glowing smiles. Here they were, as good as lost in a vast wilderness, stuck in a foreign country with a murderous uncle on their trail and the entire French army not far behind. *So why was he feeling like the luckiest man in the world?*

"But Alex—"

His head jerked up.

Octavia did her best to imitate his growl. "Don't *ever* do anything as damn foolish as that again!"

He had to choke down a burble of laughter as she gave him a wink and then set her mount into a brisk trot.

Chapter Thirteen

*S*quid stomped his boots, trying to regain some measure of feeling in his icy feet, then slowly unwound the scarf from his neck.

"Well?"

The valet chafed his hands together. "Colder 'n a witch's tit out—er, sorry m'lord." He swallowed hard as the marquess stopped his pacing in midstride to stare at him. "I'm afraid I keep forgetting my place, and that it is not Mr. Alex that I am conversing with," he continued, taking great care to place his vowels and consonants in the correct places. The result was a very credible sounding King's English.

From his seat near the fire, Alston gave a chuckle. "Don't bother altering your speech, Squid. I find your descriptions more informative than most. Indeed, after your colorful way of putting things, my own valet's words will pale in comparison." He slanted a look at the marquess and was surprised to see that his brother's lips were also twitching. "But do tell us if you have found out anything."

Squid grinned. "Aye, I have, sirs. Finally sussed out where Mr. Alex dossed—"

"Discovered where Alex stayed," translated Alston in a low voice.

The marquess took on an injured expression. "I am not quite so featherheaded as you imagine, Thomas." He signaled to the young valet to go on.

"Er, well, he was looking shabby and such, so he's sticking to the plan of masquerading as a poor tutor, I reckon. Made inquiries about coach travel to the south. Sent me haring off across the city, the clerk did, but I found the place." He paused to deliver the most important bit of news he had learned so far. "One thing we can be sure of is he ain't here in St. P. anymore. He left nigh on a month ago."

There was a moment of silence as the two men digested the news. "Well done, Squid," said Alston.

The marquess's lips pressed together in a tight line. "Hell's teeth, then he could be *anywhere* in this cursed land."

Alston nodded grimly.

" 'Course I left instructions—along with a bit of incentive—to send word here if Mr. Alex reappears."

"Good Lord, I hope Alex has had the sense to keep his wits about him—this is not one of his reckless games, like venturing into the stews of London on a wager, where a mistake might only result in a blackened eye or a broken bone."

"Oh, even when deep in his cups, Mr. Alex has extricated himself from situations way worse than this," said Squid loyally, though the crease of worry on his brow belied the jaunty confidence of his words. The dark smudges under his eyes also indicated he was far from unconcerned about his employer's situation. "Is there aught else you can think of for me to do?"

"You've done all you can for now," answered the marquess. He resumed his pacing up and down the narrow sitting room. "Get some rest. Perhaps Lord Chittenden will have some more recent news for us when he returns from the embassy."

Squid gave a reluctant nod and slipped from the room.

With a sigh, Alston picked up a copy of the latest dispatches from the front while the marquess continued to wear a path across the faded oriental carpet. Suddenly he stopped, and a faint chuckle escaped his lips. Alston's head snapped up.

"Witch's tit, indeed," repeated the marquess with a dash of amusement. "I have to admit, dressing for the evening would prove quite entertaining with a fellow like that knotting one's cravat. Poor Syms seems rather tame in comparison." He gave a ghost of a smile. "Perhaps Alex is not, as Squid would put it, as addled in the nodcock as I thought."

Alston regarded his older brother thoughtfully for a moment. "Why, William," he murmured, "you actually still have a sense of humor. Thank God."

The marquess's jaw tightened. "I know you—all of you—think me a stiff-rumped bore, but I *must* be serious. It is a great responsibility to be head of the family. And one that I had not ever expected to shoulder. Father made it quite clear on Jack's death that I must not fail in my duty to uphold the standards of the Sheffields." He hesitated a fraction, then went on in a voice barely above a whisper. "At times, it is an almost overwhelming burden, trying not to make a mistake."

"No one is perfect, William. Not Jack. Not me. Not any of us. And especially not Father. I, for one, have come to see he was wrong about many things. His own rigid expectations caused more harm than good. Because Jack was the heir, Father refused to admit he could have any faults. Believe me, Jack suffered the burden of such unrealistic demands, but it was Alex who truly bore the brunt of it." Alston shook his head. "Do not try to imitate Father's ways. I daresay the Sheffield honor is not quite so fragile as he would have had us believe. Surely we may be mere mortals rather than gods, without any censure from the heavens."

The marquess's hands clasped behind his back, and he turned to stare into the fire. After a lengthy silence, his mouth tugged into a rueful grimace. "To think I used to box your ears when we were pups, and now it is you who are teaching me a well-deserved lesson. I shall try not to be such a . . . pompous ass in the future."

His words caused his brother to grin. "Well, let us not expect miracles."

"Jackanape." But the marquess was grinning as well. His steps picked up again, and he moved alongside the leather wing chair. Gazing down at the papers in the viscount's lap, his expression sobered considerably as he took out his spectacles. "Any news that may be of use?"

His brother handed him a number of the pages. "You may have a look at these, but as of yet, the news is nothing but grim. The Russians were defeated in a bloody battle at Borodino, and Boney's troops marched into Moscow seven days later." He heaved an exasperated sigh. "The city is in flames, Kutusov's army is in full retreat, and to top it off, the snows have begun early, even for this land of ice and wind. Somewhere in the middle of such madness is Alex. That is, if he is still alive."

The marquess took the dispatches and sat down. "Perhaps Uncle Ivor will have some news when he returns from the embassy." At the look of doubt that flashed in the viscount's eyes, he cleared his throat. "No, I suppose there is no use pretending that Alex will get help from any quarter. God help him—he is going to need it."

"Keep your head down," growled Sheffield as his hand forced Octavia's shoulders to the ground.

"You needn't manhandle me. I am quite aware that we do not wish them to see us," she retorted, though her voice remained a whisper. She brushed away some flakes of snow from her cheek and raised her chin just a fraction, so she could once again regard the column of soldiers marching down the narrow road.

"French," he muttered, running his eyes over the sky blue coats and frogged braid of the uniforms. "Damnation. I hadn't imagined they—" He broke off his words as a rattle of musket fire exploded from the far side of the road. This time his hand shoved Octavia down with even more force as the troop of soldiers below them scattered for cover.

"Who—" she began.

Another oath slipped from his lips. He quickly slithered off the crest of the ridge, Octavia in tow, not pausing until they had gained shelter behind an outcropping of granite fringed by a number of stunted hemlocks.

"Of all the devilish luck," he swore. "First thieves, then murderers, and now we have stumbled into a whole damn war." His lips compressed. "I fear we will find precious little chance of shelter this way."

Octavia didn't answer right away, but took the small brass compass from her coat pocket. "Why do you imagine they are headed west?" she asked after a bit.

"West?" He turned from keeping watch on the way they had just come. "Hmmm. It may be due merely to the vagaries of the road, or—"

Another volley of shots rang out.

"Or they may be in retreat," finished Octavia.

Sheffield nodded grimly. "Kutusov may finally have rallied his men to make a stand. Wait here. I am going to take another look."

Before she could protest, he disappeared behind the low screen of trees. Giving vent to her own silent curses, her gaze turned upward. It had begun snowing several hours ago, and the thick gray clouds gave no hint of any change in the weather. Night was fast approaching as well, bringing with it an even greater drop in temperature. Alex had reason to look so worried, she thought. Her eyes shifted back to the dark outline of forest where Emma and Nicholas lay hidden, along with the horses. The children couldn't endure too much more of the cold, and their supply of food was nearly gone.

Her thoughts were interrupted by Sheffield's return. "It's not the Russian army, but partisans," he said, dropping down beside her. "The French managed to drive them off, but not before losing a few of their own." A musket and a tattered knapsack were in his hands.

Octavia gave a sharp intake of breath.

"They have moved on," he continued. "Judging by the look of the fellow I took these from, their rations have been as meager as our own."

"That was a foolhardy thing to risk," she said, eyeing the new items.

"There is at least a handful of millet and some dried beans there," he replied. "And we may find ourselves in need of all the weaponry we can muster."

She bit her lip and looked away. "Do you think we ought to retrace our steps? The other road may still be free of soldiers."

"I dare not risk it, not with our food running out. I'm afraid we have little choice but to continue along this way and pray that we may slip through the fighting." He leaned back against the rocks and pulled the creased map from his coat. "We must try to make our way in the direction of Bologoye. That will bring us to the main

road to Novgorod, and from there, on to St. Petersburg."
The snow was coming down even harder now and icy
crystals were beginning to form on his unshaven cheeks.
"Come, we had best return to the children and get
started."

The scent of wood smoke drifted through the trees, penetrating the snow-laden boughs to reach where the four
of them sat huddled against an uprooted larch.

"Can we not light even a small fire, Alex?" Emma's
voice sounded very small from deep within the folds of
wool enveloping her slight form.

Sheffield grimaced. "I'm sorry, sweeting, it's too dangerous. We must try to bear the cold as best we can."
He stood up and removed the blanket from around his
own shoulders, then wrapped it around the girl. "Perhaps this will help."

"I . . . I c-c-can s-s-share mine with her," volunteered
Nicholas, trying to still the chattering of his teeth.

Octavia brushed the snow from her lap. She and Sheffield had not wished to stop so close to where a small
detachment of French soldiers—they had counted ten
men and what looked to be an officer of rank—had set
up their tents for the night, but the children had simply
not been able to go any farther. Too exhausted and too
numb to complain about their empty stomachs, they had
curled in their blankets, but the bitter cold was making
sleep difficult. In fact, she couldn't help but wonder
whether they all might be in peril of freezing before
dawn.

The enemy camp, primitive though it was, looked ever
so inviting when she and Sheffield stole up to the edge
of the clearing to take a closer look. A large kettle hung
over a roaring fire was giving off the most enticing
aroma, and two shelters of ratty canvas, despite their
grime, had seemed a snug respite from the swirling
snows. Why, the man in command even had a small
sleigh. . . .

She dropped back into the thick pines and motioned
for Sheffield to come closer. "I have an idea."

As she explained what she had in mind, his expression

grew darker and darker. "Are you mad!" he exclaimed when she had finished. "Put such a corkbrained plan out of your head this instant. I won't hear of it."

"Alex, we have no choice but to consider something drastic. Do you truly think we can survive without shelter in this weather through the night?"

His jaw clenched.

"We need transportation as well. We will not reach St. Petersburg with only two horses and the few supplies we have left."

He moved slightly to his right, stamping his feet as much from frustration as the need to keep his toes from freezing. "Very well. But I shall be close by, and if anything goes the least amiss—"

"If anything goes amiss, you must take Nicholas and strike out for St. Petersburg," replied Octavia with some heat. "There can be no argument over that, for the boy is your first responsibility. Emma and I will be safe enough in the hands of a French officer, but an Englishman, especially one not in uniform, might be taken for a spy. . . ." Her words cut off abruptly as she drew in a ragged breath. "Come, you know as well as I that with just the two of you, there is a much greater chance you will make it."

A low oath slipped from between Sheffield's clenched teeth.

"Let us not waste any more time. I shall rouse Emma and explain what we must do, but first, give me one of the pistols."

"Bloody hell," he growled. "You have about as much chance of hitting what you aim at as—"

"That may be so," she countered. "But *mon cher capitaine* over there has no notion of that fact." Her gloved hand was already outstretched. "Pass it over."

"Bloody hell," he repeated under his breath, slapping the polished butt of the weapon into her palm. "Always determined to race in where angels fear to tread," he added as she made to go by.

Stung by the odd roughness of his tone, Octavia started to voice a retort, but suddenly his lips were pressed against hers with a fierce urgency, their heat melting through the biting cold. They lingered there for

only a brief moment before he broke away and turned
his steps in the direction of their hidden camp.

She stumbled after him, her senses reeling from the
passion of the embrace, however fleeting. Why, if she
hadn't known there was not a drop of spirits among their
supplies she might have thought he was foxed again! Surely
only someone addled by drink could be so angry one moment and so . . . possessive the next. *Men!* she fumed.
They were the most exasperating of creatures. She doubted
she would ever understand the way their minds . . .

Her foot caught on a frozen root, nearly sending her
sprawling. With a tired grimace, she reminded herself
that she had best push such thoughts aside if she was to
hope of not making a misstep in executing her plan.

It took little time to explain to Emma what was required of her. To her credit, the girl's eyes took on a
certain shine, despite her obvious exhaustion. "Oh, it's
a clever plan," she said through chattering teeth. "I shall
manage just as you say. I promise."

Nicholas looked somewhat miffed that he was not included, but his disappointment quickly disappeared as
Sheffield told him what role he was to play.

"Well, then, let's get on with it," said Octavia, taking
up Emma's hand and moving off toward the faint scent
of smoke.

The French soldiers were huddled in a group around a
single campfire, either too cold or too disheartened to
have posted a proper sentry. The two cloaked figures
ghosted out from among the trees and were within a
dozen paces of the crouched men before someone gave
a cry of alarm.

"*Grace a Dieu! Ne tirer pas!*" cried Octavia, her hands
flying to her breast as several muskets were leveled at
that exact spot. Little exaggeration was necessary to appear a female on the verge of hysteria, she thought wryly
as she continued on. "*Oh, ma petit, nous sommes sauve!*"

Emma gave a very credible shriek of relief, then col-
lapsed in a swoon worthy of any Radcliffe heroine.

The French officer was already on his feet, pistol in
hand, and approaching the two women.

"The partisans attacked our platoon—my daughter and I became separated from my husband in the fighting," explained Octavia in hurried French, hoping that any odd pronunciation would be thought the result of a mouth too frozen to move properly. For good measure, she caused a few tears to run down her reddened cheeks, an easy task as the cutting wind was already making her eyes water. "P-perhaps you know him—Colonel Levesque, from Rouen?" she added, kneeling down beside Emma's prostate form and chafing the girl's hand between her thick mittens.

"*Non, madame,*" replied the officer rather warily. His gaze flitted uncertainly from Octavia's distraught face to the small form lying in the snow. "What regiment?"

Grateful that she had paid some attention to the newspaper accounts of Napolean's movements across Europe, Octavia immediately came up with a name. She could only hope that the long march into Russia and the recent battles had created some measure of confusion within the French ranks.

Apparently satisfied that the two forlorn figures presented no threat, the officer slowly returned the pistol to his belt. "I fear our troops have become sadly disorganized in the past few days—I had not realized they had been shifted to this flank of the army." He bent to assist Emma in getting to her feet. "Please, allow me to help with the *pauvre petite.* I have a daughter nearly her age at home." A shy smile and a whispered *"merci"* from the girl caused his voice to grow even more wistful. "Thank the Lord you stumbled upon us, Madame Levesque, and not some band of those bloodthirsty Russian savages." He gave a pained grimace. "Come closer to the fire. Our fare is naught but a thin gruel but at least it is hot."

"How kind," murmured Octavia, feigning a slight swaying as she, too, rose. "O—Oh . . ." Just as she hoped, the officer was quick to offer his support. "Many thanks, sir," she added, taking firm hold of his arm. Out of the corner of her eye, she noted that Emma had dropped back several steps and followed close on her heels. "I knew I might count on the honor of a Gallic gentleman to help two ladies in need."

He smiled, then turned to give a brief order to his men. Octavia stumbled again, falling with an awkward lurch sideways that twisted the man's arm behind his back. An exclamation of concern interrupted his words, and his head jerked back in her direction. Its progress, however, was quickly arrested by a muzzle of cold steel pressed up against his temple.

"No one move, else your captain will suffer the consequences." Octavia was pleased that her voice sounded a good deal more calm than she felt.

Recovering from his initial shock, the officer swore and started to pull away from her hold.

"Freeze!" The metallic click of the hammer being cocked was quite audible above the hiss and crackle of the burning pine. "If you wish to see that daughter of yours again," she added in a lower voice, "I suggest you do as I say. No doubt she would infinitely prefer a live father to a dead hero."

Although another oath sounded he ceased all movement.

"A wise decision. Now order your men to lay down their weapons over there." She indicated a spot several paces away from the fire. "Then have two of them harness the horses to the sled."

"Madame, are you mad?" he began to argue. "Think on it. If the cold doesn't kill you and the child, the wolves—or worse—will. Whoever you are, you would be wiser to remain with us. Even if you are Russian, I give you my word—"

"Watch out—his pistol!" Emma clutched at the officer's sleeve, preventing his hand from stealing around to the weapon tucked in his belt.

Mouthing a silent curse at herself for having forgotten such a crucial detail, Octavia quickly snatched it away from his grasp. Several of the men had edged toward their muskets during the brief distraction, and although they were now still, she noted the furtive glances they were exchanging with their commander. Sensing that control of the situation was in danger of slipping away, she acted without hesitation.

The barrel of the second gun smashed across the officer's cheek, hard enough to draw blood. She then jabbed its barrel none too gently up under his throat. "No more tricks! If you think I won't pull the trigger, you are dead wrong. As you can see, I am very desperate and very angry—not a good combination in a female, especially one who holds a weapon at your head."

He swallowed hard, then slowly repeated her orders to his troops.

As soon as the muskets were stacked and the soldiers had retreated back to the fire, two shadowy shapes slipped out from among the surrounding trees. "About bloody time," muttered Sheffield, handing one of the weapons to Nicholas while keeping his own gun trained on the huddled men. "A pretty speech indeed, but must you always indulge in a flair for the dramatic?"

"Forgive me if I stumbled a bit in my role," she snapped with some sarcasm. "I have had precious little practice in subduing a platoon of enemy soldiers."

He moved to her side, a lopsided grin coming to his haggard face. "All things considered, the critics give you a standing ovation. I shall, however, take over the lead from here." Taking one of the pistols from her numb fingers, he pushed her gently aside. "Help Emma gather up some of the blankets and rations."

"You are . . . English!" stammered the officer in some disbelief. "What in the name of the Holy Virgin are you—" A nudge of the pistol caused him to fall silent.

"Don't ask," sighed Sheffield as he watched the two ladies stow several armfuls of supplies into the sled. "I doubt you would believe it, even if I were to tell you the truth." Ignoring the man's look of complete bafflement, he motioned to Nicholas. "Put the muskets into the sleigh as well."

"*Mon Dieu*, y-you don't mean to leave us unarmed in this—" exclaimed the officer.

"No. Not if you and your men do as you are told. Don't attempt to pursue us and I shall drop your weapons just before we turn onto the main road."

"God help you—the two of you really are mad," repeated the officer with a dazed shake of his head.

A gust of wind shivered the heavy pine boughs, and a flurry of snow swirled around the small encampment. Sheffield glanced at the men's tattered boots and worn cloaks, and his lips compressed in a tight line. "I have a suspicion you are going to have just as much need of the Almighty's help in making your own way home." The horses shifted in the traces, clouds of vapor muffling their snorted complaints. With a shrug of his shoulders, he signaled for the others to climb into the waiting conveyance.

Octavia didn't budge. "Alex . . ."

"The devil take it, must you always argue—" She cut off his snappish words with a mute gesture at the kettle of soup. "You are quite right. But hurry."

Octavia took up two of the battered bowls from near the fire and ladled out a generous helping for the two children, who fell upon the steaming contents with undisguised relish. After a quick bite for herself, she fixed another portion and carried it to where Sheffield held the officer at gunpoint. "You must eat as well. I'll keep my pistol trained on the prisoner."

He said something rude under his breath.

"Must you always argue?" She mimicked his own earlier tone of exasperation with frightening accuracy. "Don't be an obstinate ass! Do you really wish to pass out cold from hunger and exhaustion?"

The Frenchman's lips gave a wry twitch. "It does not appear, *monsieur,* that your wife is a lady to argue with. Er"—he gave a nervous glance at the gun that was being waved uncomfortably close to his head—"please do as she says."

Sheffield gulped down the soup. "If the lady *were* my wife, I doubt I should have even a shred of my sanity left." He tossed aside the empty bowl and took hold of the officer's coat, pulling him out of Octavia's line of fire. "Come along with me."

Octavia thought she heard a whispered prayer of thanks. Stifling an indignant retort, she hustled the children into the interior of the cab. *Men!* she thought with some asperity, slamming the door shut with more force than was necessary. *How dare they claim the workings of the female mind were incomprehensible!* What had she done—other than secure transport and supplies—to provoke the mercurial Mr. Sheffield's odious temper? It would serve him right if she—

Catching sight of two pairs of eyes regarding her with a mixture of awe and curiosity, she moderated her black scowl somewhat. "Try to get some sleep," she counseled, arranging yet another blanket around their slight forms. "We still have a long journey ahead, but perhaps the worst is behind us."

Her words proved true enough. Several times during the night, the sled was slowed by sentries patrolling the roads, but a vague mutter, accompanied by much pointing and gesturing caused the soldiers to wave them on. By the time dawn glimmered on the horizon, they had not sighted a soul for several hours.

Octavia insisted on taking over the reins, sending Sheffield inside to grab a bit of rest. No doubt the only reason he agreed, she told herself on climbing up to the driver's seat, was because his jaw was too frozen to voice a protest. There was silence all around, save for the swoosh of the iron runners through the powdery drifts. The miles continued to slide by, and as the sun stole out from behind the thick clouds, the snow-covered landscape took on an ethereal beauty, the sharp northern light setting the vast expanse of white to winking and glittering as if it were covered with diamonds.

Precious indeed was each step closer to St. Petersburg, mused Octavia. Once there, she and Alex could each feel a well-deserved measure of satisfaction in having succeeded against overwhelming odds. And what of their odd little group?

Of course they would go their separate ways.

He would be eager to catch the first ship back to England and deliver the young count to his relatives. She, too, was determined to go on to London, though it might take a little longer to arrange. However, she doubted the Renfrews would dare raise much of an objection when she threatened to expose their misuse of Emma's funds. Once she had made sure the girl was comfortably settled in a proper household, she could begin to think about what might lay ahead for her.

Right now the future did not seem nearly as bright as the sparkling snow. With no references, the chances of securing any respectable position did not seem overly good. Her mouth scrunched up in a strange grimace. Well, one thing was certain—whatever the future might hold, it did not include a certain ill-tempered, impecunious tutor. She should be glad of it, she assured herself, for he was the most aggravating, arrogant, and sardonic man she had ever met.

So why was she feeling a strange little lurch of her insides at the thought of never seeing Mr. Sheffield after they reached their destination?

She was merely . . . hungry, she told herself. Besides, she could be sure that *he* was feeling no such qualms at the prospects of being parted from his traveling companion. It was clear he thought her a managing, overbearing shrew! Why, the wretch had had the nerve to imply that any man would have to be dicked in the nob to find her—

Such lowering thoughts were interrupted by the sight of movement up head. She slowed the horses to a walk, and made ready to grab for the pistol tucked away in her pocket. It was, however, only an elderly peasant shuffling along with a large sack of firewood slung over his back. A few hurried inquiries revealed that the fighting lay well to the south. Further questioning caused the fellow to pause and tug at his long beard.

When it finally came, the answer brought a smile to Octavia's lips.

"What's the matter?" demanded Sheffield, his stubbled face finally making an appearance from inside the cab. "Why are you stopping?"

She gestured at the old man. "He says his wife would be happy to cook a hot meal for us at a reasonable price, and that we might also take a few hour's rest in his barn. But there is even better news. . . ."

He blinked.

"We are some miles to the northwest of Novgorad. That means we should reach St. Petersburg in two days."

Chapter Fourteen

*T*he journey was completed without further adventure. It remained arctic in temperature, but the main roads were well traveled and afforded a number of decent taverns where they were able to stop for hot tea laced with sugar and the opportunity to thaw out from the biting cold.

Would that he could dispel the unaccountable chill that had developed between himself and Miss Hadley, thought Sheffield glumly, as the sled drew near the outskirts of the city. Ever since the night of their encounter with the French troops, they had treated each other with excruciating politeness, but an underlying tension had robbed their exchanges of any real warmth. Emma and Nicholas had not missed the subtle change, and their own behavior had become more and more subdued. The animated readings of Mrs. Radcliffe's novel and the spirited debates over the foibles of the various characters had given way to long silences and searching looks. He had avoided the unspoken questions in their eyes, for in truth he was not sure he understood what had happened any more than they did.

Did Octavia think him a lout for daring to kiss her with such fiery abandon? He would never have given in to such emotion if she hadn't been so resolutely determined to march headlong into the jaws of danger with nary a care for herself. Good Lord, he had wanted to shake her, to scold her, to smother her with kisses, all at the same time.

Kisses be damned—what he had really wanted to do was to strip the travel-worn clothing from both of their bodies and mold his heated flesh to every delicious curve of her form. He had wanted to make slow, sensuous love to her, and hear her cry out his name as their passion exploded in a shower of white-hot sparks.

Ha! When she had spoken to him, it was to call him an obstinate ass! His hands gave an involuntary jerk on the reins. So much for imagining that flowery romance existed outside the pages of a dratted book! In reality, it seemed she was counting the minutes until they reached St. Petersburg, so anxious was she to be rid of his odious presence.

After all, she had made it clear from their first meeting that she thought him no more than a debauched wastrel. The brief interlude of what had appeared to be a more . . . intimate friendship had no doubt been engendered by mere expendiency. There had been precious little choice but to get along with each other in order to survive.

And now? He would be off to London with Nicholas and Octavia would set herself to finding a caring guardian for Emma. A sharp twinge knifed through him at the thought of the impending separation, causing his mouth to twist in a odd grimace. Surely a hardened rake such as himself was not going to miss a shrewish spinster and a pigtailed twelve-year-old? But somehow the idea of their intrepid little family breaking up had his spirits sinking to a low ebb. *A family.* Perhaps he had thought of them as such because he had none other to call his own.

Perhaps he didn't deserve any.

After all, he would only disappoint anyone who was foolish enough to trust in him. How could it be otherwise, when even *he* didn't trust in himself?

A string of shouted curses caused his head to jerk up, just in time to avoid collision with a cart loaded with turnips. Several other drivers contributed their own rude comments on his prowess with the reins, and Sheffield found he had no alternative but to devote his full attention to the crowded streets. Progress slowed as the sled made its way toward the snaking Neva River, lumbering at a snail's pace past the pastel-colored buildings and long canals that had earned the city its other moniker of "Venice of the North."

After what seemed like an age, he turned the horses into a narrow side street and pulled to a halt in front of the seedy boarding house he had used during his first visit to St. Petersburg. Although it seemed highly unlikely that Nicholas's uncle would dare try any desperate acts at this late stage, Sheffield decided there was no harm in being cautious. Until he could establish contact with the embassy, they would remain hidden among the anonymous dockyard workers and shop girls of the rough waterfront neighborhood.

He climbed down from his perch and cracked open the door to the cab. "Wait here while I arrange for a room."

"Two rooms," replied Octavia, rather too quickly for his liking.

His jaw tightened. "Until we can move you to a more genteel part of town, it would be wise to continue the masquerade of traveling together. You would find the men here no more apt to respect your person than those you encountered back in the inn."

She made a face but nodded a reluctant assent.

He returned shortly and led them up three flights of rickety stairs to a large room with two smaller bedchambers overlooking a shadowed alleyway. The furnishings were cheap and well used, but at least the place was moderately clean and possessed a small cast-iron stove in the far corner. "I've paid for some wood and a jug of water to be brought up," he informed Octavia. "As we have no further need of them, I had better go down and see to disposing of the horses and sled."

"While you are out, perhaps you should also see to purchasing some staples for our supper."

He gave a curt nod. "Anything else?"

Eyes averted, she toyed with the strap of her valise. "D-do you intend to stop by the embassy?"

"Time enough for that in the morning," he growled. *The devil take it!* Was she that anxious to be rid of him? The cold realization caused an icy knot to form in the pit of his stomach. Without further words, he turned and stalked out the door.

Biting her lip, Octavia fell to helping the children out of their heavy coats and boots, then settled them at the scarred pine table, along with their book. They raised no complaint, but it was clear from the halfhearted murmurs that their minds were engaged with something other than concern for the fate of Emily and Valancourt.

She was unpacking a few of their meager possessions when Emma suddenly closed the pages and looked up. "Are you and Alex . . . angry with us? Have we done something wrong?" The girl's voice was hardly more than a tentative whisper, and from the look of concern on the boy's pinched face, it was clear she was speaking for both of them.

Octavia brushed a lock of hair from her pale cheek. "Oh no, my dear. We couldn't be more proud of both of you. No hero or heroine from a book could have faced such dangers with half of your courage and grit."

"Then why does Alex look . . . like a bear with a thorn in his paw?" ventured Nicholas.

Because he had a thorn in his side—a prickly governess, to be precise.

Although it was the unfortunate truth, she kept it to herself, searching instead for a reason the children might understand more readily. "It has been a long and difficult journey," she answered after some consideration. "And one that is still far from over. What you see in him is not anger, but worry. No doubt his nerves are much frayed from the constant concern for your safety. H-he cares very much for both of you." A slight tremor had crept into her voice. "Does that answer your question?"

They nodded, but a certain doubt remained etched on their faces.

"Come, let us start the stove and put on a kettle for hot water. I am sure Alex will be ready for a hot cup of tea when he returns."

But when the door flung open some time later, it appeared that tea was not what Sheffield had in mind to chase the chill from his bones. As he stomped the snow from his boots and headed for the small table, his unsteady steps revealed that he had already had more than one glass of vodka. Quite a few more. And to Octavia's dismay, she spotted the corked tip of a bottle sticking out from his coat pocket.

"Alex! I've kept the water hot for you." Emma was out of her chair and halfway to the stove. "Shall I fix you some tea?"

He let the packages in his arms fall to the table in a heap. "Don't want any tea," he growled. "Just want to be left alone for a bit, without a pack of plaguey women and children pulling at my coattails."

It was the first time he had ever spoken harshly to the children. Emma recoiled as if struck, and her lower lip began to quiver.

Oblivious to her wounded feelings, Sheffield took up one of the blankets from the neatly folded pile on the floor and stalked toward the near bedchamber. "I'm devilishly tired. Perhaps I shall be allowed some peace and quiet." With that, the door was kicked closed.

Octavia was too shocked to do anything but stare, mouth agape, at the rough hewn pine boards. It was Nicholas who slid from his seat and went to put an arm around the girl's quaking shoulders. "Don't be upset. Sometimes men act very badly," he counseled, his adolescent voice so grave that Octavia nearly smiled in spite of herself. "Alex isn't . . . quite himself at the moment. In the morning, I am sure everything will be fine, and he will make a very handsome apology to you."

A watery sniff was the only response.

"Come on, let's finish the end of the chapter. We cannot leave off with Emily in such a perilous position. . . ."

Emma allowed him to guide her back to the table, where he took the book onto his lap and began to read with a forced cheerfulness. After a moment, Octavia sat down as well. Rummaging in her valise, she extracted a needle and thread and began mending a small tear in her cloak.

The parcels of food lay untouched. No one seemed to be the least hungry.

"We may be in luck, sirs!" In his haste to convey the news, Squid burst into the sitting room of the rented quarters without so much as a knock.

The marquess dropped the papers he had been reading, while his uncle nearly sloshed half of his tea over his waistcoat. Alston, who had been searching for an atlas among his belongings, stuck his head out from one of the bedchambers.

"A lad just appeared downstairs with word that a man answering to Mr. Alex's description has taken a room near the waterfront, in the same place as he stayed before." The valet's eyes were alight with excitement. "And there's a nipper with him. I shall go at once—"

Chittenden rose. "We all shall go."

"Indeed we shall." The marquess held up a note from the embassy. "As luck would have it, there is a convoy leaving for London on the ebb tide this evening. If it is really Alex, perhaps . . ." He looked expectantly at his uncle and then his brother. "I, for one, would not be adverse to quitting this land of snow and ice as soon as possible. Surely Alex will be just as eager to be on his way back to England."

His uncle stroked his chin. "Hmmm. I suppose it would do no harm to have the trunks taken around to the docks and the naval attaché ready to make room for us on one of the ships."

Alston had already gathered up their overcoats and hats. "Let's be off, then."

Squid flagged down a passing hackney and managed to convey to the driver where they wished to be taken. The man's shaggy brows waggled in surprise as he eyed the elegant dress of the three gentlemen standing behind the valet, but he merely shrugged and gestured for them to climb inside.

A few coins pressed into the landlady's gnarled hand convinced her to divulge exactly which room the tall stranger had been given. Unable to contain his impatience, Squid took the narrow stairs two at a time and was already rapping on the door as the three gentlemen reached the landing.

"Ssssh. Not a sound," cautioned Octavia in a low whisper. Another flurry of knocks shook the door, with even more urgency than before. "Both of you—go into the bedchamber and close the door." Nicholas began to mouth a protest, but Emma tugged on his sleeve and led him away.

Tossing her mending aside, Octavia groped for one of the pistols hidden among the folded blankets. There was no time to rouse Alex—if indeed, he was in any state to be roused. Given the fact that the bottle in his coat pocket had been quite full, she decided her aim would be better than his at this point.

The flint and priming looked to be in order, so she moved to the door. "Who is there?" she demanded in a low, raspy growl she hoped would pass for a man's voice.

"A-Alex? Is that you?"

The question had been spoken in English, but she hesitated, thinking it might only be a ruse.

"It's me, Squid!"

Squid? It was quite unlikely any Russian would come up with such a name. Tightening her grip on the weapon, Octavia opened the door a crack. A slightly built young man with a thatch of golden curls peeking out from under his fur hat stood only inches from her, his fist poised to deliver yet another knock.

For an instant it was difficult to tell who was more surprised by the encounter.

The young man's arm hovered in midair; then a wide grin spread across his face as he turned to speak to the others behind him. "Leave it to Mr. Alex to have a pretty wench willing to warm his sheets."

"Let us hope he has had as much success in locating our nephew as he has had in finding a doxy for his bed," remarked the marquess, his eyes raking over Octavia's rumpled gown and the tumble of errant curls that had escaped her hairpins. "Ivor, have you some money to give this . . . female for her services?"

"But we still do not know if it is really Alex who is inside," pointed out Alston. "Squid, can you ask her if—"

"If you are looking for Mr. Alex Sheffield, he is here. As is young Count Scherbatov." Recovering from her initial shock, Octavia responded rather loudly in English,

her speech clearly mirroring the same cultured tones as
those of the marquess and his brother.

Squid gave a strangled cough, and the three gentlemen
each turned a different shade of pink.

"Y-you are English?" exclaimed the marquess.

She nodded, only then remembering to lower the barrel of the pistol.

"Er, I beg your pardon, ma'am, for voicing such inap-
propriate speculation," began the earl. "We had no idea
you were, er, not one of the local—"

"You can hardly be blamed for assuming the worst,
sir." Her chin rose a fraction as she regarded the group
before her. It was most peculiar, but for an instant she
couldn't help but feel there was something strangely familiar about the two dark-haired gentlemen. . . . Quickly
banishing such odd thoughts from her head, she continued in a rush. "However, despite present appearances,
I am no doxy, but a respectable English governess.
There is a reasonable explanation for my presence in
Mr. Sheffield's rooms. We agreed to join forces and
travel north together for the sake of the young people
in our care, as it seemed . . . the sensible thing to do.
Although the highest sticklers may not approve of the
arrangement, nothing improper has occurred between
us. Together we have managed to bring our charges to
safety. Through, I might add, some very harrowing
circumstances."

If anything, her show of quiet dignity caused the gentlemen to appear even more embarrassed. For a moment, the only sounds were the shuffling of booted feet
and several more muted coughs. After an exchange of
rueful glances, it was the earl who broke the awkward
silence.

"Once again, Miss, er . . ."

"Hadley. Octavia Hadley."

"Once again, Miss Hadley, let me offer you our sincere
apologies for the crude comments that were made. . . ."
A brief inclination of her head indicated that the apology
was accepted and he should go on. ". . . I believe our
man Squid has introduced himself, but let me make the
rest of us known to you. I am Lord Chittenden and these

two gentlemen are my nephews, Lord Killingworth and Lord Alston."

Octavia blinked. *The Earl of Chittenden and the Marquess of Killingworth!* Why, even a country miss such as she knew they were two of the most influential—and moneyed—men in London. That certainly explained how such a daring rescue attempt for their young relative had been planned. But it did not explain what the gentlemen were doing here in Russia themselves. After all, if they had paid for someone else to risk . . .

Another discreet cough interrupted her thoughts. "Miss Hadley, might we step inside?"

A dull flush rose to her cheeks. "Yes, of course," she stammered, quickly stepping aside so that the gentlemen could file into the room. "N-naturally you are anxious to meet with your nephew."

"Quite." The marquess's eyes had already made a sweep of the spartan quarters. "I am also anxious to have a word with my brother."

It took a moment for the statement to sink in. "*Brother?*" she repeated faintly.

"Yes. Alex is our younger brother," added the viscount. "Did he not mention the family connection?"

Octavia felt the color drain from her face as the words of the garrulous Mrs. Phillips came echoing back. *Alexander Sheffield. Are you perchance related to William Sheffield, the Marquess of Killingworth?* No wonder the two younger gentlemen had looked rather familiar!

"No. He did not." Her voice had taken on a rather brittle edge. "I imagine he saw no reason to reveal the truth to a . . . mere stranger." Drawing in a sharp breath, she added, "Indeed, the only reference he made to his family was to indicate his estrangement from them. He said that they did not care in the least what might happen to him."

"He was wrong." The marquess's lips crooked in a rueful expression. "Not that he was given much reason to think otherwise."

Turning abruptly, she moved to one of the closed doors and threw it open. "Nicholas, you must come out and meet your . . . other relatives."

The boy slowly stepped out from the shadows, followed closely by Emma. However, rather than approach the three gentlemen who stood expectantly in a tight semicircle, he rushed straight to Octavia.

"Surely a brave fellow who has faced murderous Cossacks, deadly blizzards, and a troop of enemy soldiers can't be nervous at the prospect of meeting his family," she murmured close to his ear. Giving him a small squeeze of encouragement, she urged him forward. "Now go give your uncles a proper greeting."

Squaring his thin shoulders, the boy approached the strangers and made a very credible bow. "I am very pleased to make your acquaintance, sir. I—" Before he could finish, Killingworth had enfolded the lad in his arms. "Hello, Nicky. You cannot imagine how glad we are to see you. . . ."

Octavia took tight hold of Emma's hand and watched with a pensive smile as Nicholas was introduced to the rest of his English family. But her thoughts were focused on the one Sheffield who was not present in the room.

The wretch! It turned out that lies were also to be included among the litany of Alex's sins. Why, he had played her for a fool from the very beginning, letting her think he was an impoverished tutor, as alone in the world as she was! Her sense of betrayal was so overwhelming she feared for an instant that she might fall into a swoon worthy of the worst sort of Gothic heroine.

Her disillusionment was, however, quickly replaced by seething anger. Why, she fumed, if Alex had been able to stand on his feet, she would have been sorely tempted to plant a fist smack on that patrician nose of his!

Speaking of the devil, it was the viscount who suddenly looked up from his young nephew and inquired, "Er, by the way, where *is* Alex?"

"He is sleeping." Her lip curled up slightly. "Or, to use the term that gentlemen are wont to employ, he is sleeping it off."

"Ah." Alston exchanged a rueful grimace with his older brother.

"Don't worry, milord. I have a good deal of experience in tending to Mr. Alex," piped up Squid. "He'll be dead to the world for another few hours, but once we have him aboard the ship, I'll see that he wakes without too sore of a head."

The earl took a discreet peek at his pocket watch. "I'm afraid that we must make haste if we are to make it to the docks before the convoy weighs anchor." He slanted a look of concern at Octavia. "It was difficult enough to convince the admiral to make room for our group aboard the naval vessel leaving tonight. Two additional people, and females at that . . ."

"It was only for the sake of expediency that your brother and I traveled together this far. You needn't feel any obligation for me, my lord. I assure you, I am, quite capable of dealing with formalities here and seeing to the arrangement of a passage to England for myself and my charge."

"But we can't leave Miss Hadley and Emma behind!" cried Nicholas on realizing what was being discussed. "Alex would not—"

"Alex would not hesitate for an instant. The most important thing is for you to be out of Russia as soon as possible," said Octavia. She turned to the earl, her expression inscrutable. "Please, I insist that you not miss your ship."

Chittenden's mouth compressed in a thin line. "Under ordinary circumstances, I would not consider leaving two females alone in a foreign land. But you are right—we cannot be sure the threat to the boy is over until we have set sail."

There was a flurry of thumps and thuds as the young valet emerged from the second bedchamber with an unconscious Alex draped over his shoulder. "Leaping Lucifer," muttered Squid. "Russian vodka appears to have even more kick to it than French brandy."

It was only with great difficulty that Octavia restrained the urge to aim a potent kick of her own at Sheffield's passing posterior.

"You are a stalwart young woman, Miss Hadley," continued Chittenden with a harried sigh. "I shall of course send word to the embassy asking that they assist you in finding a quick passage home."

"That is more than kind of you, sir. But there is no reason for concern. I am well used to looking out for myself."

The marquess shifted his weight from one foot to the other. "What of money, Miss Hadley? May we offer—"

"No," she said rather sharply. Somehow the thought of accepting any payment from Alex's family made her feel rather soiled. "I have sufficient funds."

He gave a reluctant nod. "As you wish." Alston had already moved to help Squid manuever Alex's limp form out toward the stairs. The earl gave a gentle tug to his young relative's sleeve. "Nicholas, we really must be going."

The boy hesitated, then broke away to throw his arms around Octavia. "Good-bye, Miss Hadley," he said, struggling to keep his voice from breaking. "We will all meet again soon, won't we?"

She hugged him, but refrained from answering.

His gaze then turned to Emma. "I shall miss—learning what happens to Emily and Valancourt."

The book suddenly appeared from the folds of her skirts. "Here, you take it!" she cried, thrusting it into his hands.

"But Emma—"

"Don't worry. Octavia has other books, while you do not."

"I—I shall return it to you in London."

"Yes." She blinked back a tear. "Of course."

The book clutched to his chest, Nicholas allowed the earl to hurry him off toward the stairs. With a final brief bow, the marquess followed after them.

Thwock. The door fell shut with a bang.

She had to hand it to him—when it came to making an entrance or an exit into her life, Alex Sheffield was nothing if not dramatic.

Chapter Fifteen

*I*t was as if a gale-force storm was raging in his head. His brow felt like it had been pounded by an ocean of angry waves, and there was a howling in his ears, like wind tearing through rigging, that would not moderate, no matter in which direction he rolled. Even now, he was being buffeted by . . .

"Mr. Alex, come on now, it's time you opened your eyes." Squid gave him another brisk shake. "Look, I managed to bribe the cook's mate to brew up a cup of your favorite hair of the dog."

The dull roar sounded like his valet's voice, but that was impossible. No doubt it was mere wishful thinking, for a swig of the fellow's special concoction would have tasted nothing short of ambrosial at the moment. Another lurch of his queasy stomach caused him to emit a low groan.

"I think he's finally coming around, milord."

Sheffield finally managed to pry one bleary eye open. The mop of blond curls, the faint scar along the cheekbone—his valet appeared to be more than a figment of his imagination. "What the devil . . ."

Squid bent closer. "Feeling like a regiment of Boney's soldiers tramped over your bone box in their hobnail boots, eh?"

The other lid came up as Sheffield sought to bring his swaying surroundings into focus. "What in the name of Hades are *you* doing here in Russia?" he croaked. "And how the devil did you find us—stop moving about while I am trying to speak to you! It is making me . . . seasick."

A bark of laughter burst forth. "We ain't in Russia

anymore, Mr. Alex. We are near halfway out through the Gulf of Finland, with a fair wind toward Denmark."

"Not in Russia!" Sheffield sat up so abruptly that he cracked his head on the overhanging bunk. "Bloody hell! Where is—"

"Calm yourself, Alex. You and young Nicholas are safely aboard one of His Majesty's frigates, thanks to your courage and resourcefulness."

Sheffield wondered whether the blow to his cranium had further addled his senses, for the voice that came from one of the blurry shapes behind his valet sounded exactly like that of his brother William. He closed his eyes and pressed his palms to his throbbing brow, hoping to force his brain into proper working order. "Octavia," he muttered hoarsely. "Octavia and Emma . . ."

There was a brief silence, save for the groaning of the ship's timbers.

"Er, I believe he is referring to the governess."

Hell's teeth! An excess of Russian vodka must induce not only a wicked intoxication but a number of strange hallucinations as well! Now it seemed to be his Uncle Ivor who was speaking.

"Ah, yes. Miss . . . Hadley, wasn't it?"

Sheffield's lids snapped open at the mention of her name. The figure looming over him was no longer an amorphous shape, but now clearly bore the familiar features of his eldest brother, as well as his voice.

"As to that, she quite agreed that it was time to part ways, given the circumstances," continued the marquess. "It would have been impossible to accommodate two females in these cramped quarters."

"You left them in St. Petersburg?" Sheffield's voice was barely more than a whisper.

"Why, yes, of course. Miss Hadley indicated that was what she had expected all along. She assured me she had adequate funds and was quite capable of managing for herself." Killingworth gave a harried chuckle. "Indeed, I do not doubt it. An unusual female. One who is not easily intimidated—"

With an inarticulate roar, Sheffield lowered his head and lunged at his brother, his shoulder catching the marquess square in the midriff. The force of the attack sent both of them crashing to the deck of the tiny cabin. It took the combined efforts of the earl and Squid to separate the younger man's fingers from his sibling's neck and wrestle him back to the narrow bunk.

"Mr. Alex, have you gone mad?" cried the startled valet, still trying to control his employer's thrashing arms.

As the marquess rose to his feet rather shakily and began to finger the purpling bruise on his cheek, the earl regarded first one nephew, then the other, with a look of grave concern. "Alex, we know what an extraordinary amount of strain you have had to bear lately—"

Sheffield ceased his struggling and slumped back against the rough planking. "I haven't lost my mind, Uncle Ivor." He drew in a ragged breath. "Just whatever shred of self-respect I still possessed." His troubled gaze then turned on his brother. "No doubt you are well pleased to see your low opinion of my character is so justified," he said with a bitter sneer. "Once again I have left another person to founder."

Killingworth's brows drew together in consternation. "Why, surely you don't think I meant to—"

"Damn you! Get out—all of you!" Sheffield didn't care that he was perilously close to shouting. "Except for Squid. And you, you traitorous little whelp of the sea, may take yourself off as soon as you have fetched enough brandy to keep me well under the hatches until we reach England."

Squid's remonstrance was cut short by a gruff snarl. "If you wish to remain in my employ, you'll do as I say." His lip then turned up in a sardonic curl. "But perhaps you have already decided to seek a more gentlemanly sort of company."

The earl nudged the young valet and made a wordless sign for him to leave off any attempt at argument. Catching Killingworth's eye as well, he motioned at the door. "Come, let us join Thomas and the lad up on the quarterdeck," he said in a low murmur. "Perhaps later, when he has had a chance to recover from the shock of the news, he will be more willing to listen to reason."

Squid nodded glumly, but the marquess's features

took on a stubborn set. "I abandoned Alex once before when he was in need. I'll not do it again. This time, if he tells me to go to the devil, he will have to toss me into Hell with his own two hands."

A faint smile creased Chittenden's lined countenance, but he refrained from any comment as he backed into the darkened passageway, drawing the valet along with him.

With a harried sigh Killingworth turned toward his brother.

The violent outburst had left Sheffield utterly drained. He felt neither anger nor outrage, simply a yawing void within his breast. The spirits might fill it for a brief time, but he knew, with frightening certainty, that the emptiness would not be banished so easily. Oblivious to whether his rants and curses had been paid any heed, he leaned forward and buried his head in his hands.

"Alex," said the marquess haltingly, not quite sure of how to begin.

A muffled groan was the only response.

He moved closer and, after a moment's hesitation, lay a tentative hand on his brother's shoulder, as if expecting it to be knocked away. "Damnation, Alex," he blurted out. "I should have realized you would not wish to leave your . . . friends behind, not after all you had been through together." A heavy sigh sounded. "It was not my intention to cause you any pain, but I see that I have. I'm . . . well, I'm sorry. Truly sorry. I was wrong to assume I, of all people, knew what was the right thing to do."

Sheffield was moved to look up, an expression of disbelief slowly replacing the remorse etched on his haggard face. Was he truly hallucinating now, or had his rigid martinet of a sibling just unbent enough to admit to an error in judgment?

"Good Lord, William. Don't tell me that a Marquess of Killingworth actually thinks he might be capable of making a mistake." His voice, though still sharp with irony, had lost a bit of its earlier razored edge.

"I suppose I deserve that." The marquess crooked a grimace. "I have made more than a few mistakes, Alex. The shame is not in being fallible, but in being too blind or too self-assured to recognize it. Or perhaps too afraid, thinking it a sign of weakness rather than of being merely human. The trouble is, we Sheffield men had it drummed into us that mistakes were not allowed." His mouth compressed. "How absurd. It was Father who made the biggest mistake of all, for which we have all paid very dearly."

Sheffield's throat became so constricted that speech was nigh impossible. What had it cost his brother to utter such sentiments aloud? Whatever the toll, the words were a priceless gift. He blinked several times, wondering if his own face betrayed the same poignant vulnerability that now shaded his brother's lean features.

Slowly, still without a word, he leaned forward until his cheek came to rest on the marquess's silk waistcoat.

He felt the hand on his shoulder tighten its grip, and suddenly he was being held so hard up against the other man's chest that it was difficult to breath. A choked sob somehow escaped, but whether it came from his own lips or Killingworth's he was not sure.

"D-do you remember the day Mama died, you found me hiding in a corner of the nursery?" he asked rather thickly. "I was afraid to let anyone know I had dared do something so unmanly as shed a tear."

"Good Lord, you were seven years old," murmured the marquess.

"You held me that day as well, William. And you never teased me about it or told anyone else. I-I have never thanked you for that."

"That should not have been the only time I reached out to you, Alex."

"The fault is more mine than yours. I did my damnedest to push you all away with my outrageous behavior. It is a wonder you didn't wash your hands of me entirely."

"Neither of us can change the past. But as to the future . . ." He paused to clear his throat. "For too long I have lived with the loss of two brothers. I should like to have one of them back from the dead."

A wry expression pulled at Sheffield's lips. "I think I am ready to come back, for I am tired of living in a hell of my own making. But I am no saint, William. God knows, the climb will not be easy. No doubt I shall trip and stumble along the way."

"Then reach out to me for help, instead of a bottle of brandy." Killingworth managed a weak smile. "Only think of how much of your quarterly allowance you might save in the bargain—I am much cheaper than spirits, Alex. And I trust I will leave you with less of a headache."

A rumble of muffled laughter sounded against the slubbed silk. But as Sheffield sat up, the humor faded from his face. The mention of seeking solace in a bottle had brought back thoughts of his last encounter with Octavia. She must think him the worse sort of cravenly cad, and with good reason. "The devil take it," he mumbled. "I wish Squid would return with his promised elixir." The throbbing at his temples had suddenly intensified with a vengeance. "Not that the brew will be able to assuage the real problem," he added softly. "You may be willing to overlook my egregious sins, but I am afraid that there are others who may not be quite so . . . forgiving."

His brother took a seat beside him. "Surely things are not quite so bleak. From what I have heard, er, most females find it hard to resist your charms."

"Ha!" Sheffield's mouth quirked in a rueful twist. "There is certainly one female who has no such trouble. Miss Hadley finds me odious, arrogant, and overbearing. That is, of course, in addition to being a drunken scoundrel."

"Is that all?" Killingworth repressed a twitch of a grin. "In that case, figuring out how to overcome such paltry obstacles should be child's play." He paused to clear his throat. "Er, is there a particular reason you wish the young lady to hold you in greater esteem?"

"I wish to . . . ensure that she is not left to fend for herself when she arrives back in England. Her family is a malicious pack of curs who have already thrown her to the wolves once. And she will not have any references from her current employers as she has unmasked their ill-treatment of their ward." Despite his aching head, Sheffield stood up and began to pace the narrow confines of the cabin. "She and Emma were left to the mercies of the invading French army, you know. She took it upon herself to save the child, daring to attempt the journey from Moscow to St. Petersburg. If I hadn't come upon them . . ." A flash of humor stole across his features. "Actually, she probably pulled my irons out of the fire as often as I helped her."

"Miss Hadley sounds like quite a remarkable female," murmured the marquess.

"That is putting it mildly. Why, she is the most intelligent, caring, resourceful, and courageous person I have ever met—man or woman."

"Hmmm." Killingworth regarded his brother's agitation with a gleam of speculation, though his expression remained impassive. "Just how do you intend to see that she does not have to fend for herself?"

"Why, er . . . ." Sheffield felt his face turn rather warm as he stumbled for words. "I-I thought Olivia and Augusta might help me find a suitable position for her. One where she might be treated with the esteem she deserves."

"Ah." The marquess toyed with his cuff. "I am sure your sisters-in-law would be delighted to get involved. They are hopeless romantics—no doubt they will enjoy this tale far more than any of those published by Minerva Press."

"This has nothing to do with romance, William. Good Lord, I have no illusions about being some storybook hero," he muttered. *Damnation,* that was not true, he realized. He *did* wish to clasp the heroine in his arms at the end of the tale, but after the awful mull he had made of things, that seemed quite unlikely to happen, except in his dreams. "It has to do with friendship and loyalty and . . ." His voice trailed off as he shoved his hands in his pockets and quickened the pace of his steps. "And trust," he finally added, ducking just in time to keep from cracking his head on one of the beams. "The devil take it! After what happened back there in St. Petersburg, I doubt she will ever speak to me again, much less trust me. Or allow me to help her. She is too proud to accept—"

"Alex, sit down before you make yourself seasick by

spinning in such circles. Just watching you is having a deleterious effect on my own insides."

"Hell's teeth!" The oath came out in a whoosh of air as he threw himself down on the hard bunk. "I don't know how I am ever going to convince her that I am not a worthless wastrel."

"Well, it is a long voyage home, and there are three married gentlemen willing to offer whatever advice we can. Surely if we all put our heads together we can come devise some sort of strategy to soften her feelings." He gave a slight chuckle. "Although, speaking from long experience, I am not sure that any of us can claim to fully understand the workings of the female mind."

". . . Three, and that makes four."

Octavia stepped back and surveyed the corded boxes, satisfied that the porters had not left one behind. They had precious few belongings as it was, but a number of necessities had been purchased, including some much-needed new clothing, and she did not wish to embark on the voyage without them.

"Come along, Emma. Mr. Twilling has promised to escort us to our cabin before he bids us good-bye." The young man from the embassy had proved enormously useful over the past week. Not only had he quickly settled any lingering objections the Renfrews might have had about relinquishing custody of Emma, but he had managed to arrange a comfortable cabin for her and the girl aboard a large merchant vessel attached to a naval convoy returning to London, much to the irritation of a number of important gentlemen who had also been awaiting passage home.

There was no doubt as to the reason for such preferential treatment, she admitted as she strolled up the gangplank. It was clear the Sheffield name inspired a good deal of awe among the diplomatic corps. Awe, however, was not exactly the sentiment she would use to describe her own feelings about that august moniker.

Sheffield. Just repeating the syllables in her head caused a wave of anger to well up inside her.

Her brow furrowed. No, the emotion was more complex than mere anger or loathing. It was . . . disappointment. A disappointment as fierce as a Baltic Sea storm, the depth of its turmoil made greater by the fact that it so unexpected. She had thought that despite his outward show of sardonic detachment, Sheffield had come to care for them—or at least for Emma, if not herself.

Good Lord, she must have listened to the reading of far too many chapters of that cursed book to have succumbed to such sentimental fantasy. What a fool she had been to imagine a hardened rake would have any real feelings for an orphaned child and an aging governess! It was only his upbringing as a gentleman that had prevented him from abandoning them along the way. Mere duty, rather than anything else, that had dictated his actions. And as soon as they had reached relative safety, he had announced just how onerous that duty had been by promptly drowning himself in—

Mr. Twilling's discreet cough made Octavia realize she hadn't been paying the least attention to what he had been saying. "Forgive me," she sighed, forcing her eyes from the chunks of ice bobbing among the leaden waves. "I fear I was . . . letting my thoughts wander."

"That is most understandable, Miss Hadley. You have had a great deal to think about over the last little while. I was merely inquiring whether there is anything else you might need before the ship weighs anchor?"

"You have done more than enough for us, sir. I am well aware that without your help we would be spending a long, cold winter in St. Petersburg."

Twilling inclined a bow. "Well, then, I shall take my leave. Good-bye, Miss Hadley." A quick wink was directed at the girl. "And Miss Emma as well. I wish you Godspeed and good luck in London."

Ha, thought Octavia. She was going to need more than luck in navigating her way through the coming weeks. As she didn't know a soul in the city, she had no idea where she and Emma would stay while she sought consultation with the trustees of the girl's estate, or how long her funds would hold out. . . .

Well, time enough to think of that during the voyage. She forced a smile. "Good-bye, Mr. Twilling. And thank you again."

With another tip of his hat, the young man turned and hurried off, weaving his steps between the burly sailors carrying the last of the spruce spars and barrels of pine tar up from the docks.

"London," murmured Emma, her mittened hands coming to rest on the varnished railing. For a moment she, too, seemed engrossed in studying the flock of gulls hovering over the frigid waters before she ventured another word. "Do—do you think Nicholas and Alex might be there to greet us?"

Octavia bit her lip. "I should not count on it, Emma," she answered, deciding it was best not to encourage such hopes.

"Oh." The girl stared straight ahead. "I thought they were our friends."

"Of course they are. But they will have a great many other obligations, for Mr. Sheffield's family is very important—"

"And we are not?"

How was she to answer that? wondered Octavia. She drew a deep breath. "It is not as simple as that," she began. "I, that is, they . . ." There was an awkward pause while she searched for some way to explain what she meant. "They must begin a new chapter in their lives."

"And we are not part of it?"

"No, we are not," she said bluntly. "Emma, dear Mrs. Radcliffe may use artistic license to create all manner of trials and tribulations for her characters and then blithely pen a happy ending. It makes for entertaining fiction, but unfortunately real life does not often follow such a perfect plot."

Emma kept her gaze locked on the swirling currents, but the tilt of her profile did not quite hide the quivering of her lips. "I think I understand what you mean." She gave an exaggerated shrug of her shoulders. "Anyway, boys are nothing but a nuisance."

Amen to that, thought Octavia to herself as her arm slipped around the girl's waist. "That's right," she said with a forced laugh. "Nothing but a nuisance. We are much better off without them, aren't we?"

"Right."

Tactfully ignoring the small sniff that accompanied the girl's reply, Octavia leaned down to pick up the valise by her side. "Mr. Twilling was able to locate a copy of *The Castle of Otranto*. Perhaps you would like to go below and have a look at it. I believe you will like it, even if the author is a male."

"If you don't mind, I think I will just lie down for a bit," answered Emma in a small voice. "It has been an awfully busy day, and I find I am not much in the mood for reading at the moment."

Chapter Sixteen

*T*he cries of the circling gulls mingled with the snap of the riggings and oaths of the stevedores as the elegant vehicle approached the bustling wharves. Sheffield shifted against the soft leather squabs of his brother's equipage, feeling his stomach take a decidedly seasick lurch at the prospect of the coming meeting.

Unlike the male members of the family, his sisters-in-law had not been fooled in the least by his prevarications. His halting explanation of wishing to find a suitable position for Octavia had been met with raised brows and the withering scorn it deserved. He was naught but a craven coward, they had exclaimed in short order. Not for any lack of physical courage, but for being afraid to admit what was patently obvious to any observer with a grain of common sense.

He was in love with the lady. And, they added, he would be the biggest idiot between the Thames and the Volga if he didn't acknowledge it and do whatever it took to win her heart. Begging and groveling were among the first suggestions.

For some reason that eluded him, they seemed to think he had a chance of success.

In the face of such formidable forces, his defenses had quickly crumbled. But rather than engendering any sense of defeat, the admission of his feelings had been more liberating than he had ever imagined. Freed from the shackles of the past, he dared hope for the future.

Hope, however, had seemed a dim prospect when he considered the obstacles in his path. With a sigh, he had said as much.

From there, his family had sprung into action with

dizzying efficiency. The earl had used his considerable influence with the government to learn on which vessel Octavia and Emma had set sail, while his brothers had pulled all manner of strings to help him deal with a number of important matters in Town. In the meantime, the ladies had passed the days preparing Killingworth House for additional guests, as well as spending considerable time behind closed doors making arrangements they refused to discuss with the gentlemen.

Frequent updates from the Admiralty on the progress of the ships and their naval escort kept them alerted as to when the convoy was expected to tie up at the Greenwich wharves. Even now, as Sheffield craned his neck to peer out of the paned window, he could see a billow of white canvas ghosting in with the current. Swallowing a gulp, he turned to the other occupant of the carriage and forced a show of nonchalance. "Well, Nicholas, it looks as though they will soon be here."

The boy's nose pressed up against the glass too, his nervous anticipation not nearly as well hidden. "Oh!" he exclaimed. "I can hardly wait to . . . find out what will happen to Emily and Valancourt."

Sheffield gave a low chuckle in spite of his own over-wrought nerves. "I should have thought you would have finished that book long ago."

Nicholas squirmed in his seat, causing the corner of a much-worn leather binding to peek out from the folds of his coat. "I-I did not think it right to go on without Emma," he replied in a hesitant voice. "Perhaps you think me—how do the English say it—less of a man for caring about the opinion of a mere girl, but . . ."

Alex reached over to ruffle the boy's hair. "On the contrary, lad. Loyalty to one's friends is one of the qualities of a true gentleman. And Emma has shown herself to be more than worthy of your esteem, regardless of her skirts and braids." A sudden jolt of the wheels indicated that the horses had pulled to a halt. Sucking in a deep breath, his hand groped for the door latch. "I think it best if you wait here to greet Emma while I have a few words in private with Miss Hadley. There are, er, a number of things that the two of us need to discuss regarding . . . plans."

Nicholas regarded him with owlish intensity, then gave a solemn nod.

Offering a silent prayer to the heavens, Sheffield turned up the collar of his coat, stepped down to the muddy cobblestones, and pushed his way through a bevy of swearing sailors trying to wrestle a load of salt beef off of a nearby wagon. It was some time before the heavy hull of the merchant ship was manuevered into place alongside the barnacled pilings and the thick hawsers snugged around the iron stanchions. His pacing grew more impatient as the gangplanks seemed to take an age to be set in place. Finally, after a line of officers had descended from the quarterdeck, he spotted two females, half hidden by the tarred shrouds, their familiar profiles silhouetted against the scudding gray clouds.

They disappeared among the jostling of the other passengers seeking to disembark, then were visible again just as they stepped onto dry land. Sheffield hung back, waiting for them to move away from the milling crowd. Even at that distance, he could recognize the tilt of her chin and the determined set of her slender shoulders. He even imagined he could see the exact shade of her eyes, and how they were alight with . . .

In that instant Octavia turned toward him. She froze, her whole frame going rigid as an icicle. Then taking firm hold of Emma's hand, she continued on, her gaze locked on the small cluster of hansom cabs gathered near the end of the wharves.

Hell's teeth, he swore to himself. How was he ever going to melt the coldness he had glimpsed in her eyes?

There was no ice in Emma's reaction. Catching sight of Sheffield, she tore away from Octavia's grasp and ran at him with a shriek of delight. "Alex, Alex! I knew you would not forget us!"

He swung her up into his arms. "There hasn't been a day that I haven't thought about you, sweeting," he murmured, a fierce constriction in his chest making him realize just how true his words were. Good Lord, how he had missed those thin arms wound around his neck and that soft cheek pressed up against the hard line of his jaw.

The girl's companion made to go by, but he turned to

block her way. "Octavia," he began, placing Emma back down on her feet. "Please wait—"

"What for?" she countered, falling back a step to elude the hand reaching out for hers. "You made it abundantly clear how quickly you wished to submerge the memory of your sojourn—and the company you were forced to endure—in Russia. Well, I, too, wish to forget that unfortunate interlude." Her jaw was set in the stubborn tilt he had come to recognize all too well. "Please move out of my way now. There is nothing more we need say to each other, Mr. Sheffield." There was a fraction of a pause. "Or is it really 'my lord?' It is hard to keep track of all your lies."

"I never lied to you," he said quietly. "And actually I have a great deal I wish to say to you, if only you will listen for a moment."

Octavia's gaze seemed to waver for an instant before regaining its martial light. "Why should I? Indeed, a better question is why did you even bother to show up here? Now that you are back in London, I am sure you have more interesting things to occupy your thoughts than an aging governess and an orphaned girl." A slight quiver of her voice showed that she was not quite as composed as she wished to appear. The realization seemed to make her scowl grow even blacker than before. "No doubt you are back to your usual revelries—drinking and . . . and gaming . . . and visiting your latest mistress. . . ."

Emma's eyes went very wide. "Alex has a mistress?"

"Of course I don't!" he said through gritted teeth. "Damnation, Octavia, please—"

"Don't swear. Have you forgotten there is a child present?" she scolded.

"How can I!" he exclaimed with mounting frustration. "They have rarely been out of our company, making it deucedly hard for me to tell you how much I—" His words cut off with a harried sigh. "Emma, you see that black and yellow carriage standing over there? Hurry along and climb inside it."

The girl pulled a face. "Why do adults always send us away just when the conversation is getting interesting?"

"NOW!"

"Oh, very well."

"There is someone inside who is anxious to see you," he added as she started to stalk off with deliberate slowness.

A radiant smile replaced the petulant pout, and the girl broke into an exuberant dash. His own lips curved upward. "At least the children seem happy at the prospect of being reunited," he murmured, searching Octavia's face for the least glimmer of welcoming warmth.

She looked away, just enough to throw her features into shadow. "Well? Make it quick, Mr. Sheffield. I have a great many arrangements to make this afternoon."

"Lord, you aren't going to make this easy for me," he whispered, half to himself. "Not that I deserve any quarter." Despite the obvious lack of encouragement, he forced himself. "Let me begin by addressing the accusations you have just raised—"

Alex got no further as Octavia's eyes suddenly narrowed and two hot spots of color appeared on her cheeks. "Speaking of high flyers," she said with a barely concealed sneer. "There are two very fancy females waving handkerchiefs and blowing kisses in our direction. As they are complete strangers to me, they must be friends of *yours*. Quite intimate friends, by the look of it."

He looked around quickly, and couldn't help from swearing under his breath at the unfortunate timing.

"Aren't you going to wave back?" Her tone couldn't have been more scathing.

"Those two very fancy females are my sisters-in-law." He was somewhat gratified to see that his explanation caused her mouth to scrunch in embarrassment, but before he could go on, his relatives had swept down upon them.

Octavia was having a hard time regaining her equilibrium—it was as if there were still a lurching deck beneath her feet rather than terra firma. The mere sight of Alex had set her heart to turning somersaults, and on seeing the wistful tenderness that shaded his expression when he took up Emma, she had to restrain the urge to throw herself into his arms as well.

Drat the plaguey man! If such emotions were not bad enough, she had also been thrown off balance by the fierce stab of jealousy that had knifed through her breast on seeing the two elegant ladies seeking to attract his attention. Though why she should feel the least—

"You must be Miss Hadley." One of the ladies flashed a brilliant smile as she reached for Octavia's hand.

"Allow me to introduce Lady Killingworth," began Alex in a slightly dazed murmur.

"Oh, you must call me Augusta. And I hope we may call you Octavia. We have heard so much about you from Nicholas that I feel we are already . . . friends."

"From Alex as well." Olivia's eyes held a mischievous twinkle. "I am Olivia. Knowing how exhausted you must be from the arduous sea journey, we decided to come fetch you ourselves."

Octavia bit at her lip, too overwhelmed for the moment to reply.

"But I had planned—" Alex made another attempt to speak, only to be silenced yet again by Augusta.

"And no doubt overlooked any number of practical details. Men have not a clue about such things." She gave an airy wave of her hand. "Run along with the children, Alex. We will bring our guest back to Killingworth House after we have made several stops in Bond Street."

"Yes," chimed in her sister-in-law. "I imagine Octavia could do with a few new gowns and sundries after all she has been through. We have already made a number of purchases. There are just a few final fittings to be done."

"G-guest . . . g-gowns?" Somehow Octavia managed to recover her wits enough to stammer a reply. "S-surely you can't mean for *me* to stay with *you*. Or to incur such extravagant expenses on my behalf. After all, I am a complete stranger, naught but a country parson's—"

"Nonsense! As far as we are concerned"—Augusta stole a sly look at Alex—"you are part of the family."

"You journeyed through the wilds of Russia with two cold, tired children and Alex, all the while braving wolves, kidnappers, and Bonaparte's army," added Olivia, her lips taking on a humorous twitch. "My dear, you deserve more than a few gowns—you deserve a medal. On second thought, a whole row of them."

Octavia's gaze darted from the two smiling faces to Alex's countenance. His wore a more enigmatic expression. What were his feelings about the prospect of being together under the same roof, if only for a short while? There was, she admitted to herself, little question as to her own emotions. While she had managed to feign an outward indifference to his presence, the thought of a reunion, however temporary, had her insides sliding around like jellied aspic.

Her jaw tightened. Only a naive gudgeon would fail to see that real life rarely provided a storybook ending. There was no point in starting another chapter, one that would only result in more . . . disappointment.

"It is a most generous offer, but I am afraid I cannot possibly accept it."

Neither of the ladies batted an eye at her refusal.

"Of course you can," replied Augusta firmly. "Both you and Emma would be much more comfortable with us at Killingworth House rather than in some hotel surrounded by strangers."

As there was no credible arguement to that, she stared down at the tips of her half boots, hoping to hide the flicker of longing that lit in her face for just an instant.

"Besides, Nicky would be quite devastated. The stack of books he has picked out for his young friend reaches nearly to the ceiling of the schoolroom."

"But—"

"No more 'buts' about it." Octavia suddenly found herself between the two ladies being whisked toward the waiting carriage. "Come along. We must hurry. One of the first little rules you must learn here in Town is not to be late for an appointment with Madame Celeste."

Hell's teeth!

Alex listened in glum silence as his sisters-in-law regaled their guest with yet another pithy bit of gossip about Prinny and the Carlton set. If they were trying to help improve his standing with Octavia, he groused to himself, they were certainly going about it in a deucedly peculiar fashion! Why, he had not had the chance to exchange a private word with her since her arrival at Killingworth House four days ago. If truth be told, he had scarcely set eyes on her, what with the flurry of sightseeing activities and shopping expeditions that his relatives had organized for her and the children.

At the moment, however, his eyes *were* riveted on the lady in question. From his seat at the far end of the breakfast table, he had clear view of the stylish new sprigged muslin day dress she was wearing. Despite its modest cut, it still exposed a good deal more of her creamy flesh than he was used to seeing. The design also emphasized the natural curves of her figure instead of shrouding them in a billow of sacklike folds. The sight was rather . . . mesmerizing.

". . . Isn't that right, Alex?" Augusta turned, one brow rising in pointed question.

His knife ceased cutting the slab of bacon on his plate into mincemeat. "Er, yes," he mumbled, although he had absolutely no idea what had just been asked. "Of course."

"You see!" She looked back to Octavia with a triumphant smile. "There is no need to put off the planned drive through Hyde Park just because Olivia and I must call upon poor Lady Crenshaw, whose gout has taken a turn for the worse. I told you Alex would be delighted to serve as escort to you and the children."

The thought of the four of them together, just like old times, caused his throat to constrict for a moment. It was not exactly the private moment he had been hoping for, but given the swirl of Sheffields that had surrounded her of late, it was, at least, a step in the right direction. Octavia must have caught the tightening of his expression, for her own face became a bit pinched. "Perhaps Mr. Sheffield had other plans—"

"Of course Alex had no other plans. And if he did, he would simply have to change them." Olivia took a bite of her toast. "It is a *perfect* morning for such an outing. Nothing like a bit of bright sunshine and fresh air to clear the head and invigorate the spirit. Now run along, both of you, before any gray clouds blow in to spoil the opportunity."

As Alex rose, he could have sworn that both of his relatives gave him a surreptitious wink.

The carriage was brought around without delay, and the little party was soon tooling through the gates at Park Lane. Olivia's pronouncement was indeed correct—the day was mild for so late in autumn, the sun a large, buttery orb whose radiance took all the chill from the brisk breeze. Alex found himself wishing his mood might feel nearly as bright, for while the children kept up a steady patter of exuberant comments, Octavia had yet to utter so much as a word.

Perhaps his sisters-in-law had better regroup and come up with a different strategy. . . .

"Oh look!" Emma leaned out of the open landau to get a better view of the ducks paddling about the Serpentine.

Nicholas took out a sack of breadcrumbs from his coat pocket. "Would you like to stop and feed them? Aunt Olivia says they will come eat right from your hand."

Her hands clapped together in delight. "Really?" she asked, her eyes going wide as saucers. "May we, Alex?"

"Of course we may."

No sooner had the coachman drawn the team to a halt by the graveled path than the two children scrambled down from their perch and lit out for the water's edge.

For a moment, the two adults sat in awkward silence. Sheffield tugged at a corner of his scarf, cursing himself for a coward. Daunted by her refusal to meet his gaze, he hesitated, but knew he would despise himself forever if he didn't make some sort of move to thaw the coolness between them. "Er, would you care to take a stroll? I imagine they will be occupied for some time."

Octavia considered the suggestion for what seemed to be an age before giving a frosty nod.

Repressing a sigh, he handed her down from the carriage and offered his arm. They walked on for a bit, the only sound between them the brittle crunch of their steps on the stones. A sideways glance at her rigid profile caused his shoulders to sag just a touch. *Hell's teeth!* It might be an easier task to chip through the frozen Neva River than to melt her chill reserve.

However, after another few steps, it was Octavia who finally broke the ice. "Your family has been quite wonderful, what with the kindness they have shown to a total stranger. I am extraordinarily grateful to them for all their thoughtfulness."

"Yes." A faint half smile played on his lips. "So am I."

The enigmatic comment sparked an odd flash of emotion in her eyes. Then she blinked and it was gone, leaving him to wonder whether he had only imagined a spark of their former rapport.

"The earl has been most generous in his assistance with Emma's situation. He thinks it may soon be resolved," she continued softly. "And your sisters-in-law have told me not to worry about my own future, as they are in the process of arranging a new position for me."

He stopped in his tracks. "Position?"

"Why, y-yes. Something more . . . permanent, they said. There is no guarantee that Emma's new guardian will want to retain me as her governess." From a distance came a peal of laughter from the children, and she turned to watch them scatter crumbs across the placid water. "I shall miss them a great deal—even the pouts and squabbles." Her mouth quirked upward. "Indeed, I shall even miss those hours spent listening to Mrs. Radcliffe's prose, despite its penchant for waxing melodramatic."

A lock of hair had blown free of her bonnet as she spoke. Sheffield reached out to tuck it back in place, then let his hand linger on the curve of her cheek. In that instant, he decided to throw caution to the wind. "Octavia, please—will you consent to listen to a few fumbling words of mine? Lord knows when I shall have another chance to speak to you alone. And while my command of the English language will no doubt pale in comparison to that of the children's favorite novelist, there are things I *must* say to you, no matter how awkwardly they are phrased."

Octavia felt a flash of heat run through her as his fingers grazed her skin. How she had missed the warmth of his company! Not just his physical presence, but his quirky humor, his gentle kindness, his fierce compassion.

Even his all-too-human weaknesses, for he had the courage to face them, despite his efforts to appear the unrepentant rake.

She finally looked up, and the sight of his sensuous lips, lean jaw, and dark, ruffled locks caused the breath to catch in her throat. On second thought, she had to admit that his physical presence had a great deal to do with the fact that her knees were in danger of folding like an overcooked souffle!

He seemed to take her inability to speak as a sign to continue.

"I never lied to you, Octavia. At first it seemed prudent to keep my family connection a secret from everyone. Then, when I knew I might trust you with our lives, I remained silent out of concern that the knowledge might put you and Emma into danger if we were apprehended by Nicholas's pursuers."

"I . . . suppose that makes some sense," she allowed.

"And to be totally truthful," he went on in a near whisper, "I also feared breaking the camaraderie I felt had developed between us. I thought you might like me less were you to know I was from a prominent family, rather than someone dependent on wits and pluck to survive in the world, like yourself."

Her brows arched in utter surprise. This was not at all what she had expected to hear. "You cared whether I . . . liked you?"

Sheffield could no longer attempt a measured, rational explanation. His words spilled out in a flood of emotion. "Why do you think I sought to drown myself in a sea of vodka at the end? You had frightened me half to death by charging into danger with no thought for your own safety. And then the thought of being parted, of never seeing you again . . ." His jaw set. "Like a cravenly coward, I ran from the idea, sinking myself so low in your eyes that—"

"You are no coward, Alex," she interrupted softly. "Far from it."

"Oh, not in any physical sense, I suppose," he replied with a bittersweet smile. "But I lacked the courage to tell you my true feelings and therefore deserve to have you despise me. I have no doubt you would have rejected me out of hand, but at least I might have retained a shred of your respect had I told you then that . . . I love you."

"*L-love?*" stammered Octavia, feeling her face turn as white as a Russian snowfall, save for two spots of color high on her cheekbones. He was speaking so softly she knew she must not have heard him correctly. "Surely you didn't say *love*. That's impossible! Why, you think me shrewish, stubborn, opinionated, meddlesome—"

"Wrong, my obstinate darling. I think you compassionate, caring, principled, and entirely too brave for your own good."

Onlookers were beginning to show a decided interest in their conversation, some of them staring quite openly. "P-perhaps we should continue this conversation in the privacy of your carriage." Feeling none too brave at the moment, she sought some delaying tactic to regroup her defenses. "Let us call to Nicholas and Emma—"

"Privacy? Ha! There is not a snowflake's chance in hell that I am going into that carriage with you, not until I have finished saying all I wish to say without the children comparing my every word to that of some damn storybook hero. With my luck, they would probably be reading the passage where Valancourt, bumbling idiot that he is, manages to win his lady's heart with some eloquent speech, making me feel even more of a stuttering fool than I already do."

Sheffield paused long enough to take hold of her arm and pull her behind one of the stately elm trees lining the path. "Flowery sentiments do not flow off my tongue as easily as they do from Mrs. Radcliffe's pen, my dear. I'm not some perfect hero, but a man with so many faults you have probably ceased counting. . . ." A strange sound caused him to halt in midsentence. "You . . ." He peeked under the brim of her bonnet. "Octavia, you aren't . . . crying, are you?"

"Of course not." Her sleeve scraped against her cheek. "It must be the spray from the fountain. . . ."

She had no chance to finish. Sheffield's mouth came down hard upon hers. "Lord, you are more intoxicating than any of the spirits I have ever tasted," he whispered as his lips drank in the salty tears and the sweetness of her shy smile. With a muffled groan, he pulled her closer. "Dare I hope, sweeting? After all, you have not yet felled me with a jerk of your knee."

Rather than lash out, Octavia allowed the passionate embrace to wash away the last of her resistance. Her lips parted to deepen the kiss, and her fingers, which had been poised to deliver a resounding slap, crept up to twine in the silky softness of his unruly locks. "Oh, Alex. I imagine I can recite every one of your faults, starting from the time you accosted me with that first drunken kiss. They are what make you human, rather than some character with no more depth than a sheet of foolscap. And they are far overshadowed by all your admirable qualities." She lowered her lashes, which were still wet with tears. "Now it is my turn to be honest—I think you the most wonderful man in the world."

His arms wrapped her in a bear hug.

"But, Alex," she managed to squeak, even though he was holding her so tightly she could scarcely breath. "Things are rather more complicated than our own feelings. There is your family and position in Society to consider. And all the details of seeing that the children are settled with the right family."

Sheffield smiled. "I have been busy in Town these last few weeks, but not in the manner that you implied when I met you at the docks. With my brother and my uncle lending their influence, I have managed to convince Emma's trustees that she would be better off with a guardian that truly cares for her welfare, even if he isn't a blood relative."

"*He?*" she repeated.

"Me, actually. She seems to have grown rather fond of Nicholas, and as I also mean to look after the lad, I thought she might prefer being with us to the company of strangers."

Octavia felt her heart give a lurch. "You wish to give up your life of a carefree gentleman about Town to take on the responsibility for two children?"

"Well, I hoped I might have a little help." He gave a crooked grin. "You see, one of the reasons Emma's trustees agreed to the arrangement was that I told them I soon hoped to be a respectable married man."

Her insides were now doing full-blown somersaults.

"And as for my previous existence, it no longer holds any appeal for me," he continued. "William was kind enough to offer me one of the minor Sheffield estates in Devon when I told him I wished to serve as guardian for Nicholas. I thought the four of us might enjoy a comfortable country life together, without being attacked by armed ruffians, frozen in raging blizzards, or squaring off against Bonaparte's army."

"The four of us?" Octavia knew she was sounding rather slow-witted, but the idea was taking a little while to sink in.

"Well, I imagine we will be adding to that number soon enough." A twinkle came to his eyes. "I have always wanted . . . a dog."

She couldn't repress a burble of laughter. "You are an incorrigible rogue."

"No. Not anymore." His face became serious again. "For too long I had been a castaway, lost at sea, adrift in a raging storm. But then I finally saw the bright beacon of a safe harbor in all the darkness, one that has helped guide me back to solid ground." He pressed a kiss to the palm of her hand. "You are truly the light of my life, Octavia. I should like to spend the rest of my days with you. And Emma and Nicholas and children I hope we may have of our own."

"I cannot think of anything I should like more." Her cheek came to rest on his shoulder. "For one who claims no talent for words, you have certainly written a story-book ending."

Sheffield gave a chuckle. "We really must see that the children take to reading less sensational literature. Something from the Bard, perhaps." He thought for a moment. "I have it—*The Tempest*!"

Octavia looked up and brushed a kiss against his cheek. "I was thinking more of *All's Well That Ends Well.*"

Signet Regency Romances from

BARBARA METZGER

"Barbara Metzger deliciously mixes love and laughter." —*Romantic Times*

MISS WESTLAKE'S WINDFALL
0-451-20279-1

Miss Ada Westlake has two treasures at her fingertips. One is a cache of coins she discovered in her orchard, and the other is her friend (and sometime suitor), Viscount Ashmead. She has been advised to keep a tight hold on both. But Ada must discover for herself that the greatest gift of all is true love....

THE PAINTED LADY
0-451-20368-2

Stunned when the lovely lady he is painting suddenly comes to life on the canvas and talks to him, the Duke of Caswell can only conclude that his mind has finally snapped. But when his search for help sends him to Sir Osgood Bannister, the noted brain fever expert and doctor to the king, he ends up in the care of the charming, naive Miss Lilyanne Bannister, and his life suddenly takes on a whole new dimension...

To order call: 1-800-788-6262

S435/Metzger

Allison Lane

"A FORMIDABLE TALENT...
MS. LANE NEVER FAILS TO
DELIVER THE GOODS."
—*ROMANTIC TIMES*

THE NOTORIOUS WIDOW
0-451-20166-3

When a scoundrel tries to tarnish a young widow's
reputation, a valiant Earl tries to repair the damage—
and mend her broken heart as well...

BIRDS OF A FEATHER
0-451-19825-5

When a plain, bespectacled young woman keeps
meeting the handsome Lord Wylie, she feels she is not
up to his caliber. A great arbiter of fashion for London
society, Lord Wylie was reputed to be more interseted in
the cut of his clothes than the feelings of others, as the
young woman bore witness to. Degraded by him in
public, she could nevertheless forget his dashing
demeanor. It will take a public scandal, and a private
passion, to bring them together...

To order call: 1-800-788-6262

Signet Regency Romances from
DIANE FARR

FALLING FOR CHLOE
0-451-20004-7

Gil Gilliland is a friend—nothing more—to his
childhood chum, Chloe. But Gil's mother sees more to
their bond. And in a case of mother knows best, what
seems a tender trap may free two stubborn hearts.

ONCE UPON A CHRISTMAS
0-451-20162-0

After a tragic loss, Celia Delacourt accepts an
unexpected holiday invitation—which is, in fact, a
thinly veiled matchmaking attempt. For the lonely
Celia and a reluctant young man, it turns out to be a
Christmas they'd never forget...

"Ms. Farr beguiles us."—*Romantic Times*

To order call: 1-800-788-6262